ADVANCED CHEMISTRY

A SOUTH ROCK HIGH NOVEL

A.J. TRUMAN

1

CHASE

"You can't have chemistry without catalysts," I said to my fifth period class, who were having a hard time focusing. It wasn't hard to understand why. I didn't need the scientific method to determine that their lack of attention was directly correlated to the warm, sunny weather outside. Trying to teach students in May was a fool's errand, but I soldiered on.

"There are elements that live a humdrum life, doing their proverbial thing, until they come into contact with certain other elements and create something dynamic and new. Chemicals are permanently altered, reconfigured into some other substance. Take iron, for example. For most of its life, iron is iron. It's a mineral we can eat. It can be used to make metal. It has many purposes for our everyday lives, but nothing out of the ordinary. Until it comes into contact with nitrogen and hydrogen during the Haber Process, and all three elements turn into..."

I paused and turned to the class, waiting for a bevy of raised hands that never came.

"Come on!" I wrote H + Ni + Fe on the markerboard. Why was I the only one excited about this? "What do you get when you add iron to hydrogen and nitrogen? This shouldn't be a stumper as it was clearly delineated in last night's reading."

A good number of blank stares blinked back at me, while the rest of the class was turned toward the sunlit windows.

"Once the class is over, you have your lunch period and you can frolic outside to your heart's content," I borderline pleaded.

For some inexplicable reason, getting any of my students to answer a question was like Annie Sullivan trying to get Helen Keller to say water in *The Miracle Worker*.

Billy, an unsure gentleman in the second row raised his hand. "Ammonia?"

"Correct!" I needed to invest in a bell to ding. That would make students participate more in class. Young adults loved loud noises. "Isn't that fascinating to think about? Three disparate chemicals coming together to form a completely new substance. We ingest iron all the time, but then, in the presence of two other chemicals that we breathe in every day, we suddenly get a lethal substance."

More blank stares. Teaching advanced chemistry was not for the faint of heart, which was a shame since it was such a fun subject.

"Billy, can you explain how the Haber Process works?"

Billy squirmed in his seat.

"Can I use the bathroom pass?"

I slumped my shoulder. "Sure."

Was it an excuse to get out of answering my question? I didn't want to take a chance and damage a young man's bladder. He scurried into the hall.

"How many of you have bottles of Hydrogen Peroxide in the back of your medicine cabinets?" Suspecting that nobody would chime in, I continued on. "Hydrogen Peroxide takes years and years to decompose. The bottle your parents bought when you were babies is still good. Unless..." I held up a finger, getting to the good part. "It comes into contact with a tiny amount of manganese. Then it will decompose instantly! How wild is that?"

Not wild at all, according to my class's reaction.

"It's analogous to a class of blank stares all period long, and then at the end, the teacher pulls out a giant bag of potato chips." I opened the bottom drawer and reached inside. The drawer was empty, but my students didn't know that. They instantly perked up, moving to the edge of their seats.

"See, you've all been activated now, your compositions changed into bright and alert. Unfortunately, that was just a rhetorical example. I don't keep snacks at my desk because using a marker with greasy hands never goes well."

Students let out audible sighs and returned to their slumped positions.

"The bottom line: it is impossible to have a chemical reaction without a catalyst. There would be no advanced chemistry without catalysts. Could you imagine your lives without this class?"

The bell was mid-ding, and my students were already out the door, unintentionally answering my question.

———

I WEAVED my way through the crowded halls. The warm weather streaming into school had made everyone extra giddy. I didn't feel their excitement. I was an indoors kid, so warm weather only reminded me of being picked last and being forced to play sports at summer camp.

In the teacher's lounge, I grabbed my lunch from the fridge: tuna fish sandwich, baby carrots, and as always, a Twinkie for dessert. While I understood that Twinkies were chemically engineered "food," I allowed myself this one indulgence. They were too good to resist, and after they'd been previously discontinued, I never took them for granted.

As I sat down at an empty table to eat, my phone buzzed.

Everett: Impromptu lunch picnic?

Julian: Yes! Should we go on the roof?

Everett: Let's make it a real picnic and eat on the grass. I have a blanket in my car.

Amos: Here for it! It's so nice out! I swapped lunch periods with Mr. Selner this week, so I'm available.

Everett: Meet you on the soccer field in five?

Julian: Done.

Amos: Yep!

Everett: Chase?

I stared at the quiet, empty teacher's lounge, realizing I was in the minority of people wishing to stay inside.

Everett: Earth to Chase?

Chase: Wouldn't it be more comfortable to sit at a table and eat?

A few minutes later, I joined my friends on a blanket in the middle of the soccer field. Groups of students were sprawled on the grass around us, enjoying lunch and the fresh air. There were only a few weeks of the school year when it was possible to enjoy being outside without it being too cold or too hot. I supposed I might as well enjoy the low humidity, sunshine, and warm breeze.

Amos, Everett, and Julian, and I were all gay teachers at South Rock High School. Amos taught history, Everett drama, and Julian French. We started around the same time and quickly bonded. It was one of those odd chemical reactions considering how different we are. Julian and I were on the quieter side, Amos was bubbly, and Everett was...volatile.

"I can't believe Principal Aguilar won't let me use live explosives on stage. That man has no appreciation for the arts." Everett picked at his salad, his pale skin turning as red as his hair.

"Actual explosives?" Amos asked, his eyes bugging out. With his mop of tight, curly hair and lanky body, he sometimes reminded me of a puppet off his string, but in a good way. I once told him this, mistakenly thinking he would take it as a compliment.

"Yeah. But not a lot." Everett rolled his eyes at the question. "It's for this play I'm circling to direct for the fall show. There's a flashback scene that takes place during war. How much more realistic and heart-pounding would it be for actual explosions to be going on in the background?"

"Heart-pounding for the wrong reasons," Julian said.

"I'm with J. That sounds like twelve lawsuits waiting to happen." Amos lay back and put on sunglasses for maximum outdoor enjoyment.

"I would have full control over the explosives. They're fake explosives anyway."

"Fake explosives how?" I asked. "What is the chemical incendiary element? If something is built to combust, then it can't be fake."

"I saw it on the internet." Everett waved away my line of questioning.

"Even if the chemicals aren't flammable, the act of explosion could cause particulates to fly into the air, compromising your actors. I don't want to sacrifice your artistic vision, but wouldn't it be easier to use sound effects?" I stared at Everett while chomping into my sandwich.

"That would be half-assing it," Everett said.

"Better than half a student's face getting blown off." I shrugged. My friends cracked surprised smiles.

"I believe what you just experienced was Chase sassing you," Amos said.

I had never considered myself funny. Sarcasm wasn't my default mode. In Star Trek parlance, I was more Spock than Kirk.

But being friends with these guys had brought out my humorous side over time. At first, it wasn't intentional. I would state factual observations, and they somehow found them hilarious. Then I eventually discovered my sassy gay side. It had been stuffed deep down like layers of igneous rock in the earth's core, only coming to the surface thanks to erosion and the determined drills of oil companies.

"Fine. I won't blow anything up on stage. You're all killjoys." Everett sighed. "If audience members call the play a snoozefest, it'll be your fault."

"Okay. I can live with that," Julian said. He turned to Amos and me. "Can you guys live with that?"

We nodded yes.

Amos perked up. "Are we good here, or did you need to sulk more, Everett?"

"Let me have one more histrionic sigh." He cleared his throat, then released a very pronounced, loud sigh. "Okay, I'm done."

"Good! Because I have news." Amos rubbed his hands together. "Someone's getting married."

Everett jolted up, as did Julian and me. For the past year, Amos had been dating his boyfriend Hutch, who coached the South Rock soccer team on the very field where we were eating. They'd been living together for months. Was this the next logical step?

"Congratulations!" Julian said, hand partially over his mouth.

"Holy shit. That's awesome." Everett squeezed Amos's shoulder.

"This does make sense. You and Hutch have been dating and cohabitating for a substantial amount of time. Marriage is the next logical step," I said.

"Um, so it's not me and Hutch getting married, but I love the support." Amos turned red at his unfortunate misdirection. "Pop is."

Pop was Hutch's dad, a very kind man who'd also been dating

his girlfriend for about a year. Even though he wasn't our father, he had us call him Pop. Except for Amos, it was likely none of us knew his actual name. It was an exciting development—less exciting than if Amos was the one getting married—but still exciting all the same.

"It probably would've been better for you to say right off the bat that Pop was getting married," I said, trying to explain our reactions. "Rather than asking us to guess. Something to keep in mind the next time you have big news."

The guys blinked at me, much like my students. I was very much used to these looks.

"Chase is right, but this is still great news," Julian said.

"We love Pop. We are pro-Pop around here. Has Hutch gotten over the fact that his dad is dating and now marrying his doctor?" Everett asked. Pop had a heart condition last spring, and when he was discharged from the hospital, he left with a clean bill of health and a new girlfriend. It sounded like one big HIPAA violation, but they were very sweet together. The man very much had the gift of charm that people like me were not born with. It was no surprise that he swept his doctor off her feet while hooked up to tubes.

"Hutch will be okay. We love Dr. Kumar. I guess we can call her Sarita. Or, I guess...we'll be calling her Mom?" Amos scratched his head. "No, I think we'll still call her Dr. Kumar. But I haven't even gotten to the best part: Pop wants us to be his groomsmen!"

Everett and Julian cheered the news, while I waited for more information on what it would entail.

"He loves you guys and wants you to be part of the wedding," Amos said. We'd spent many dinners and barbecues with Pop. I had no relationship with my dad, so it was possible to interpret him as a sort of father figure. He never knew what I was talking about with my chemistry lessons, but he always acted interested.

"I'll try not to upstage him," Everett said. "I pull off suits very well."

Julian laughed to himself. He had lush brown locks of hair that framed his full face. "When's the wedding?" he asked.

"Mid-July," Amos said.

"That's only two months away. They can plan a wedding in that time?" Julian asked.

"Pop doesn't want to drag this out for obvious reasons," Amos said.

"Because he had a heart attack, mortality is constantly on his mind?" I asked to make sure I understood the obvious reasons.

"Oh Chase." Amos clapped my shoulder.

"What?"

"Nothing."

"You know what this means?" Everett twiddled his fingers together, the telltale sign of mischief. "It's time to find Chase a wedding date."

I shoved my Twinkie in my mouth, letting the sugar high drown out their voices.

"Yes!" Julian excitedly nodded his head, as did Amos.

"We're going to scroll through our available inventory of guys for you," said Amos. "Statistically, taking a date to a wedding has a higher chance of ending in love."

"According to who? What is your sample size? Are they demographically representative of the general population? Are you employing a control group?" My friends were wonderful people, but they had little respect for the field of statistics or the scientific method in general.

"Raleigh and I got together at a wedding," said Everett of him and his boyfriend, a gym teacher at South Rock.

"Seamus and I finally got together at an anniversary party, which is like a wedding," said Julian of his boyfriend, who taught Spanish.

"That's just a coincidence," I said. "Correlation is not causation."

"You never know what could happen." Amos had a playful smirk on his lips.

"You can say the same thing about waking up and coming to school." I was not one of those people addicted to whimsy and fate. I preferred the hard, cold logic of science that our world was actually based on. I brushed sugary crumbs off my lap.

"Let us help you find a date to the wedding at least," Everett said.

I had a feeling I'd be getting more of this pressure lately. A year ago, we were all single and mingling. But now, my three friends were in serious relationships. I had no interest in succumbing to peer pressure.

"I appreciate the offer, but no thank you."

"You don't want to go..." Julian started.

"Alone? I really don't mind. I can still have fun without having to make awkward smalltalk with a gentleman I don't know. I'll be there with you guys." Even though I was technically the lone single man in our group, I never felt like the odd man out. I loved hanging out with my friends and their boyfriends. We were one big family. And unlike them, I got to go home and relax in my apartment alone, another plus!

"Please don't try to set me up with anyone. I like things the way they are," I said.

"I know you're a very literal-minded person, Chase. That's what we love about you, but I don't get why you're so averse to dating," Everett said.

"I'm not averse. I'm apathetic. Why add unnecessary mess to my life when things are a well-oiled machine?" I'd seen firsthand how awful things could get when one introduced mess into their lives. "Statistics—actual statistics here—show that more than half of marriages end in divorce, and we can extrapolate that the stats for all relationships are probably the same, too. Which, I don't see that happening with any of you or Pop, but just pointing out numbers."

"You and your well-oiled machine and your numbers and your logic." Everett picked at the grass.

"I think what Everett is saying is that it's okay to shake things up," said Julian, the peacemaker of the group. "I never thought I was the type of person to fool around with my friend, but I took a chance, and now Seamus and I are together."

"Unleash your inner freak more often. Twinkies shouldn't be the only thing you're deep throating." Everett threw grass at me, as if we were eight. I'd shared stories with my friends of past sexual encounters, and it always blew their minds, as if they thought I was genuinely incapable of having fun.

"Speaking of Twinkies, did you want to go to SpringFest this weekend? There's a booth that has deep-fried Twinkies and other confections," I said, trying to change the subject to something more palatable.

"I'm going to Staten Island for Seamus's family thing," said Julian.

"Hutch and I are going zip-lining this weekend. Wish us luck." Amos shrugged his shoulders.

"Can't. There's something called the NFL Draft that Raleigh wants to watch, which is just a butch way of saying football is announcing their casting for next season's show. I swear, men can be so dramatic when it comes to their sports." Everett sipped his can of Sprite. "And then after that, we'll probably hit up some estate sales."

"Do you really need more stuff? Your apartment is packed to the gills as it is," Julian said. Everett was addicted to heavily discounted secondhand merchandise. Getting a good deal was like foreplay for him and Raleigh.

"I'm not giving up hope," said Amos, turning back to me. Alas, my attempts at topic-changing were a bust. "We'll all be keeping our eyes open for a suitable date for you."

"That sounds like a colossal waste of time," I said. "Your energy would be much better spent on other efforts, in my opinion."

My friends shared silent looks with each other that I could easily decipher.

"You're not being as stealthy as you think. I know what you're all telepathically saying to one another. 'Why doesn't Chase want to be fixed up with anyone?' I just don't. I'm happy with how things are. I have my friends. I have a fun job imparting the wisdom of chemistry to impressionable students. I have apps that provide me with moderately attractive strangers with whom I can have no-strings-attached sex with whenever I feel the urge. My life is one perfectly balanced chemical equation. Trying to add in an unknown, untested element could destroy that balance. Look what happens when you remove one oxygen atom from carbon dioxide. You get carbon monoxide, which can kill you in your sleep."

They couldn't argue with science.

2

ANTON

First, we hit the gym, then we hit the phones.

That was my daily mantra, and so far, it'd worked well for me.

"C'mon, man. You got this. You got this. Push!" Sebastian yelled above me.

Two hundred pounds of solid weight hung in the air, the only thing stopping it from crushing me was my body's strength.

There was no better moment in a workout than when I summoned my strength and pushed the barbell filled with way too much weight way over my head. Heat lanced my pecs.

"One more, man. You can give me one more. Don't quit on me."

I flexed my arms, controlling the weight as it sunk closer to my chest. I heaved and grunted loud enough for the entire gym to hear. My pecs were spent, so I had to ask my triceps to pitch in. Sure, I could give up, let Sebastian rack the weight for me. But that wasn't my style.

An actual roar flew out of me as my muscles strained, using the last drops of force to push the weight back into the air.

"There it is."

My arms collapsed as Sebastian racked the barbell. I sat up, my chest and arms on fire. I felt strong and alive and fucking ready to seize today.

"Uh, dude. That was a PR," he said.

"Was it?" I wiped my arm across my sweaty forehead.

"Yeah, you just did 200 for twelve reps. Last time, you could only do five reps before quitting."

"I didn't quit. I gave out. Big difference." I swiped the towel from the floor because my arm wasn't cutting it.

Sebastian was the number keeper of our partnership and friendship. He was the brains, and I was the pretty face—although Seb had a nice mug, too, especially when his eyes squinted with a super wide grin. It made him look Muppet-like, but in a cute way.

Sebastian scribbled our stats in his notebook, making sure we were doing progressive overload. Now that we weren't on the wrestling team anymore, we didn't have to obsess over making weight.

Sebastian was a tank of a man, short but compact and filled with big muscles. His olive complexion and dirty blond hair gave him a surfer boy look, but he was as far from a laid-back, hang ten bro as a person could find. Sebastian was always on, always thinking and calculating. I wasn't born with that skill, but flying by the seat of one's pants had its perks.

"Good workout," I said. We pounded fists. "Now–"

"We hit the phones."

"You know it." I stood up, chest puffed the fuck out. I felt like the Lord of the Weightroom. I would never be one of those guys who was jacked, but I was toned. If anyone challenged me to a fight, they'd be sorry. Not like I was the type of guy who got into fights. I preferred to make friends, not enemies.

"Anton, are you sure we should be hitting the phones on a Saturday?"

"Did you read that article I sent you, Seb? Business owners and executives check their phones and email on weekends. They're as hungry as we are. They don't want to miss anything." The article interviewed top salespeople who all admitted to calling C-suite prospects on the weekend as a way to cut through the clutter. Prospects are inundated with sales calls throughout the week. The sales guys said that most people were receptive to receiving weekend calls, but I completely understood how it could backfire on us.

"Listen, we'll try it this one time, and if we get chewed out by a prospect for the Saturday phone call, we won't do it again. But it's worth a shot. Everything is always worth doing at least once. What do we always say?"

"Let other people tell you no." Sebastian sighed. He knew I was right.

I wasn't the smartest guy out there. Far from it. My high school report card was one big woof. But like many other non-booksmart guys, I had gone into sales, where grit mattered more than brains.

I chugged down my water bottle, then led us to the treadmill for our cool down walks.

"I just hope we don't call a top prospect and burn that relationship because he's at his daughter's dance recital."

"Seb, if the man is answering a work phone call during his daughter's recital, then we are not the asshole in the situation. Look, if people are answering the phone, that means they're open for business. It's all about big moves."

I peeked over at Sebastian's treadmill screen. His speed was set at 3.5 miles per hour. I bumped mine up to 3.7.

"You're great at looking at both sides and being cautious. That's why I love being friends and business partners with you. We balance each other out perfectly. But a dash of my crazy ideas hasn't hurt us yet."

"Begrudgingly true," he said, his lips creasing into a knowing smile. "Don't paint yourself as some Steve Jobs genius and start wearing turtlenecks and shit. I've helped land sixty percent of our biggest clients." Sebastian upped his speed to 3.9.

"I love that you know it's sixty percent." And I bumped mine up to 4.0. "I remember the first time I met you freshman year of high school, when we had to wrestle each other during our first practice. I said to myself, 'This guy knows what's what.'"

"Did you say that before or after I pinned your ass to the ground?"

"During. Also, for the record, I let you have that victory since you were the new kid in town. Like the free space on the bingo card."

"Sure, Anton. Whatever you say."

"Have I led us astray yet?"

I wasn't going to jeopardize our business, especially since I knew how much we'd sacrificed to give it a shot.

While we initially bonded over being the two gay guys on the South Rock High wrestling team, our real bond formed around our love of business. We devoured business and sales podcasts on drives to and from school. We read stories about successful startups. After listening to a podcast about how easy it was to start a vending machine business, we purchased our first junior year. We had a nice, small business going, but after graduation three years ago, we decided to hold off on college and pursue it full-time.

That was more of a no-brainer for me since school was never my strong suit. Sebastian was smart, though. Really smart. Watching the gears in his mind turn was like peeking inside a Swiss pocketwatch. Sometimes, I didn't know what he saw in me as a friend. The last book I read for fun was *Goodnight, Moon*. He had gotten a partial scholarship to a school upstate, which he turned down to operate vending machines with his knuckleheaded friend. I would never forget what Sebastian gave up to pursue our business. I wouldn't have been able to do this on my own. I was eternally grateful for our friendship.

And best of all, we never let the fact that we both had hot bodies get in the way of that friendship, even though there were times when I definitely got curious about what he looked like naked.

Kids at school always wondered about us, but we were just friends who happened to be gay. Yeah, Seb was hot. I knew it. Anyone with functioning eyes knew it. But we never crossed that line. Seb needed a guy with brains, not just brawn. A guy who could keep up mentally, not just on the treadmill. Even when I hooked up with guys and knew they couldn't measure up to Sebastian, that was their problem for being lacking, not mine.

"You must be hungry after that intense workout," Sebastian said.

My stomach growled in response. "Yeah. I could go for something."

"Here you go. You can eat my dust."

Sebastian kicked up his speed to 5.0. His power walk was now a brisk jog.

"Oh, shit. Seb with the throwdown."

Two could play that game. I kicked up my speed to 5.5. My power walk was now a full-fledged run.

Sebastian responded by bumping his speed up to 6.0, which I beat with a 6.2. Very soon, our cool down walks morphed into intense sprints, and we were huffing and heaving to fill our lungs with much-needed air.

Who was going to quit first?

Were we not out of breath, we would've been shit-talking each other.

I decided to take the L this time. I lowered my speed back to a walk, wiped my forehead with my shirt and my towel. Both were needed.

"You are a machine," I said.

Sebastian shrugged and lowered his speed, yet the thrill of victory flashed on his face.

Just in case calling prospects backfired today, I wanted Sebastian to experience at least one victory.

But for the record, I totally could've outrun him.

AFTER THE GYM and grabbing omelets to go from Caroline's, we headed to our office to hit the phones. We shared a small office just off the warehouse where we housed our vending machines. For our first year, all it had were two desks, two chairs, and one mini-fridge. Our moms came in and forced us to add a picture to the wall and an indoor plant by the window.

Sebastian and I pulled up our call lists and got to it. There was nothing quite like the thrill of the cold call. Yeah, we might've been living in the age of email and texts and social media DMs, but the phone still reigned supreme. The phone lets two people connect live in real time. It was easy to reject someone via email, less easy to do so via phone—though not impossible. I'd received tons of hang ups.

We were on fire, passion and confidence infusing every call, even if all we got were rejections.

"Oof," I said, hanging up the phone after a brutal rejection.

"What happened? Looks like you were having a good conversation with him."

"This guy listened to my entire pitch, asking me questions. It was going well. Then he said 'not interested.' He was just talking with me to pass the time while he was on the can."

"Maybe this was a bad idea," Sebastian said, crossing off

another prospect on our shared document. "I've been getting voicemails and hangups all morning."

"Patience, young grasshopper."

"I'm two months older than you."

"One yes erases the failure of ninety-nine no's," I told him, bowing as if I were a wise monk.

"A quote from The Book of Anton?" Sebastian raised his eyebrow.

"From the latest *Top of Sales Mountain* podcast ep."

"I gotta get caught up on that."

"Remember, sales is a numbers game. We're getting our reps in."

Sebastian was the nervous one between us, the thoughtful one. Sure, I was getting a little nervous myself that this was a mistake. A business couldn't survive off no's. We needed more yeses if we were going to grow and make this work long-term.

"One name left," Sebastian said. I followed his eyes to our joint spreadsheet. "Craig Wimmer at Hollis."

I gulped back a lump in my throat as I read over the name. There was a reason Hollis Property Management was at the bottom of the list. I was saving the best for last. Ninety-nine cold calls could thicken my skin to dial the big whale. Craig Wimmer was in charge of procurement for Hollis, which oversaw twenty multi-story office buildings in the region. Each floor in each building needed a vending machine.

"Let's call together," I said.

Sebastian came around to my desk. We huddled over my phone. I pounded a good luck fist on his muscular thigh. I dialed the number; Sebastian hit send.

"Hello," said a gruff man after two rings.

Adrenaline spiked my system, and I was off.

"Hi Craig, this is Anton and Sebastian from Vending Solutions. I know we're calling you out of the blue, but I was hoping we could have twenty-three seconds of your time to tell you why we're calling and see if you're interested."

Craig groaned out a phlegmy sigh that lasted an eternity. I came up with the twenty-three seconds part to pique interest.

"Sure," he said.

Sebastian's face lit up. I pointed at him. *All you, dude.*

"Thank you, Craig. We provide and stock high-quality vending machines to businesses which keep employees refreshed and more productive throughout their day. How are your properties' vending machines currently working for you?"

I gave Sebastian two big thumbs up. The man could pitch.

"They're fine," he said unconvincingly. The f-word made my ears perk up almost as much as the other f-word. "I haven't heard any complaints."

"Fine, hmm..." I flashed Sebastian a smile. "Craig, what's stopping these vending machines from being excellent or outstanding?"

"They work. They're a little outdated, but like I said, no complaints from tenants."

Sebastian leaned over the phone. "Craig, we've talked with hundreds of building managers. Many of them never hear complaints from tenants, but then are blindsided when a tenant doesn't want to renew their rental agreement. Has that ever happened with Hollis?"

"Actually...yeah. Two this year so far."

"I'm sorry to hear that. Is that why you're working on a Saturday?" I asked. "You should be out on the golf course on a day like today!"

Our initial, non-stalker research on Craig showed that the man loved to golf. He seemed like one of those guys who was counting down the days until he could retire to Florida and play year-round.

Craig let out a chuckle. "I wish. I'm going to try and get some holes in on Sunday."

"On Sunday, God rested and retreated to the nearest golf course," I threw in. Worry flashed across Sebastian's face for a second.

What? I mouthed.

Sebastian muted the phone. "Don't talk about religion."

"It's not religion. It's God."

"Craig could be an atheist or a polytheist. Or he might think you're taking the lord's name in vain."

I rolled my eyes, secretly loving how much Sebastian thought through things.

"God has the right idea," Craig said. I smiled triumphantly at my partner. "But I don't think it was because of the vending machines in their break rooms."

"We get that," I said. The words rolled off my tongue smooth as butter. Was there any better feeling than a sales call where you could feel momentum growing? "Rent and office head count are usually the biggest factors in whether a company renews their agreement. But what we've found is that just underneath those two factors, there are several little factors that can, over time, turn a renter against their office space. If employees keep logging frustrations over things like cleanliness, temperature, or outdated vending machines, then it'll inspire their boss to evaluate the company's relationship with their office space, and make them take a hard look at rental terms and head count. With working from home becoming more popular, companies are evaluating any reason to downsize their physical footprint. Were there any hints from the two companies that didn't renew?"

"Now that I think about it, I'd heard whisperings about one of them being annoyed by the hot air blower in the bathroom not working consistently."

"How difficult is it to find new tenants versus keeping current ones satisfied?" I asked.

"It's much more difficult, but I think you know that already."

Oh hell yeah, we knew that. Anyone in sales knew that.

"Craig, if you could provide a delightful vending experience for your tenants, say with sparkling, brand new machines stocked with healthy options that appeal to Gen Z and Millennial employees, how would that help strengthen your renewals?" Sebastian asked.

"It would make staying in our building more appealing," Craig asked, stammering for an answer. "I guess if employees raved about awesome vending machines that were installed, it would make them like coming to the office more, which would keep clients renewing their rental agreements."

Sebastian and I gave each other fist bumps. The best salespeople didn't talk at prospects. They asked the right questions that made prospects come to the right conclusion themselves.

I winked at Sebastian. *Time to close.*

"Renewing their rental agreements sounds like a huge win for Hollis," Sebastian said. "Because you're looking to improve client experiences and reduce unwanted churn, we'd love to meet with you to discuss Beverage Solutions' offering in more depth. Would Wednesday at nine a.m. work for you?"

"Why don't you fellas just email me and we can take it from there," said Craig.

Oh, Craig. We weren't letting you get away that easily.

"We'll send you some information after this call, but in our experience, we've found that it's a much more efficient use of your time to have a thirty minute meeting rather than spending weeks trading emails back and forth," I said.

Emails were a blow off black hole.

Craig let out another phlegmy sigh. "Can we do eight-thirty on Monday? I have a busy week, and I don't want this meeting creeping into my workday. Like I said, our vending machines are fine, but I'm willing to hear you gentlemen out."

It was a good thing this wasn't a video call because Sebastian and I were dancing in our chairs like we'd won the lottery.

"Eight-thirty works for us," I said. "We'll send you a calendar invite with some information recapping what we discussed. Enjoy your weekend, Craig. We hope you can make it to the links tomorrow."

Craig wished us a good weekend, and we hung up. I double-checked the phone to make sure the call was officially over.

Then we celebrated.

"YES!" We said in unison as we leapt out of our chairs and gave each other a sloppy high-five that folded into a monster hug while we jumped around the room. We were one combined ball of unstoppable energy.

"We have a meeting with Hollis this week," Sebastian said, dumbstruck.

"We have a fucking meeting with Hollis this week. I told you, Seb, all it takes is one yes."

"We don't have a yes yet. We have a scheduled meeting with a mid-level executive who isn't the decision maker."

"If we impress Craig—excuse me, *when* we impress Craig, then we'll get on the radar of Perry Hollis himself."

Perry Hollis, a legend among business owners in the area, was the white whale we were chasing. Wait. Were they chasing whales or sharks in *Moby Dick*? I should've paid more attention in class.

Our call whetted my appetite, and there was no going back. Hollis Property Management was within reach. I wasn't going to let it go.

"We need to celebrate." I knelt on my office chair and spun around like I was a kid. "We need to go out."

"We need to prepare for our meeting in less than forty-eight hours."

"SpringFest is today. Let's check it out. We'll walk around, grab some drinks, listen to the bands." I put my hands on his shoulders, feeling the corded muscle under my fingertips. I leaned my forehead against his for some friendly mind melding. His hazel eyes sparkled back. "Seb, let's take one afternoon to bask in our potential success. One afternoon where we allow ourselves to count our chickens before they hatch. Tomorrow, we can go back to business."

3

SEBASTIAN

It was a good rule of thumb not to fall in love with your best friend. An even better rule of thumb was not to give up a wrestling scholarship and start a business with said best friend you were in love with. My whole life, I was so good at following rules.

But I failed completely when it came to Anton Akbarian.

Was it pathetic that I fell for him the first day we met?

Probably.

It wasn't so much that he looked good in his wrestling singlet, which he did, his dark Middle Eastern skin, intense eyes, and spiky black hair popping against the red uniform. But then he had the audacity to stretch his thin, red lips into an easygoing smile directed squarely at me. He had this confidence that rattled me, a warmth that drew me in, and this sublime trust in the world that things would work out. Unlike me, he never thought about worst case scenarios, or any other scenario with a less-than-ideal outcome.

From our first interaction, we just vibed, as if we were already in the middle of our friendship. I couldn't really explain it, but it was the same instinctual feeling of knowing when two puzzle pieces were a match seconds before putting them together.

Anton came out freshman year of high school, and I followed suit in the summer. He was the first person I told, under the fireworks blanketing the sky on the Fourth of July. I thought that would be the evening where we would have our first kiss. The setting was perfect. But my coming out didn't change Anton's feelings for me. It didn't inspire him to reveal that he, too, had a secret crush on me.

"My first gay friend!" he'd exclaimed that night, genuinely thrilled for me, for us.

But a gay friend was still in the friendzone.

From then on, I buried my feelings for Anton deep down inside me. He was an amazing friend—loyal, kind, never missing a chance to remind me how awesome I was. I wasn't going to toss that away just because he didn't want to be anything more. We remained the best of friends, our friendship strengthening with each passing year.

When he proposed we work on Beverage Solutions full-time in lieu of college, I locked my feelings away permanently and hoped they suffocated from lack of air. I didn't agree to partner with him because of a crush; I said yes because it was a great opportunity, because I knew what my life would hold if I went to college. This was the road less taken, and I wanted to see where it went. If we flamed out, I was young enough to go back to college.

I wasn't going to fuck up a business partnership with feelings. Now that I was an adult, I signed up for apps, I dated, I hooked up with a few guys, convinced that getting out there would ensure that I didn't fuck up our friendship or partnership.

So far, I hadn't met any guy who could remotely stack up to Anton, and those locked-away feelings hadn't suffocated to death yet. But I remained hopeful.

And Anton remained...Anton.

"Cheers." He held up his plastic beer cup branded with the Stone's Throw Tavern label, his smile unleashing his two dimples that were weapons of mass attraction. "To victory and legally drinking alcohol."

We'd both recently turned twenty-one, but thanks to the wild antics of our wrestling teammates, we were no strangers to drinking.

"There's no victory yet. It's one meeting."

"We're going to close them. I can feel it." His confidence would be unnerving if we weren't on the same team.

I hated how much it turned me on.

We stood around a high top table watching the flurry of activity at SpringFest. Harried parents chased after kids with painted faces. People ducked in and out of local craft vendor tents while snacking on freshly made food from downtown restaurants. I'd lived in Sourwood for six years, and there was no other place I wanted to be.

Anton downed half his beer in one powerful gulp.

"Easy there," I said.

"I don't want to take it easy, Seb. I want to celebrate! We'll rock out with the live band later. Maybe the mayor will even play some guitar. We're going to ride SpringFest hard."

"Don't forget that we have work to do tomorrow."

"Relax." He put a hand on mine, unleashing a flutter of feelings that were supposed to be repressed.

I knew that I sounded like a killjoy compared to Anton's burst of life and energy. I was the responsible one; Anton was the free spirit. That was our dynamic, and it suited us. But it was also a form of self-preservation, a way to fight off succumbing to his charm and revealing things that needed to remain unsaid.

"Thank you," he said.

"For what?"

"For taking this chance on BS."

Part of why we named our company Beverage Solutions was so that we could call it BS as a nickname, which ensured we never took ourselves too seriously.

He leaned on the table, gazing at me with his dark eyes, his arms bulging against the fabric of his tight T-shirt.

Resisting his charm was the fight of my life.

"So what happened with Kamran?" I changed the subject to his current hookup to remind myself that Anton was incredibly off-limits.

Anton rolled his eyes, teasing that there was quite a story he had no interest in rehashing. "Kamran is gonna Kamran."

"What the hell does that mean?"

"Seb, he said the M-word." Anton gritted his teeth. "Moving in together."

"Already?" A flash of jealousy raged through me, which was what I deserved for bringing up Anton's love life. In addition to being a friend and business partner, Anton was also my roommate, so I was technically invested in this outcome, and thus could continue digging. "How long have you guys been together?"

"We were never together. We were dating, hooking up, hanging out for like what? A few weeks?"

"Those are all suitable synonyms for being together." Scarlet and crimson were synonyms for red, the color lighting up my brain at the thought of other guys getting to hook up with Anton.

Anton was probably a really good kisser. He probably knew that about himself, too.

Ugh. So confident. So fucking hot.

"Being together implies being a couple, and we both know that's not my speed. I thought we were having fun. But then on Tuesday night..." Anton steeled himself to keep going. "He invited me over, and he *cooked* for me, and we *cuddled* on the couch and watched the final two episodes of *Bridgerton*."

Anton shuddered, as if he survived a hostage situation that would haunt him the rest of his days.

"You're acting like those are bad things."

"It was so...normal and boring and...couple-y." He shuddered. *Shuddered.* As if those adjectives were fates worse than death. "Like we were some old, married husbands squared."

"It sounded sweet." What I wouldn't give for a good cuddle? I was a wolf in the boardroom, and a cuddleslut in the bedroom.

"Seb, you know me."

I nodded. The only thing that Anton liked sweet was candy. This was a common occurrence for him. We'd had this conversation many times before.

"You keep finding yourself in these situations. You start hooking up with a guy, but then you get upset when you find out that you're actually dating. Is that technically a Catch-22?"

"Why can't things stay fun? Why do guys have to get clingy? That's not my style."

"A home cooked dinner and watching TV isn't clingy. That sounds nice!"

"That sounds like my parents." Anton made a retching sound.

"Your parents have been happily married for thirty years. You poor thing. The generational trauma you must be walking around with..."

Anton lovingly flipped me the bird.

"I'll happily trade you happily married parents for my broken home."

"Shit. I'm sorry, man." He bowed his head, contrite and unsure how to respond to my joke. Dark humor was what helped me survive watching my dad walk out, but it would never resonate with people from happy families.

"It's okay. I'm used to you sticking your foot in your mouth." Even his boneheaded statement came out suave. "I still don't understand why you're so against getting serious with a guy. Are you really that scarred by your parents' happy marriage?"

Anton shifted in his seat slightly. To anyone else, it wouldn't register. But I knew my friend well enough that it signaled internal discomfort, like we were treading close to a sensitive topic.

"Relationships either turn toxic or boring. I don't want either. I want option C: excitement, thrills, heat. I want to be kept on my toes. I see my parents, and they were madly in love once, but now they're roommates. Dad never sweeps Mom up in a kiss. He kisses her on the forehead, like she's his daughter or something. They have discussions about coupons for paper towels and making grocery lists and putting dishes in the sink."

Was it weird that I found that incredibly sweet?

"To each their own, but I don't want my life to fall into that kind of lull." Anton shook his head to underline his point. "Like, is that all there is? Having an ongoing dialogue about whose responsibility it is to load the dishwasher? Life is about living and risk and rush. You know how the top of the muffin is the best part of the muffin? After that, the stump is...fine, but it's not what you came here for. Those first few weeks of dating someone, when there's still mystery and desire, that's the muffin top. After that, it becomes Stump City and wasted carbs."

"I'm more of a croissant guy," I deadpanned.

"Actually, you love muffins. I saw you wolf down three corn muffins at that small business conference we went to last year." He tipped his head, acing a victory in his mind. In my defense, those were *really* good corn muffins. "Kamran is a good person, but he became a big, old stump."

Maybe it was for the best that I never acted on my crush. The last thing I wanted was to be a half-eaten discarded pastry in Anton's eyes.

"Goodbye, Kamran." I shrugged and gave him a half-hearted toast before taking a drink.

We downed the rest of our beer, then got refills. Mitch, the no-nonsense bear of a man who ran Stone's Throw, gave us a questionable look, a silent warning not to overdo it. We made our way through SpringFest en route to the live bands section. I followed Anton, who cut through the thick crowds with laser focus. He was determined to party, as if he had something to prove.

On stage was a cover band of dad-type guys jamming out to a Dave Matthews Band song. Anton stopped just before we entered the throng of dancers.

"Yo, is that Mr. M. from high school?"

I followed his gaze to our old chemistry teacher Mr. Mathison, standing alone under a tree shoving a deep-fried Twinkie in his mouth. We'd bumped into him a few weeks ago while refilling a vending machine at a winery. He looked the same as he had when he was our teacher. The same neat, blonde hair. The same twinkling, crystal blue eyes hiding behind thick-framed glasses. The same tall, lean figure and general obliviousness in public settings.

"He still looks good," Anton said with a pleased smile.

Mr. Mathison was always nerdy-cute. Anton and I used to joke about having a crush on him. Whenever Mr. Mathison would turn his back to the class to write on the markerboard, Anton would give me a wink and pretend to take a bite out of his ass.

"The man sure loves his Twinkies," I said, watching as Mr. M. inhaled the sugary treat, as if it was a really good corn muffin or something.

"Let's go say hi." Anton had a glint in his eye, the same glint that let me know when he'd found a new challenge. "It'll be good to catch up."

Anton beelined through festival attendees. I hurriedly caught up to him.

"Mr. M.! How's it going?" Anton clapped Mr. Mathison on the shoulder, nearly causing him to choke on his snack. "How's the Twinkie?"

"Delicious. It's deep-fried in chocolate."

"Yum," Anton said, though only in hell would he willingly eat something so decadent. "Are you out here enjoying SpringFest by yourself?"

"I came with a neighbor, but she left. I wanted to get another Twinkie. Why they don't make these year-round is a mystery. They could make a killing."

"Speaking of, I know I said this when we saw you at the winery, but you still look good, Mr. M." Anton gave Mr. Mathison a thorough once over. He had the uncanny ability to make blatant flirting come off as charming. Or maybe I was so pathetically in the bag for him that I found anything he did charming.

When it came to Mr. Mathison, Anton's assessment was on point for the most part. The dark, thick glasses made his eyes and pink lips extra vibrant. His T-shirt that read "I Tell Jokes Periodically," with "Jokes" broken up into element symbols, clung to his chest. I doubted the man hit the weightroom, but he seemed to at least know the benefits of daily pushups.

"Thank you," Mr. Mathison said bashfully at Anton's compliment. "You both still look like you're in top physical form."

"We love hitting the gym regularly." Anton shrugged, getting in a subtle arm flex. His muscles were more subdued than mine, which was just how our genetics shook out since we work out equally.

"What are you two doing now? Home from college, I presume."

"No college for us. I remember one time, you handed back my test and said you'd never used so much red pen before." Anton beamed with pride. It technically was a record he broke. He knew how to be self-deprecating while bragging at the same time.

"I guess a career in the sciences wasn't the most opportune choice," Mr. Mathison said.

"Anton could've been a kick-ass scientist if he put his mind to it." Despite us all laughing, I meant every word. Anton liked to joke about how he didn't have an academic bone in his body, but the truth was when he put his mind to something, he excelled. Both his parents were professors, which I think turned him off to school. He wanted to forge his own path. If he really wanted to be a scientist, he had the grit and work ethic to pull it off.

"We started a business operating vending machines. It's going well," I said, refusing to let our former teacher think we were slacking off.

"Can you fix the vending machine at South Rock? I have to push down hard on the F key to get it to work. It's a hindrance to getting a midday snack."

"Noted," I said. South Rock was one of our first clients.

"Mr. M., now that we're out of the classroom, I can tell you that your chemistry class was my favorite. It had the best view." Anton's lines sounded more obvious and less convincing than an actor in a porn scene.

What the hell was he doing? It was one thing to joke about having a cute teacher, but now he was blatantly hitting on Mr. Mathison. Was he just fucking around? How strong was his beer?

"I'm lucky that my classroom has a nice mountain view and doesn't overlook the parking lot."

I snorted a laugh. Was Mr. Mathison this oblivious, or was he flirting right back with Anton, making him work for a reaction?

Anton, never one to step back from a challenge, leaned closer. "I wasn't talking about the mountains, Mr. M."

The red hitting Mr. Mathison's cheeks told me he wasn't that oblivious.

"Now that we're no longer your students, we're allowed to be honest with this shit, right?" Anton clapped him on the back. "Seb, you thought Mr. M. was a stone-cold fox, right?"

For a brief moment, his flirty gaze was turned on me, making my mouth go dry.

Anton had a playful glint in his eye. I had no idea what he was up to, but if he wanted to have some fun, fine. I could have some fun, too.

"One hundred percent. Should we tell Mr. Mathison what we used to do whenever he wrote chemical equations on the board?" I flashed both guys a smirk. It seemed flirting was contagious. The weird pheromones buzzing in our little circle went straight to my head.

Anton raised his eyebrows, shocked I would bring that up. If he wanted to fuck around, I'd keep him on his toes.

"I hope the answer to that is solving said equations," Mr. Mathison said.

"Unfortunately not. We were checking out your ass, Mr. M." Anton put his hands in his pockets and lifted his shoulders. His downright cockiness toward our former teacher was intoxicating. I just...went with it, letting his vibes carry me to wherever we were going.

"We weren't very good students," I added.

"If I recall, you got an A-minus," he said.

"Uh, that's right," I said, dumbfounded as his airtight memory.

"And Anton, you squeaked by with a C-minus."

"Mr. M., that brain of yours is something to behold." Anton massaged his shoulder.

"We're no longer in the classroom. You can call me Chase."

The band switched up songs, segueing into something upbeat that got people on their feet. The space by the stage filled up with dancers.

"I love this song. Let's go dance!" Anton said to both of us. "You want to cut loose, Chase?"

"I would prefer..." Chase thought about it for a moment, a sense of realization coming over him. "Actually, I see no reason why not."

"Seb, as Bowie himself implored, let's dance." He pressed a

gentle hand at the small of my back for a fleeting moment, but it was enough to trigger a torrent of want and dirty hopes and dreams in my head.

Anton snaked a hand around Chase and led us to an opening in the parking lot-turned-concert hall. The sun was shining, the air was warm, the smell of beer and sweat enveloped us. The perfect day infused our bodies as we danced. I was usually so wound up, but there was something about the energy between the three of us that made me let go and enjoy myself. Maybe it was Anton's fun flirtiness or watching Chase slowly give in. Our arms and hands bumped into each other in a sweaty mess, sometimes by accident, or in Anton's case, sometimes intentional. There was flirting going on, but overall, we were just three guys having fun, probably having the most fun of anyone in that mess of bodies. We sang along to the music, jumped up and down, threw in some corny moves remembered from middle school dances. I tossed my head back and allowed myself to unclench for a few minutes and live in the moment like Anton. My hand grazed his lower back at one point—accidentally or intentionally, I didn't know—and his lips turned up in bliss, pleasantly surprised.

He put his hands on my shoulders, leaned his forehead against mine. "We did it, Seb. BS is going to blow up."

"Chickens. Hatching," I said.

He cupped my cheek. "Seb...relax."

Was it just me, or did his hand linger on my skin for a second longer than it should have? Before I could second-guess, the first rain drops plopped on my head. The weather turned, as the rain became heavier.

"Well this sucks," I said.

"There was a twenty percent chance of rain in the forecast, so we can't say we weren't warned," Chase said.

"It's just some water." Anton shrugged, uninterested in running to shelter like those around us. He was still possessed by the energy we had on the dance floor. "Let's hang out back at our place until the weather clears up. What do you say, Chase?"

Chase rolled it over in his head. "Sure."

"Seb?" Anton turned to me. "Sound good to you?"

Anton had something up his sleeve. The wheels continued to turn in his head. But would he really try to put the moves on a former teacher? Wasn't that too far, even for him?

I should've held back, but something deep in me wanted to see what happened, how far this game could go.

"Sounds good."

4

CHASE

As we made the trek back to Anton and Sebastian's apartment, I kept thinking about how my friends teased me when we initially bumped into them at the winery a few weeks ago. They kept telling me how hot these two former students were and that they were hitting on me.

I thought they were seeing things that weren't there, except for the hotness factor because Anton and Sebastian were very attractive.

But perhaps my friends were onto something. If we went by standard flirting criteria—big smiles, touching, complimenting someone's looks—then objectively, Anton was flirting with me. But flirting was such a nebulous space in human interaction. One person could see flirting, and another person could be friendly.

The guys lived in an older apartment building a few blocks off the downtown drag. We were soaked by the time we got back and walked up the three flights of stairs to their place. My T-shirt clung like a weight to my chest.

Anton and Sebastian whipped off their shirts right away and flung them over dining table chairs. The wetness from the rain prickled on their firm chests. Despite being so similar, Anton and Sebastian had very different body types. Anton was tall, dark, and toned, his long torso crested with a six-pack.

Nope. Make that an eight-pack.

Sebastian was several inches shorter than him. He was squat and wide, but built like a tank, with beefy arms and a broad chest. He also had an eight-pack, but it was more compact.

I technically had a six-pack, too, but only because of natural thinness caused by genetics. Not because I actually worked out. My ancestors weren't warriors. We were the medics tending to the warriors.

I got by with bodyweight exercises to keep myself spry and ward off potential health issues down the road. Studies showed that body weight could be as effective as working with heavy weights. Still, looking at these two gorgeous bodies in front of me, I had to wonder if maybe the gym had its benefits.

I told myself not to gawk at Anton and Sebastian since they'd been in my classroom only a few years ago. The temptation was very hard to resist.

Sebastian passed by me en route to his bedroom. When he left, I could feel indeterminable energy crackle between Anton and me, like we were particles that could combust by being in proximity to each other.

"You want something to drink Mr.—I mean, Chase." Anton leaned against the entranceway to the kitchen, the muscles in his arm fully on display. "It's gonna take me a while to get used to that."

"I'll take water if you have it."

"Of course we have water. We also have beer, too." Anton cocked his head slightly, as if he were daring me.

"I'll take a beer."

"Sweet. I didn't want to drink alone." He adjusted his crotch, then went into the kitchen. Was that adjustment for him or for me?

Despite not attending college, their apartment had the broke-college-student decor down to a T. The living room was modestly furnished with a futon, a coffee table, and a TV plus gaming system on another coffee table with the wires hanging behind. On the wall were a mix of sports posters for local teams, a mismatched cluster of framed pictures of family and friends, and posters with business plans for their vending machine venture. They were doing a lot of manifesting, and I admired their motivation.

Sebastian came back wearing a dry South Rock Wrestling T-shirt. His dirty blond hair was rumpled, presumably from being rubbed with a towel.

"How's the business going?" I asked.

"Good. We're continuing to grow, and we have potentially big things on the horizon."

"Not potential. Actually happening!" Anton yelled from the kitchen.

Sebastian signaled me to ignore his friend.

"Is it tough being in business for yourself?" I wanted to sit down but remembered my shirt was wet.

"We like the hustle. Yeah, it can be scary, but the upside is unlimited. It's not just about vending machines. We're building something from scratch, you know? All companies started from nothing."

It was impressive. I had no doubts that Anton and Sebastian would go far. I supposed I had *some* doubts, since the majority of businesses failed, but they were smart and driven enough to figure things out.

"Everyone has a business inside them," Sebastian said, eyes glowing with the same passion that took over me when I got into demonstrating an experiment.

"I'm not sure I do. I like teaching."

"Teaching is a business. You're the CEO of your classroom, deciding how to run it, how to best sell knowledge to clients, your students. You've built this reputation within South Rock."

I cocked my head. I'd never seen it that way, but I did enjoy the autonomy that came from teaching, even though that autonomy was perpetually encroached upon by overbearing administrations and parents.

"I'll bet you have a business inside you, Chase." Anton returned with three beers and a half-plundered family size bag of potato chips. He handed Sebastian and I beers and plopped the chips on the table. A slight sheen of sweat glistened on his skin.

"Dude, did you do push ups in the kitchen?" Sebastian asked him.

"Just a few to stay awake." Anton's pec bounced. His eyes flicked to me making sure I caught it. My dick twitched in my pants. Yes, as a matter of fact, I did see it. "I like to do push-ups randomly during the day. It keeps me fresh."

"Fresh for what?" I asked, trying to ignore the erection forming in my jeans.

"Here." Sebastian threw his roommate a T-shirt. "I pulled one from your dresser."

"I'm good. I'll air dry."

Sebastian rolled his eyes. "Fine."

"Did you want a dry shirt, Chase?" Anton pulled at my sopping wet T-shirt. "You're soaked. You're going to catch a cold."

I doubted that. I was feeling hot all of a sudden. But pneumonia wasn't something to ignore. Anton handed me the shirt he refused to wear, our fingers touching for a second under the fabric.

"The bathroom is the first door on the left," Sebastian said.

"You can just change here. We've all been in locker rooms before." Anton sipped his beer while remaining in place.

"Anton, the man wants some privacy. You can change in the bathroom." Sebastian's face tensed for a moment before pointing me down the hall.

I had to smile at the fluffy blue toilet seat cover in the bathroom. That had to come from a mother or concerned aunt.

I whipped off my wet shirt and toweled myself dry. Unfortunately, all the friction from the towel only made my erection more prominent. There was something sexy about being shirtless in someone's apartment when they were also shirtless. I began rattling off elements on the periodic table to keep myself from thinking about Anton's chest and Sebastian's arms. *Are you there, Hydrogen? It's me, Chase.*

Anton sat on the futon flipping through his streaming menu when I returned. Sebastian sat in a wheeled office chair to the side. The rain came down in sheets outside, which inexplicably made me more aroused. I'd lived in my body for thirty years, and yet it remained a mystery to me.

"Chase, pop a squat. I was looking for something to watch." Anton patted the empty area next to him, setting off a lash of desire within me. For a moment, I forgot I was in the company of former students and could only focus on being in the middle of two muscular, very attractive men. Nothing about this afternoon had gone according to my schedule, and all the unpredictability was causing me to have very dirty thoughts.

I plopped down beside him leaving an ample, but not insulting, amount of space between us. He had a magnetic pull to him that couldn't keep me far.

"Anything here look good to you?" Anton asked. "I don't watch a ton of TV."

A familiar foursome of faces popped up on screen.

"Have you ever watched *Schitt's Creek*?" I asked.

He and Sebastian shook their heads no.

"I've heard of it," Sebastian said.

"It's funny. You'll want to start on season two. The first season's a little slow. The characters and humor need some time to come into their own."

"Is that the mom from *Home Alone*?" Anton asked.

"Correct."

"Works for me. Seb?"

"Yeah. I may go out and get something to eat." Sebastian shrugged, the tension from before continuing to linger on his face and tighten his jaw. As proof that horniness had zero logic to it, his stonefaced demeanor turned me on. Perhaps all the pheromones Anton was pumping out were messing with my head.

"In this weather? It's still cats and dogs out there." Anton clicked on *Schitt's Creek*. He turned to me with a raised eyebrow. "Season two. Let's fucking go."

His mighty, outstretched hand navigated the remote to the season two tab. I nodded and rested my hands in my lap in the hopes they would hide the shenanigans still happening in my pants.

My friends loved to joke about how oblivious I could be, but I didn't need an electron microscope to determine that Anton was hitting on me.

Anton shut off the floor lamp, leaving the apartment shrouded in gray. He turned on *Schitt's Creek*. The Rose family helped me calm down. *Schitt's Creek* was my happy place. I was able to concentrate on the show and stop wondering about the guy next to me.

Each episode was approximately twenty-two minutes, and it took people on average three episodes to decide if they liked a show, so that meant I had sixty-six minutes to figure out what was happening here. Did I want things to progress, or did I want to be the responsible adult in the room?

So far, judging by the howls of laughter, Anton seemed to

enjoy the show. He'd rub my knee here and there, as if to say *Can you believe this family?*

The squeak of Sebastian's desk chair broke through a few times during the episode.

"Sebastian, you don't seem comfortable. We can make room on the futon," I said.

"I'm fine."

"You don't seem fine," Anton said.

"I'll scoot down." I shuffled closer to Anton. He wrapped his arm around my back and pulled me flush against him, which I did not mind at all. My objections against getting too close to a former student became weaker and weaker. More dirty thoughts played in my mind. My pants got even tighter.

"Seb, come on," Anton coaxed. "Watch some TV with us."

Sebastian blew out a resigned breath and squeezed in next to me. Three grown men on one futon was a challenge, but we made it work.

"There we go. You good, Chase?" Anton asked, his thumb massaging circles on my shoulder.

Was I good? Well, the gravitational pull of collapsing stars in the galaxy was so strong that it could transform carbon molecules into oxygen. But collapsing stars had nothing on the pull of being sandwiched between Anton and Sebastian.

Anton was looking at me, waiting for my answer. Was I good? I gave him a thumbs up.

"Awesome." Anton turned the episode back on.

I was in a testosterone sandwich, the pheromones and hormones circling around me, impacting my brain chemistry. The darkness and rain and Anton's glimmer and Sebastian's steely frame all combined into a powerful concoction. In other words, holy fuck was all this close proximity making me horny.

Anton moved and let his hand rest against my leg. He kept looking over at me, making me meet his stare.

Then, as the second episode started, his hand dragged up my thigh.

Let's look at this logically, Chase. You are a gay man scrunched in between two gay men that you find attractive. It's only natural to be stimulated, but that doesn't mean you need to act on your impulses.

Brain, you make a good point. I'm still going to ignore you, the way I ignore my dentist when he tells me to lay off Twinkies.

I couldn't wait until we reached sixty-six minutes.

So I put my hand on his crotch.

Anton's eyes burst open. Whatever was on his flirting agenda, it was not this. I stroked him over his shorts, his thick cock pulsing under my touch. I let myself get sucked into the collapsing star and go Type II Supernova. Who knew astrophysics could be so sexy?

Anton tried to be quiet, but a moan escaped his lips. I glanced over at Sebastian, feeling a twinge of guilt for letting horniness override my manners as a guest. But he seemed intrigued by what we were doing. He stared at Anton's crouch, pupils wide.

And because natural selection had blessed me with two working hands, I grabbed Sebastian's crotch and unzipped both their flies at the same time.

5

SEBASTIAN

What the fuck was going on? On screen, siblings David and Alexis bickered while in the apartment, it was dead silence.

Chase watched *Schitt's Creek* while his hands went to work. I looked over at Anton, whose shocked and excited expression matched what I felt. He gave a head nod and a thumbs up.

I should've been questioning this whole thing, but...it felt too good. It'd been a while since I hooked up with someone. Anton let out a low moan as Chase reached inside his pants. It was a sexy, beautiful moan, one that I'd dreamed about hearing.

Chase unbuttoned my pants. My cock strained against my white boxer briefs. A sexy grin lined his thin lips. Was there anything hotter than a nerd with a wild side?

I peeked over to see what was happening on the other side of the futon. Anton yanked open his shorts so fast the top button almost came off. He shoved them down to the floor.

And there it was. Despite sharing a locker room with him all through high school, I never sneaked a peek. That would be a breach of friendship. But in this case...this was new terrain.

Holy hell, what a beautiful dick. Long and thick, standing up tall and eager, a trimmed bush around the base. It was better than what I'd dreamed about, capped off with his lips puckered into a transcendent moan.

"Fuck, Mr. M. Yeah." Anton pulled Chase to him for a quick kiss, a kiss that I found incredibly hot while gashing my heart.

Chase spat into each of his palms and went back to work. His slick hand glided up and down my cock. I arched my back to meet his strokes. This was all so unexpected and strange, more so because of the background noise of the *Home Alone* mom's weird accent, but damn was it hot. I was a planner, and getting jerked off by my old chemistry teacher was not in the schedule for today.

I whipped off my shirt. Anton and I grabbed a side of Chase's shirt and pulled it over his head. We each palmed his milky, smooth skin, fingers sliding over the modest grooves of his chest and flat stomach. Chase stroked us harder. My cock strained for release, yet I didn't want to come before Anton and have him see me as a premature ejaculator.

"Stand up," Chase said, voice husky. He fell to his knees between us, hungry for us, his eyes blazing with heat.

He took me in his mouth, and I nearly melted on the spot. His tongue rolled around my cockhead, waves of pleasure hitting me, made even sexier as I watched him stroke Anton. Anton's incredible body was on display for me, his cock ragingly hard and thick. He checked out my body and my dick, too. I hoped he liked what he saw. His eyes widened at me, as if to say *Can you fucking believe this?*

No, I couldn't.

Chase moaned against my cock. I threw my head back, and all the pressure of life faded away.

"Yes," I eked out in a whisper. "Suck me."

Chase looked up at me, my dick on his tongue, his thick

glasses fogged up, a sneaky smile on his lips. Teach was thoroughly enjoying himself.

He moved over to Anton, taking him down to the base. In an inverse of our body types, Anton's dick was thicker, but mine was longer. I saved it to my eternal memory. It was better than I'd imagined.

"Suck that cock, Mr. M. Just like that. Feels so good." Anton threaded his fingers through Chase's hair and pulled him closer. Chase's free hand remained wrapped around my dick, giving me light strokes that managed to bring me closer to the edge.

I thought I'd heard all of Anton's sounds by now. But the grunt he emitted was different from the ones uttered during wrestling matches, different from the ones he uttered while eating a delicious burger, different from the ones let out during a heavy bench press. These grunts filling the apartment now were hungry and primal and vulnerable, and they made my dick swell. If this was as close to having sex with Anton as I'd get, I wasn't complaining.

Anton pulled out of Chase's mouth and smacked his dick on his tongue. Rather than letting this happen to him, Anton was taking control in the sexiest way. He held Chase's head and let his cock slide in and out of his mouth.

"Lick my balls," he commanded. "Don't stop stroking." He put Chase's hand back around his shaft. Chase looked up at him with obedient eyes.

"Now back to Seb," he said.

Chase nodded and turned my way. Anton guided his head to my crotch. My balls ached for release as he took me back in his warm mouth, moaning against my shaft. My fun hot-for-teacher crush was now a full-on fantasy.

"Take him all, Mr. M." Anton firmly pushed Chase's head forward, making him deep throat me, sending me to the next level. My knees buckled with the crushing load of impending orgasm.

"Holy fuck," I cried out, unable to resist the ecstasy flooding my veins. Chase took me with ease and eagerness, his red lips spit shined.

My eyes flickered open and closed, trying to focus. They settled on Anton, watching us, watching me with an intensity I'd never felt from him before.

"So fucking hot," Anton said. "Take that thick cock again."

Anton pushed Chase forward, giving me another rush of heat as Teach deep-throated me. Anton pulled his head back, my cock drenched in Chase's saliva. Anton turned him back to his own cock, where Chase didn't need any command to take him to the base.

"Yes. That's it. Just like that." Anton let out another grunt, his voice cracking as he reached new levels of pleasure.

I didn't think things could get hotter, but then Chase brought back our dicks together in his mouth. The heat of Anton's cock-head pulsed against mine. A streak of my pre-come landed on my shaft before Chase licked both our cocks clean.

"Chase, I'm gonna come. Holy shit, I'm gonna come," Anton cried out.

I wanted to savor the victory of not coming first, but it didn't matter in the moment. It didn't matter because I got to watch Anton lose control, his cocky veneer vanishing as his body shook with orgasm. His dark eyes fixed on me, making us experience this moment together.

"Fill his mouth with your come, Anton," I commanded.

He pulled me to him and quieted me with a heat-filled kiss that turned into crying against my lips as he emptied himself in Chase's mouth.

Anton and I were kissing.

Anton was kissing me.

His taste was on my tongue, his breath filled my lungs. Years of longing for my best friend. So much for pushing down my feelings. I held him upright as the orgasm pummeled his body, my hands pressing against his slick chest. I inhaled his sweaty scent before he pulled away.

"Damn," he said, returning to his cool self.

Was he talking about the blow job or the kiss?

Before I could get an answer, Chase took me back in his mouth, where I exploded in record time, unleashing waves of release that mixed with Anton's.

Chase looked up at us, a pleased grin on his face and a drop of come on his right lens. He got to his feet and grabbed a dry shirt from the futon. Anton and I watched him, both completely naked, shorts at our ankles, dazed looks on our faces.

"Always fun catching up with former students," he said, before calmly exiting our apartment.

6

CHASE

I got to school early Monday morning to set up for an experiment I was having my classes run. I loved the quiet in the building before the rush of students. It gave me time to think and relax.

"Hey hey hey, science man. How was your weekend?" Everett popped his head into my classroom, his arms full of wigs.

So much for quiet reflection.

"It was good. You're here early," I said.

"Principal Aguilar is making me do an inventory of all props and costumes because the storage closet can't hold all of them."

That sounded like a metaphor for Everett himself. Unrestrained by a closet, exploding with drama.

"Maybe if I do a good job with it, he'll reconsider his position on using live explosives on stage." Everett looked down at his full arms. "Why did I make us buy all these wigs?"

"Character authenticity?" I suggested.

He shrugged. That answer was probably better than the real one.

"Did you wind up making it to SpringFest?" he asked.

"I did make it to SpringFest," I said.

"Did you get your Twinkie?"

"As a matter of fact, I got two." I couldn't stop the smile from curling on my lips. Not only because of my witty wordplay, but because my mind returned to that apartment on Saturday. What a time...

Everett narrowed his eyes at me. "Seems like you really enjoyed your snacks."

"Oh, I did." I strummed my fingers on my desk, deliberating on whether I should spill the proverbial beans. My friends and I had a very open relationship. The nature of my Saturday rendezvous aligned with our frequent topics of conversations in our circle. And a part of me was curious to see Everett's reaction, which was always dialed up to eleven.

"What is it, Chase?"

I made sure nobody was walking in the hall. "At SpringFest, I ran into two former students. They were big fans of my class." Bigger fans than I ever expected considering they were B and C students.

"Oh, nice. It's always fun catching up with old students."

"I actually did more than catch up with them."

Everett crinkled his brow. "What does that mean? Did y'all go out to dinner?"

"We went back to their apartment where I proceeded to fellate them while watching an episode of *Schitt's Creek*, which they'd never seen."

Everett's pile of wigs fell to the floor, fanning out in fake hair diffusion.

"Chase." His eyes bugged out. "Are you serious?"

"Yes."

"I'm speechless."

"Me, too. Who hasn't watched *Schitt's Creek*? It's a truly wonderful show."

Everett stepped over the wig pile and marched into my classroom. He stopped just short of my desk, unsure whether to continue. I had a suspicion that Everett was staging his reaction entrance in real time.

"Chase..."

"Hmm?"

I expected Everett to be surprised, but he almost seemed angrily surprised.

"You might want to pick up your wigs. You don't want them to accumulate dirt, which would be hard to get out."

"Forget the wigs." Everett collapsed against the markerboard. "Chase, if you don't give me details on what the hell happened, I am going to scream at the top of my lungs."

I knew Everett well. He wasn't bluffing.

———

AFTER TELLING Everett the story of what happened, he dragged me to the teacher's lounge, where Amos and Julian were drinking coffee with their respective boyfriends.

"Amos, Julian. Can we speak to you outside?" Everett called from the doorway, his voice tense and stern. Were we all in trouble?

Seamus, Julian's boyfriend, did the requisite Ooooooh that all students uttered when one of their own was called to the principal's office.

"What happened? Everett, you look like you've seen a ghost," Amos said once we all got into the hall. Everett led us down the quiet corridor, out of earshot of the teacher's lounge.

"Is everything okay?" Julian asked.

Everett was getting comically red. He was a pale redhead, and that skintone led itself to easily showing one's emotions. His boyfriend would call him Red Hulk whenever Everett got angry, which only made Everett's shade darken.

"Everything is not okay!" Everett said. "Chase, are you going to tell them what you did this weekend?"

"Certainly," I said, only to be cut off by Everett a second later.

"CHASE. HAD. A. THREESOME," he whisper-yelled.

"Oh?" Amos deliberated for a moment, then shrugged his shoulders. "Okay. Cool."

"Sounds like a fun time," Julian said.

"WITH. TWO. FORMER. STUDENTS."

"What?" Amos yelled, no whisper.

"Shut the front door." Julian's eyes bulged from his head.

"Usually I'm good at reading your reactions, but I must say I'm confused at the moment." I tipped my head, trying to make sense of the mix of emotions criss-crossing my friends' faces. "Is this a bad thing?"

"No, not bad. We're not mad. We're just...taken aback," said Amos.

"We're in shock. We've fallen through the ice on a frozen lake, and we're in hypothermic, motherfucking shock," Everett said.

"What Everett means to say is that we're excited to hear more." Julian could've been a press secretary in another life as he had a skill in translating Everett's histrionics.

"We bumped into each other at SpringFest. We talked, we danced, it started to rain, we went back to their apartment. I'm loath to use cliches, but one thing really did lead to another."

We paused my interrogation as our kindly old school librarian Mrs. Peterson passed our huddle.

"Hello, Mrs. Peterson," we all said as pleasantly as could be.

"Hello, boys! Happy Monday!"

We watched her go until she turned the corner. Then the inquisition continued.

"There's a gap in there. How did it go from getting dry at their apartment to getting it on?" Amos asked.

"Yeah, who initiated it?" Everett crossed his arms.

"Well...I did."

"How? You don't even like asking the waiter for extra napkins when we go out to eat," Amos said.

"We were watching TV."

"What show?" Julian asked.

"*Schitt's Creek*," Everett shot back, admonishing him for interrupting. "And what does it matter what show it was, J? Go on," he told me.

"We were watching TV and..." Here was the part that I kept getting stuck on, as pure lust had defied my internal logic. Usually I could keep myself in check, but the combination of Anton and Sebastian proved too much to resist. "I made the first move. I believe the technical, Urban Dictionary term is skiing."

Amos had to hold out his hands in fists like he was holding two ski poles to get the reference.

"And from there, I progressed things by getting on my knees. I believe the position we were all in was the Eiffel Tower. You're the French scholar, Julian, so you can confirm."

"That sounds right," Julian said, turning red.

"So it was all you. Huh." Everett scratched his head.

Huh seemed to be the appropriate reaction. I'd been forward when it came to sex before. I wasn't shy about my urges when I was with a guy. But in those instances, I had been on dates or had arranged to hook up. On Saturday, there was no similar agenda or pretense. We were merely hanging out. Yet there was this nebulous buzz in the air that hung between all three of us, something I didn't know if I could put into words for my friends. It was like the electrostatic activity that created the adhesive forces that pulled molecules of different substances together. I definitely couldn't put *that* into words for my friends.

Essentially, I didn't out of nowhere decide to initiate a three-some. Invisible tracks had been laid, even if we couldn't see them.

"Who were the guys? I wonder if I had them," Julian said.

"You met them at the winery for your birthday. They were restocking their vending machine."

"Shut up. Those two hot jocks who were obviously hitting on you?" Amos said. "Now this all makes more sense."

"I stand by my previous protestation that they were being friendly, not flirtatious." Sebastian and Anton were happy to see me a few months ago, but perhaps Amos was right. I could feel the mess of uncertainty creeping into my life.

"I know it's not ideal. It was a pleasurable time for all, but there won't be a repeat." I nodded my head to confirm my stance and continued walking down the hall into the breezeway that connected the "new" addition to South Rock that was added on in the late 90s.

My friends caught up to me. Fresh morning sun blasted through the windows of the breezeway.

"Why not?" Everett asked. "If the three of you had a good time, why not do it again?"

"They're students."

"Former students," he said.

"I shouldn't."

"Your answer isn't rooted in logic," Julian said, which felt like an especially brutal twist of the knife. He was the reasonable friend in our life, and he was on board with this?

"J is right. Let's look at this logically. The three of you are sexually attracted to each other. You're all consenting adults. Humans are wired to seek out pleasurable experiences. If you don't see them again, you're bitchslapping Mother Nature." Even Everett's logic had a flair for drama, though unfortunately, he wasn't completely wrong.

I could feel the mess boarding the train and riding on those aforementioned invisible tracks, headed straight for my orderly life.

"I'll take your sentiment under consideration," I offered. "But for now, I'd prefer that it remain a one-off experience."

"An ad hoc fuck?" Amos quipped.

"Chase, you're kicking a gift horse in the mouth when you should be putting two dicks in there." Everett brushed his fiery red hair out of his eyes.

"That's a horrible metaphor, not to mention animal abuse," I told him.

I appreciated that my friends were blunt and honest and had my wellbeing at heart, even if for them, my sexual wellbeing was what mattered most. I was meant to be a noble gas, standing alone, no need to link my molecules with others.

"Hey." A smirk spread across Julian's face as he pointed to the trophy case that happened to be right in front of us.

The trophy case commemorated the victories of South Rock's wrestling team. In the center of the case was a photo of the top two wrestlers from the school's most recent regional championship.

Anton and Sebastian.

I telepathically willed my friends not to say anything. It was a coincidence, that was all.

"Amos, you forgot your coffee." Hutch joined us holding a lukewarm styrofoam cup out to his boyfriend.

"Thanks," Amos said while trying to hold back laughter.

"What's so funny?" Hutch asked. He looked at Julian and Everett, who had similar struggles keeping a straight face.

Even Sebastian and Anton seemed to be smirking at me through the case.

7

———

ANTON

I woke up Monday morning and stared at my ceiling. The weekend was a blur.

Correction: Everything that happened after I spooged in my old teacher's mouth was a fucking blur. Everything that happened during *Schitt's Creek*: crystal clear.

I was a hungover zombie for the rest of Saturday and Sunday. Maybe I cleaned my apartment and did laundry? Maybe I made myself some chicken breast on the George Foreman grill?

My body was on autopilot. My mind was back on that futon, going over the events of Saturday afternoon.

What a day. What a fucking day. I could not get it out of my head. None of it. It was officially the wildest, hottest day of my life. It made me feel alive, a bigger endorphin rush than my best workouts.

Watching Chase go from quiet, nerdy guy to quiet, nerdy guy who was giving two blow jobs at once was insanely sexy. Anytime I'd thought of him this weekend, I'd gotten an instant boner. I kept thinking about the sneaky smiles that lit up his face, and how he could suddenly take control like when he ordered Sebastian and me to stand up so he could blow us. There was a confident calm brewing under his quirky exterior, like a burst of caramel at the center of a chocolate.

"Hey." Sebastian knocked at my door. "We have our meeting with Craig Wimmer this morning. We need to leave in twenty-five minutes."

"Cool," I yelled back.

There was also Sebastian. We hadn't really spoken post-three-some. Like, we weren't ignoring each other or avoiding each other, but we kept conversation strictly to preparing for the meeting. We played lots of video games, too, but fortunately, we only had to look at the TV screen.

It was a weird gray area for us. We were best buds, forged in the fire of wrestling and running a business. We were always talking about everything.

I wasn't sure how to approach this, though. Did I laugh it off as a one-time thing? Did we need to have The Conversation about how this shouldn't affect our friendship and/or business?

My instinct was the former. The hookup was epic shit, after all. But I didn't want it to be a one-time thing. The adult in me said that The Conversation needed to be had. Sebastian could be so damn hard to read at times. His no-nonsense expression was stamped on his face all weekend. Was he upset? Was he focused on the Hollis meeting? Was he confused?

I hopped in the shower and let the hot water wake me up. Sebastian had made us buy this nice, quasi-fancy soap at the start of the year. He'd read that it was the same brand used by five-star hotels. He wanted us to smell like successful, rich businessmen, so that we could believe our own hype on a visceral level.

But this morning, I wasn't thinking about smelling like a rich dude. I kept thinking of the way Sebastian smelled when we kissed. A little musky, a little salty, a little like beer. Flashes of his heavy-lidded eyes seared into my brain, as did the tiny gasp of surprised breath when I pulled him into a kiss.

A kiss.

I kissed my best friend.

I'd always known Sebastian was attractive, but seeing him naked, hard, and groaning with want was on another level. He was *hot*.

So hot that I was rock hard in the shower, something I took care of quickly. (The rich people soap made for excellent lubricant.) One could not go into an important business meeting with a loaded gun.

After I finished and washed off, I stepped out of the shower, wrapped a towel around myself, rubbed product through my hands, and styled my hair in the mirror. There were times over the years when I'd suspected that Sebastian might have had a little crush on me—the way his face would change when I discussed hookups, a look here and there that might've lasted just a bit too long.

Was it a crush, or was I reading into things and being a tad self-absorbed?

"Nah," I said to myself. Sebastian was my friend.

"You almost done in there?" Sebastian asked through the door.

"Yeah." I finished getting my hair in position with a little upturn in the front. I opened the door to a shirtless Sebastian. Our chests almost touched.

I'd seen Sebastian shirtless a zillion times. Why was it making my stomach flip now?

"Hey," I said.

"I need to, uh, get in there." Sebastian pointed past me, with the same deer-in-the-highlights look I had to be sporting.

"Cool, yeah." Goosebumps danced up my spine as I stepped aside. I eyed the bulge in his pants, knowing what lay underneath.

Yeah, The Conversation definitely needed to be had.

"Listen," I said.

Sebastian turned from the mirror. "What?"

"Um, yeah, so maybe we should talk…"

"About what?"

"The, uh…" If this was a sign of my verbal skills for today, we were epically fucked. All I could do was point to the living room.

"Is it about the meeting?"

No, it was absolutely not, but I took the easy way out.

"Yeah. Are you feeling good?" I asked.

I usually wasn't this much of a chicken. But this wasn't some guy I was letting down with a standard "It's not you. It's me." speech. This was Sebastian, who was sporting a frustratingly unreadable face at the moment.

"I'm feeling great," Sebastian said flatly. "We're prepared. We have a great business. Craig is going to be blown away."

"Yeah, totally."

"Cool. Well, you can't go into Hollis Property Management wearing that." He cracked a smile.

I suddenly felt very naked under my towel. I hightailed it to my bedroom before I sprouted wood in front of my friend.

I appreciated Sebastian never taking his eyes off the ball. He sacrificed a lot for Beverage Solutions. With his intellect, he could have done anything he wanted. He had unlimited paths to any career. And he chose operating vending machines with me. I wasn't going to fuck things up with weird thoughts and feelings about one wild night. Sebastian didn't have a crush on me. It was the heat of the threesome messing with my head. It was still for the best that we at least acknowledged the elephant in the room, even if just to laugh it off. But we could do that later.

This morning, we had a meeting to crush.

———

THE HOLLIS HEADQUARTERS were located at the end of a cul-de-sac in an office park with a large man made lake and fountain in front of their parking lot. We'd never tried to sell our services to a company with their own lake and fountain.

This was the big leagues.

"They're a company like all of our other clients. Doesn't matter the size of their building," I said.

"We got this," Sebastian said.

We bumped fists and headed inside.

The lobby was buzzing with employees coming to work. They weren't nervous. They were enjoying their coffee and chit chat. This was a regular day for them.

The receptionist gave us passes and instructed us to head to the third floor.

"Third floor. Not the top floor," I noted in the elevator.

"Makes sense. Craig is head of procurement, but he's likely not the final decision maker. He's the layer before the final C-suite approval," Sebastian said.

"True." Sebastian was the researcher of the two of us. He probably knew the names of every Hollis VP already. I noticed a hint of shaving cream just under his jaw. "You missed a little."

I licked my thumb and went to wipe it off when Sebastian smacked my hand away. Hard. He was tightly coiled, but was it just because of the meeting?

The elevator doors opened, and we walked to Craig's office in silence. His office was small and windowless, made to feel even smaller because of the hefty man behind the desk. He had a bushy beard, a combover, and wire-framed glasses perched on his large head. He reminded me of many of my friends' dads, a not-uncommon feeling I had on sales calls.

"Good morning." I knocked on the doorway to get his attention from his computer.

"Can I help you?" he asked.

"It's Anton and Sebastian from Beverage Solutions. We have a meeting on the books for eight-thirty," Sebastian said.

"We do?" Craig looked at his computer. "Oh, I see we do."

He looked up at us again, likely calculating the realization that he couldn't shoo us away as easily as he could hang up.

"I have a hard stop at nine. I mean it. I can't go a minute over," he said.

"Not a problem. We only need twenty minutes to blow your mind," I said.

"Okay," he said, slightly amused. "Shut the door. Have a seat."

As soon as the door shut, I clicked into sales mode. Whatever awkwardness lay between Sebastian and me waited outside of Craig's office. Sebastian pulled out his tablet. While we had a few slides prepared, we knew that the crux of this meeting would live and die on how well we communicated. Sales guys who relied heavily on cookie-cutter slides easily lost their prospects. Nobody liked to be sold to or talked at. The biggest thing I'd learned since starting this business was that more than anything, people wanted to be heard.

In the span of sixteen minutes, Sebastian and I delivered one of our best presentations in company history. We were on fire. Sebastian hit Craig with data, which I shaded in with some WII FM (What's In It For Me). Seb had this ability to crunch numbers and still make them sound compelling, whereas I went cross-eyed when I stared at an Excel sheet for too long. His brains and my charms worked wonders. Our hand off was seamless, our energy was contagious, and our pitch was compelling as hell. Craig was riveted. Somewhere in the middle of the meeting, our presentation became a conversation, with Craig chiming in with questions and background on Hollis's operations.

This was why I could never have a regular, boring job. This was why the rough patches of entrepreneurship were worth it. A nine-to-five couldn't make me feel this alive.

I kept looking over at Sebastian as he refuted objections and concerns with ease, his disarming smile and bright eyes brimming with fiery intelligence. My brain cut back to Saturday and the image of Sebastian throwing his head back in abandon as he came.

Sebastian glanced over at me, waiting for me to chime in.

Shit. Stupid brain.

"What Anton means to say is that Hollis can provide its tenants with a superior vending machine experience and improve the value of your rentals. It's the little things that people remember."

"So Craig, what do we need to do to win your business?" I asked, getting back into the groove. I loved asking this question. It was direct and caught people off guard, which was when we usually got the most honest responses.

Craig heaved out a surprised breath, then cracked a smile at the audacity. "Uh...I've never been asked that."

Sebastian and I shared a glance. We didn't interrupt or cut in. We let the silence hang in the air, forcing him to fill it. We knew that letting a prospect continue to talk rather than trying to put words in his mouth would be far more powerful.

"I like your product and your price. The real decision maker is our CEO, Jim Hollis himself. Because of ballooning costs elsewhere, he's now more involved in granular spending. Very involved. Look, what we have works well for us."

"Works well? What happens if your current supplier continues to raise prices on you while the quality of service declines?" I asked.

"We'll have to cross that bridge if and when we come to it."

"You could score points with Jim by showing initiative on ways to reduce spend," Sebastian added.

Craig see-sawed his head. "That is true. It's best that we bring in Jim for a conversation. He's a straight shooter, an interesting character. I'm game to make this change. If you can win over Jim, then you'll have a deal."

As Craig pulled up his calendar, I tried not to have pure joy burst across my face like I was a toddler getting the lollipop he so desperately wanted.

"He has a busy schedule, let me see..." Craig clicked his tongue as he scanned his computer. "He can do this day and time on the eleventh of June."

"June? That's next month," I said. The longer the gap between meetings, the quicker interest cooled.

"He's a busy man. That's the soonest he has open."

Sebastian and I traded glances, knowing neither we nor Craig had the ability to reshape Jim Hollis's calendar.

"Works for us," I said, determined to keep momentum alive for the next month.

Sebastian and I shook his hand and thanked him for his time. We pretended to be adults all the way down the elevator and all the way through the lobby. We waited until we got into my car to scream at the top of our lungs.

"HOLY SHIT!" I yelled.

"WE HAVE A MEETING WITH THE CEO!" Sebastian yelled back.

Adrenaline had guided me through our meeting, and I was just now coming back to earth.

"You were amazing in there. The way you swatted away his objections. Brilliant," he said.

"I'm not the sharpest crayon in the box, but I have my moments."

"Oh, shut up." Sebastian gave me a playful shove. "Shit. I can't believe this."

I was so overcome that when Sebastian turned to me with watery eyes, I threaded my fingers through his hair and pulled him close, our foreheads touching. We'd done this many a time in

the past: before championship wrestling meets, after we gradu-
ated. It was like our version of a mindmeld.

It all felt different now. More intimate. Our hearts were
melding as much as our minds. We were post-whatever Saturday
was. Our dicks had rubbed against each other.

Sebastian pulled back, always the sensible one.

"We have to start prepping. We need to pull out all the stops,"
he said.

But I wasn't ready to return to business, though. There was no
way I could continue with life as usual until The Conversation
was had.

"Seb," I said, a nervous lump in my throat. "We need to talk."

8

SEBASTIAN

I kept my fingers wrapped around the steering wheel. Anton wasn't one for talking about things. Correction: the guy loved to talk. He schmoozed and chit chatted and shot the shit. But talk? This kind of talk? The kind of talk that could veer into serious territory...that wasn't like Anton.

"What did you want to talk about?" I asked.

"Yo, so I think maybe..." His face twisted with internal struggle, which made it even cuter. He swept his hand as if he were clearing a table, a classic Anton move that meant a do-over. "Look, we need to air things out about Saturday. It was wild. Just get everything out in the open."

That was the problem. Everything *was* out in the open, most notably our dicks.

"Anton, we don't need to...it was..." Hot. Epically, earth-shatteringly hot. "It happened, it was a good time. And it's cool, you know."

It was a very good time. But I was not cool about it. My mind was all sorts of screwed up. Anton and I were naked together, and he kissed me, and all those feelings that I told myself to forget returned to the surface. I was still hopelessly in love with my best friend, and we'd crossed a line that couldn't be undone. For Anton, it was a wild, impulsive afternoon. For me, it was a revelation. I couldn't let my feelings jeopardize our business at such a crucial moment.

"Pull over," he said.

"No."

"No?"

"Why do I need to pull over?" I asked. We could have a conversation while driving. It was better that way. I didn't have to look at him as he told me Saturday was an epic mistake.

"Just do it, Seb. I don't want to drive back in awkward silence."

Won't there be awkward silence once we talk about it?

I turned right into the parking lot for a Revolutionary War site that we'd visited on a field trip years ago. Anton had gotten yelled at for trying to climb into the cannon.

I put the car in park and turned to my friend, prepared to face the firing squad aimed at my heart.

"Dude, we had a threesome. Our lips and our dicks touched." Anton was not one for subtlety. His best quality was cutting to the chase and being direct. A great quality in a salesman, but in a friend, it made my stomach clamp up. "We need to talk about it because things have been weird all weekend. I don't want us to keep tiptoeing around this thing. Our friendship and partnership are too important to me."

"Okay, then talk," I said. Like hell was I going first. Not when my head was still a mess.

"How are you doing?"

"That's not fair. You're supposed to talk first." I shifted in my seat, my eyes narrowing at him. "How are you doing?"

"I loved it. I loved every second of it."

"You did?" I asked, my voice trembling a touch at Anton's directness.

"I can't stop thinking about it."

What parts, I wanted to ask. *The Chase parts or the Sebastian parts?*

"I know it's weird. My old teacher and my best friend. But I don't regret it. It was freeing, like we just let ourselves be." Anton shrugged, then glanced at me. It was my turn to speak.

I needed air. I opened the door and vaulted out of the driver's seat, a warm breeze hitting my face. I walked up to the infamous cannon and ran my fingers along the slick black shell.

"Seb!" Anton jogged up to me. "What's going on?"

Now was the time to tell him. *I am in love with you, Anton. Feeling your lips on mine was a transcendent experience, better than all my dreams and fantasies.* The words were on my tongue, begging to be set free.

"Look, Seb. I know this is a weird thing to talk about, but I think we need to have this conversation. I didn't mean to make things weird. But I'm going to make them weirder: I liked what we did, and I want to do it again."

My heart raced inside my chest. "You do?"

"Fuck yeah. It was amazing. How was the experience for you?"

"Incredible," I said with a sigh as I released the word from my chest. "Really incredible."

"Do you feel weird?"

"Yeah, a little. Or a lot. But not in a bad, regretful way." I couldn't get over how Anton was staring at me, his dark eyes staring into me like I'd always wanted. Again, far better than my dreams. "I want to do it again. And again."

"Who knew our nerdy chemistry teacher was such a freak?"

"Not me."

"Yeah, me neither. Do you remember when he told us to stand up and he dropped to his knees?"

I nodded emphatically. I would never forget it for multiple reasons. Chase was cute, and experiencing him go from awkward nerd to lustful nerd was supremely hot. As was watching Anton drop his pants and being able to drink in his whole body.

"Was that your first threesome?" I asked him. Anton had more sexual experience compared to me. That was one area where I didn't feel like competing, though.

"Yeah. You guys popped my ménage a cherry."

A quick gust of relief blew within me. It was a first we got to experience together.

He dipped his head to me, wondering the same. As if it were even a question.

"Yeah. Total newb," I said.

"Figured."

"Shut up, man." I smacked his chest.

"It was hot watching you letting yourself lose control."

"You enjoyed that, huh?" I cocked a playful eyebrow and closed the space between us. A newfound boldness took hold of me. "I enjoyed...all of it. I hate to inflate your ego, but you have a very nice body. And the way you made Chase deep throat me was something I'd never forget."

Hell, I'd never forget a second of that afternoon, including the exact episode of *Schitt's Creek* that was on when Chase made his move.

Anton let a finger slink down my arm. "We'll have to do it again. See if lightning can strike twice. You, me, and Chase."

Record. Fucking. Scratch.

This wasn't about us. This wasn't about two friends coming together finally. It was about having another threesome.

"There was something about the three of us that just clicked. We'll have to see if Chase is up for it. He zipped out of our apartment like he was a fugitive. Is it cool if I talk to him about maybe hanging out again?"

Hanging out. Ugh, was there a worse expression that a hopelessly in love friend had to hear?

Anton studied my eyes. Damn him for knowing all the telltale signs of my shifting thoughts.

"Seb, how does that sound to you? Be honest with me, please. If you don't want to do it again, I totally understand."

I couldn't be honest with him after getting his hopes up. I was used to being the rational friend, but I didn't want to be the killjoy.

"Seriously, Seb. I don't want to do anything if you're not feeling it. Our friendship is too important."

Maybe over the course of another "hang out" (ugh) with Chase, we could get closer. Although it seemed obvious he wasn't in love with me, so I'd keep my hopes low and enjoy the orgasm.

"Why wouldn't it be okay? I'm game. We'll have to see if Chase is, too," I said.

"You sure?"

"Oh yeah. I can't wait to manhandle him next time." And despite my sadness, there was truth in that.

"Sweet."

"You think he'll want to, though?"

"You leave that to me," Anton said with a smile as if looking at another potential sale.

9

CHASE

The routine of school kept my mind clear of thinking about my sexual escapades. One student complained to me that there was no point in studying chemistry since he'd never use it in his adult life. I asked him how the rubber soles on his sneakers were constructed, and that stifled his dissent. *Don't mess with science.*

After four straight periods teaching, I left my classroom for lunch. I had a sandwich and Twinkie in the fridge with my name on it. Well, my name was on a tag affixed to my lunch bag, but those who ignored that were just being cruel.

Raleigh stopped me in the hall and clapped me on the shoulder. "Congrats, man. I'm rooting for you."

"Thanks?" I said, completely confused by his non-sequitur. "Do you mean in a general sense? In that case, I suppose I'm rooting for you, too."

"You're funny. No wonder you got nominated."

"Nominated?"

Raleigh crossed his fingers and held them up. "Good luck!"

He continued on his merry way, leaving me scratching my head.

My confusion didn't subside as I made my way through the halls. Students gave me thumbs up and approving smiles. I wasn't used to any of this. I wasn't the kind of teacher who bonded with his students in the traditional sense. I never sat on my desk and shot the proverbial breeze or pulled out a guitar and sang a lesson to them. Relative to other teachers at South Rock, I received few requests to sign a student's yearbook.

I stumbled into the teacher's lounge, where Julian and Amos immediately looked up from their coffees.

"I'm confused," I stated.

"Congratulations!" Julian said.

"People keep congratulating me, yet I don't know what I did."

"I forgot that you don't check your phone when you're teaching. Chase, you were nominated for Teacher of the Year." Amos handed over his phone so I could read the social media post listing the three nominated teachers.

"I was nominated?" Teacher of the Year was a special award voted on by the student body. The winner received a plaque and got to make a speech at graduation. The award usually went to the same handful of fun, cool teachers who shot the proverbial breeze and played guitar.

"Is this a joke?" I asked.

Amos and Julian exchanged a look that told me my rhetorical question was rooted in truth.

"I heard some rumors," Amos said.

"What kind of rumors?" I asked for clarification.

"Well..." Amos inhaled a breath. "Alfred Rover is poised to be valedictorian. He's out ahead by a mile, but apparently you gave him a B-plus in the last marking period."

"I didn't give him that grade. He earned it himself with a substandard lab writeup."

"Anyway, he complained to the rest of the AP crowd about how you ruined his perfect A average, but that it doesn't matter because he's still going to Princeton. Well, it's an open secret that none of the smart kids like him, for obvious reasons. So to piss him off, a few of his classmates came up with the idea to vote for you as Teacher of the Year, so that you two would have to share the stage at graduation. The idea spread through school. Lots of kids don't like Alfred, and lots of kids thought it'd be a fun lark, I guess. Enough kids voted for you that you are now in the running to be Teacher of the Year," Amos said, winded from the explanation.

It sounded to me like a bunch of kids had too much time on their hands, and that democratic systems of government were inherently flawed. But still, I couldn't help feeling a flush of pride as I stared at my name on Amos's phone.

"I doubt I'll win. Students love Mr. Simkins and Mrs. Gonzalez. They've won before." They taught music and art, respectively. Kids loved music and art. They didn't love chemistry.

"You never know." Julian shrugged. "It's pretty cool, though."

"Chase, we're getting you that award." Everett barged into the lounge, eyes loaded with determination. "There is a pathway to victory. Students have been buzzing about your out-of-the-box nomination."

"As a joke," I said.

"History will reveal that this is no joke. I have two words for you: Marisa Tomei. When she won an Oscar for *My Cousin Vinny*, she became a joke. How dare a comedic performance win an award? But over time, we've all now realized that she deserved the fuck out of that award. Her performance is legendary. Chase, we're going to turn you into the ingènue of South Rock and make students remember why they fell in love with you in the first place."

"I'm not following the metaphor here, Everett," I said. I made a mental note to add *My Cousin Vinny* to my ever-expanding and sadly neglected watch list.

"Chase, no matter what kids say, they care about the name they write down on that ballot. Voting is important to them. This might've started as a revenge scheme, but if these kids really didn't like you, none of them would've written down your name," Everett said.

Another flush of pride hit me. I wasn't the fun teacher—I didn't have that gene—but perhaps I had been doing something right. Maybe Anton and Sebastian weren't alone in their admiration of my class.

"I'm thinking banners, Q&A sessions with influential students, finding some babies for you to kiss." Everett sat on the table, his mind falling down one of his typical histrionic rabbit holes.

Amos put his hand on Everett's shoulder. "Or maybe we let voting take its course."

"Take it down a notch, Everett," Julian said.

"Sorry. I'm in the theater. Awards are my oxygen."

I had too much to think about between school, my personal life, and my cat. I didn't need to use up precious space wondering about my prospects of winning Teacher of the Year. But the plaque *would* look very nice on my fireplace mantel.

———

I HAD students tell me they were voting for me, a statement which never got old. Because the awards stuff muddled my focus during my free period, I stayed after school to work on crafting the final exams for my classes. Just because I was in the running for Teacher of the Year didn't mean I'd design an easier exam to curry favor.

I thoroughly enjoyed putting tests together. It wasn't about torturing students, though they might have believed that. It was yet another puzzle. How could I take information we learned throughout the year and twist it back to them in a way that required critical thinking?

It was a harder challenge than people realized, and when I looked up from my computer, it was already six. The high sun of the afternoon shifted to the orange hues of evening slatting through the windows.

I strolled through the quiet hallways and stopped at the vending machine outside the cafeteria, where I came upon a familiar, broad back.

"Mr. M." Anton stood up. The thick glass case of the vending machine was open, and it was like staring into a bank vault with food instead of money. At his side were boxes of candy and chips. He wore a tight polo stretched over his arms and slim pants that showed off his long legs. He was more dressed up than half the teachers at South Rock.

"You can call me Chase."

"We're at school, though." His lips turned into a lazy smile that sent a funny surge of warmth up my spine.

"Yes, but you are not a student. What are you doing here?"

"I heard that the Snickers bar kept getting stuck in the teacher's lounge machine, so I fixed it and thought I'd do a restock while I was here." He grabbed a fistful of Twix and stocked them in their rightful place. He took care to make sure none of the wrappers crinkled and that all the candy bars were facing the same direction.

"You don't have staff that do this for you?"

"We have a guy who does it. But South Rock was our first client. I like to give their vending machines extra TLC. And it's always fun coming back."

It was odd to hear a former student say he enjoyed returning to high school. Most kids were itching to get out of this place and never come back.

"The real question is what are you doing here so late?" Anton cocked his head at me, the spotlight of his gaze sending a jolt of heat up my spine.

"It's only six."

"You're the first person I've seen in these halls in a while." Our voices echoed in the emptiness.

"I was preparing for finals," I said.

"Shouldn't your students be the ones doing that?" Anton bent down to stock the packs of chewing gum. Perhaps I was reading into things, but I thought he was pushing his butt out more than he had to.

Not that there was anything wrong with that.

Anton rested his arm on the open glass case, showing off his long torso. It was a similar position he took in his apartment, and I wondered if he had the same intentions here. "You're looking good, Mr. M. I like this shirt." His fingers danced down the edge of my collar.

"Thank you." Heat raced up my neck. It was merely an uncontrollable response to stimuli, right?

"Of course, I'd like it much better if you weren't wearing it."

I choked out a laugh, amazed that Anton could say statements like that and still remain charming. He had social acumen I could only dream about. Although currently, I was dreaming of something else, a scenario in which our shirts were both not being worn.

"Saturday was a one-time thing," I said, clearing my throat.

"It's a shame. Because there are so many things I wanted to do to you, Mr. M." He sauntered up to me, disregarding any respect for personal space.

"What kind of things?" I asked, only to make sure we were on the same page when it came to things that we shouldn't do.

"Only one way to find out." He shrugged, refusing to go into further, dirtier detail. It was for the best. There had to be something in the teacher handbook about avoiding erections on school property.

Anton carefully placed bags of chips into the machine, straightening their corners. "Come grab a drink with me and Sebastian this week."

"It wouldn't be a good idea."

"Why?" Anton's directness was unnerving, as was his unblinking stare with his lips pouted just so.

"Saturday was a fluke, Anton, in every sense. Usually I spend my Saturdays writing lesson plans or doing laundry. Going to SpringFest was already an anomaly for me. Our actions were extremely out of the ordinary and shouldn't be interpreted as normal, repeatable behavior from me."

Was there a problem with the thermostat in South Rock? Surely there was no scientific proof that Anton's smoldering gaze could raise the temperature. It had to be in my head, but getting out of my head was a perpetual challenge.

"See, that's where you're wrong." His hand drifted down my chest. "I don't think our actions were as out of the ordinary for you as you think."

"I think I have a better handle on my life than you do."

"I think you have a wild side, Chase. Correction. I know you have a wild side. It's dying to get out of you. And I'm not just talking about what you did on my futon."

His last sentence caught me off guard, partially snapping me out of my horny brain fog. Anton seemed to sense my confusion.

"You present yourself as this buttoned-up nerd, but I can tell you're so much more."

"Buttoned-up nerd is a pretty accurate description of me. My life is built around structure and routine by design." Unless I had a secret Dr. Hyde alter-ego that only came out at night, which would mean going through a rigorous psychological evaluation to determine if I had schizophrenia, then there was no wild side to speak of.

"Respectfully disagree. You're wild and exciting. Underneath, there is a Chase that is bursting to be free."

Anton spoke with as much confidence about my inner life as he did about my physical self. He wasn't Wikipedia, though. He didn't know everything.

"I see a Chase who is impulsive and creative and bold. I see a Chase who laughs so hard he can barely catch his breath. I see a Chase who throws his head back in a convertible and lets the wind whip through his hair." Anton's gaze changed, the glimmer in his eye shifting from lust to something sweeter, which seemed to surprise him as much as it did me. "You are endlessly fascinating, Chase."

Disregarding the fact that I had zero interest in driving in a convertible, there was something about Anton's description that hit home for me unexpectedly. I didn't know who that Chase was, but I wanted to meet him. I wanted to spend time with someone who saw that Chase. All my life, I had allowed people to label me as weird or quirky. Nobody had ever said I was fascinating, that I was a mystery worth solving.

"You really think I'm fascinating?"

"I'm not bullshitting you."

I had an urge to hold his hand, but I resisted. Somehow, that seemed more inappropriate than sprouting an erection on school grounds.

"How can you make this bold of an assessment after one day with me? You have a scarcity of data."

"But it hasn't been one day. I spent a whole year in your classroom. I watched you get excited when talking through chemical equations and how you kept pushing us to do more complicated experiments. You were getting us to live on the edge, in a way."

"That's a generous reading."

"You are unlike any person I've met. And I've met a lot of people. I talk to people all day with my business. I'm used to sizing someone up quickly." Anton leaned against the vending machine. "I'm able to put people into buckets and tailor my talk track. There are introverts, extroverts, East Coast directness and Midwestern niceness, people who love to smalltalk and people who love to observe. But you, Chase Mathison, deserve your own box."

"I always saw it as a curse. I never really fit in anywhere." It was easy to open up to Anton. Was there a better feeling than a person taking interest in you? I was sure psychologists and specialists in human behavior could provide a better explanation, but for now, I let myself feel a glow building inside me.

"Fitting in is overrated."

"You seemed to do a good job of it. From what I observed in the halls, you seemed to be popular in high school." Teachers liked to claim that we were above following the social dynamics of our students, but it wasn't hard to see the stratifications of popularity.

Anton shrugged and played it off, the natural response of anyone who was called popular. He twinged with discomfort at the label, as much as I did at being called weird.

"You were trying to fit in. It probably wasn't easy being an out gay athlete in high school."

"It was a constant tightrope walk."

"It wasn't easy being a gay nerd either. I could talk all I wanted about how much I loved *Star Trek*, but I could never say that I found Chris Pine attractive." People made the incorrect assumption that so-called nerds were more accepting. To the contrary: they could be just as hostile and exclusionary as our jock nemeses.

"I laughed off homophobic jokes and comments in the locker room. I had to. I didn't want to be labeled as sensitive."

"You never wanted to make things uncomfortable for them," I said. Because no matter what, it was always about them.

A quiet moment of understanding simmered between us.

"I knew there was a reason why you were my favorite teacher."

"Apparently, you're not alone. I was nominated for Teacher of the Year." Even though it was a nomination predicated on revenge, and nothing that I could put on a resume, I couldn't help sharing.

"Congratulations! It's about time someone other than Simkins and Gonzalez won. If you could make chemistry interesting to an idiot like me, then you definitely deserve an award."

"Anton, you're not an idiot." I was offended on behalf of him. "You're a very intelligent, smart young man."

He scrunched his eyebrows together, as if I were crazy. "Okay."

"It's true."

"I was a C-minus student."

"I was once a C-student, too."

"No shit. Really?"

I bowed my head in confirmation. "I struggled in school, but I worked hard to improve my grades as I got older. People think that being smart is an inherent and unchanging quality within us, but really it's like any other muscle. The more you train it, the smarter you get. Albert Einstein wasn't a great student either."

"The hair guy? Seriously?"

"He struggled, too. When you were engaged in class, you did well. You would ask good questions. Some kids have natural smarts, which only gets them so far. But you're smart, and you have grit and curiosity, which will take you farther than they could ever dream."

Anton nodded, taking it all in, thoughts swirling behind his eyes.

"You really think I'm smart?"

"Absolutely."

He opened his mouth to respond, but there was no sly comeback, no smooth line. Not even a flirty smile. He did something I didn't expect at all: he blushed.

Then he did another thing I certainly didn't expect: he palmed my crotch, sending a sizzle of lust up my body.

His dark eyes bore into me with heat, but I detected a trace of fear in his pupils, like I'd hit on a dirty little secret he was desperate to cover up.

"Seb and I would really like to see you again. I mean, you didn't even get off last time. What kind of gentlemen would we be if we didn't return the favor?"

Just as my lips were about to buckle and a groan of deep-seeded want was about to fly out, Anton stepped back. The music started up again, the lights turned back on, reality was upon us.

"It was good bumping into you, Chase. Always fun catching up with former teachers." Anton clapped my shoulder and left me alone in the hall.

Though I wasn't alone. I had the tent in my pants to keep me company.

10

ANTON

The only time you'd find me on a college campus was because I was visiting my mom or dad. They were professors at this super crunchy liberal arts college where students seemed to spend more time protesting than studying. Dad taught macroeconomic theory, and mom taught comparative literature. Were there two subjects that I could have less interest in?

They'd met as grad students years ago and left each other secret notes in each other's cubbies when they first started dating. Nowadays, they interacted more like colleagues than a couple.

After stocking the vending machines at South Rock, I high-tailed it over to their house for a family dinner. As "collateral" for loaning me some money to get Beverage Solutions off the ground, I had to agree to dinner at home once a week. According to an ex-hookup, it was very *Gilmore Girls*, whatever that meant.

At tonight's dinner, we were eating chicken shawarma, but I was in a bit of a daze. I was still in shock that I grabbed Chase's dick in the hallways of my old high school. That was forward, even for me. The thing was, I didn't do it to turn him on. I did it to shut him up, and I was trying to figure out why. Why was I so rattled at Chase calling me smart?

Fortunately, it was easy to zone out at dinner. I had nothing to contribute. The topic of conversation was Dad's latest article that he'd gotten published. He and Mom got articles published in journals and magazines that I'd never heard of, but were supposed to be impressive. I was still waiting for their spread in *Sports Illustrated*.

"I loved the part where you dove into the adverse selection dynamics in Central American debt markets," Mom said, swirling her glass of wine. "Your grasp of the tenuous geopolitical climate and its effect on labor was brilliant. Just brilliant."

"Thank you, dear. It can't hold a candle to your exploration of Flaubert's earlier works for that piece in *Comparative Literature Quarterly*." Dad held up his wine glass, and they air-clinked.

Were the conversations always this boring on *Gilmore Girls*, too?

I didn't understand genetics. I looked like Mom and Dad. Mom with her olive skin and toothy smile, Dad with his height and thick eyebrows. There was no question that I was their son. Yet I didn't seem to inherit an ounce of their brain power.

"What do you think, Anton?" Mom asked.

"I think...I think this is awesome shawarma." I pointed at the platter and gave her a thumbs up. "A-plus."

"Your dad marinated the meat."

"A-plus, Dad."

I knew my parents loved me, and I loved them to death. But I couldn't help feel like an idiot around them. Did the smart gene skip a generation? Would my kids be geniuses?

Sebastian thought my folks were a cute couple. A pair of brainiacs. But was this really what he wanted from a relationship? Talking to your soulmate about economics articles and watching passion curdle into a stagnant friendship? My parents were rarely affectionate with each other, though they seemed generally happy. Whatever their deal was, it wasn't for me. To each their own.

"How was your day, Anton? Did you sell any vending machines?" Mom asked. I ignored the twinge of condescension in her voice.

"We don't sell vending machines. We install them and operate them in facilities. If you sell a vending machine, you only get paid once. But if you rent them out, you get paid every day." I looked at Dad, and he gave me a smile of modest approval. I didn't know jack shit about macroeconomics, but I knew how to make a buck. "Today, I had to do some restocking for a client."

The thought of Chase popped into my head. He looked damn good in his proper, preppy teacher's outfit. His ass was still bite-able in those khakis he wore. He was a gorgeous man.

"You know Anton, it's not too late to look into college," Dad said. He held up his hand to stop my usual objection whenever he brought this up. "You don't have to quit Beverage Solutions. You can take night classes."

"That would take away time from the business."

"It could help you. You can take business classes," Mom said, picking up the thread from Dad. "A college degree is a valuable thing to have. An education lasts forever."

"Unless I get amnesia," I countered.

"Studies show that amnesia victims have a better chance of remembering academic facts than personal information. So yes, an education will survive if you get amnesia." Dad had a gleeful gotcha look on his lips. Despite how smart he was, the man could be a goofball when he wanted to.

"How do you know that?"

"Because this isn't the first time you've used the amnesia line on us," he said.

"I love the thought behind it, but I'm doing well. I don't need college. College isn't for everyone."

They got quiet for a second, and I knew what they were thinking: *why isn't it for our only son?*

"Seb and I are doing well. We don't want to stop our momentum with night classes and writing papers."

"Sebastian never talks about going back to school?" Mom asked. "He's so bright."

As opposed to me?

"He knows the option is available if he wants to." I made sure we had that talk before we jumped in with BS. I never forgot what Sebastian gave up to join me, and I would never guilt him into staying in something that he wasn't fully invested in. But so far, so good. Sebastian showed no signs of wanting to leave. I hoped our hookup didn't change that. Not just because of the business, but because I didn't want to lose my friend.

"Why didn't you and Sebastian ever get together? He's a great guy."

"Mom!" I felt my face go red. It wasn't the first time she asked me that, but it was the first time she asked me that after I'd seen him naked.

"Your mother's right. We like Sebastian. He's intelligent and thoughtful. We'd love him as a son-in-law."

"Whoa whoa whoa. Why are you thinking I'm going to get married? That's not my speed." I was grateful that my parents were cool with me coming out, but sometimes, they were too cool with it. Boundaries, folks!

"I don't understand why you're opposed to eventually settling down with someone," Dad said.

"Why do you want me to get married at twenty-one?"

"*Eventually* settling down. You're good-looking, social, and somewhat successful." I was sure Dad had trouble with that last part. "We thought you'd bring a boyfriend around to one of these dinners by now."

"Could we go back to talking about macroeconomic theory and Flaubert?" A sharp pain hit my stomach. I couldn't storm off like I would as a child. And I couldn't grab anyone's crotch. Instead, I hit them where it hurt. "Mom, isn't it true that Flaubert's prose pales in comparison to Ivan Turgenev's? I thought I read that on the internet."

Her eyes bugged open, and she slammed her fork onto her plate. "What? Where did you read that? People refuse to give Flaubert his due. Ivan Turgenev's work is puerile and misbegotten..."

Mom launched into a lengthy takedown of Turgenev, her favorite thing to do, and mercifully got us off the topic of my lack of love life.

***

My old bedroom remained intact, and I liked to go up there to relax after these dinners. A good bedroom brought a sense of peace. Mine had a large bay window that overlooked our backyard and pool. One day, I told myself, I would be able to buy a house with a view like this.

I lay on my old bed, staring up at the ceiling still plastered with posters of extreme athletes and *Workaholics*. My bedroom was a shine to everything my parents hated: sports and lowbrow entertainment.

Even though Mom's trashing of novelists from the 1800s saved my ass from awkward dinner conversation, I couldn't shake thoughts of Sebastian and Chase. Sebastian was my best friend, and yeah we crossed a line, but that didn't have to change everything. We could still have fun with Chase. He and Chase seemed similar. They were both intelligent, thoughtful pieces of bread, and I was the piece of meat in the middle.

I hopped off my bed and pulled my old yearbook from my

bookcase, which had more toys and sports paraphernalia on it than actual books.

Seb and I might as well have been conjoined twins because we were always in pictures together. I flipped to the wrestling team's page where we posed, arms around each other's shoulders after a meet. A few pages later, I found a candid shot of us at our cafeteria table. A warm feeling lit up my chest.

I turned to the section with the teachers' pictures and smiled at Chase's neat, put-together pose. Apparently, there was a whole page dedicated to something called Science Olympiad, which he ran. There he was prepping a table of nerdy students at some kind of quiz bowl-looking competition, thick glasses framing his face perfectly. On the other side of the page was a group shot of the Math Club. Sebastian stood in the back, smiling proudly, easily the most attractive person in the club. I'd forgotten he participated in math competitions during the wrestling off-season.

My parents thought it would be a no-brainer for me and Sebastian to wind up together. The truth was, I'd had that thought before. How could I not? My best friend was sexy, sweet, and we had our rhythms down. Of course I'd wondered about life with Sebastian as my boyfriend.

And even though I told Sebastian and the whole world that I didn't want to be in a boring relationship, that wasn't the full truth.

Here was the truth, in all its ugly glory: I wasn't smart enough to date Sebastian, or any worthwhile guy.

Sure, I could wow them with my charm and good looks. And then I could wow them even more once we got in the bedroom. But once the initial high wore off, what else could I offer them? I couldn't have intellectually stimulating conversations like my parents, unless sports or beer were considered intellectual topics. I was a master at the sales smalltalk that enabled me to close deals, but I stumbled at anything deeper.

What if I let myself fall for a guy, but I only wound up boring him? How humiliating would that be, to be rejected for being an uninteresting person?

People stayed together because they found their significant other interesting. They could spend time with them for the rest of their lives. Ninety-nine percent of my friends were surface-level hangs. We did shots at parties. We liked each other's posts. We played a pickup game of basketball. But when the fun times were over, we didn't have anything to talk about except recalling crazy stories of past fun times.

Sebastian was my only friend who I had something real with. And he was smart. Really smart. College scholarship smart. Whatever feelings were bubbling up inside me from our night together with Chase couldn't be acted upon.

It didn't matter that Chase thought I was smart...or did it? Did he actually mean what he said, or was he trying to reverse psychology his way into my pants?

I stared at his picture in the yearbook, and I could've sworn he was staring back at me, nodding at me that he meant it. I looked up and caught the dopey smile on my lips. Chase was certifiably smart. And he thought I was smart. He thought I had the chops to be a chemist.

Maybe I had a nerdy side dying to get out?

I snorted a laugh at the thought. Fat chance, but it was nice to dream. I reshelved the yearbook, leaving said dream in the past.

What if Sebastian thought I was a fun friend, but not serious boyfriend material?

It was better to be a player than to face that kind of defeat. At least I was smart enough to know that.

11

SEBASTIAN

Sometimes, I thought about the path I was supposed to travel. In an alternate world, I was finishing up my third year of college. There was an alternate version of me hanging on the quad with friends, wrestling at the collegiate level, maybe rushing a fraternity. It all seemed ideal.

Until I met up with Savannah.

"Why the fuck do I want to be a doctor?" Savannah slammed her head onto her thick textbook, which was open on top of four other open textbooks, which were next to a laptop, a notebook, and a half-drunken can of Monster Energy Drink.

"Because you want to save lives?" I ask.

"Ugh."

Savannah was one of my closest friends from South Rock High. I had taken the train up to Ithaca to visit her at Cornell. Her curly brown hair was wrestled into a messy bun. Her gold necklace spelling *Savannah* in gilded cursive, found on a field trip to New York City, hung down and touched the textbook. She and I were on the yearbook committee, where we spent most of our time snarking about the supremely anal editor-in-chief Ronna

Rogalski who shot down any idea that wasn't hers with her trademark "I'm just not feeling it."

Savannah was pre-med and hating it, while also loving it in some twisted way. She and her uber-challenging coursework were in a toxic relationship.

It was finals week, so I was meeting up with her at her college's library where she told me she almost had to fight some girl for the private study room we were in. As with any girl she didn't like, she threatened to punch her in the tit. I was very curious how her personality would translate to bedside manner. Threatening to punch patients in the tit for not listening to her advice seemed not to jive with the Hippocratic Oath.

"How the fuck does he expect us to remember all of this? Maybe if I wear a low-cut top to the exam," she said. "I'm kidding."

"Of course you are," I said with a smirk. I leaned back and kicked my feet onto the table in the meager space not subsumed with books.

"You sure you don't miss this?" Savannah's voice was laced with sarcasm, but I detected a hint of genuine curiosity, too. She was as shocked as my parents when I turned down my scholarship.

Would I rather be chained to a library desk for four years or hustling in the world? I chose the latter.

"Business is booming," I said. "Anton and I are in the process of closing our biggest client ever. We had a great initial meeting, and things look very positive."

"Aw, that's wonderful. I'm proud of you guys. I mean, I think you're kinda weird for wanting to sell vending machines, but you're making it work."

Savannah came from a family of doctors. There was one path that'd been laid out for her since birth, and she couldn't fathom anyone who diverged from the college pipeline.

"I think you're kinda weird for holing up in a library for weeks at a time studying..." I peered over at her textbook, but I didn't know what half the words meant. "Science."

"It's organic chemistry. You took chemistry in high school, right?"

"Uh, yeah." I gulped back a lump.

"Did you have Mr. Mathison? Great teacher, but super odd."

"Yeah, I think I had him." Oh, I had him all right.

Savannah cracked open another can of Monster Energy. I didn't have to be a med student to know how bad that shit was for her.

"How late are you planning to stay up to study? It's only three in the afternoon," I said.

"I didn't sleep last night. I was here." She chugged the can. "Well, not here. I was in another section of the library until this room opened up. These econ bros were being so fucking loud. I think one of them was looking at porn on his phone. It had to be porn. I threatened to punch them in the man tits if they didn't keep it down."

None of this was in the college brochures I flipped through. And I thought being an entrepreneur was a rough life.

"Anyway, my life has been boring because I've been here for the past two weeks. I haven't even had a chance to see Mathias." Mathias was her boyfriend, a pre-law student presumably doing a similar amount of cramming. "He texted me a dick pic a few days ago, but I've been so busy, I haven't had a chance to look at it." She tossed me her phone. "Can you open it and respond back?"

The phone landed in my hands like a live grenade.

"Write back something complimentary about his dick. Like 'OMG so big.' And add some emoji. Eggplant, winky face. Make it flirty, but not so flirty that he thinks we're going to be having sex this week."

"Um, I'm going to let you handle that one." I slid back the phone, preferring not to Cyrano with her boyfriend's junk.

"Thanks, friend," she deadpanned. "Sebastian, I think you need to enroll in college if only because it'll help you shed your prudishness."

"I am not a prude."

She cocked her head to the side, a sharp rebuke of my claim. "Even the characters in a Jane Austen novel think you're too prudish."

"I've had sex."

"People who've had sex can still be prudes," she shot back. "Sex is the most prudish sexual act there is."

"That doesn't make any sense."

"Super religious people have sex. They don't eat ass."

"I think your energy drink is messing with your head."

"C'mon, tell me the most exciting thing that's happened in your life lately. I need to feel alive. Look at me, Sebastian, I'm surrounded by books. The only penetration I've gotten this week has been a paper cut."

Fortunately for her, I did have interesting news to share on the sex front. I wasn't going to say anything because it was a sensitive subject for me, but when she held up her poor index finger, wrapped in a band-aid, it was too pathetic to ignore.

"If I tell you this, it has to stay between us. I am absolutely serious." I picked up her organic chemistry textbook and made her swear on it.

"What is it?" She leaned forward in her seat, her eyes aflame with anticipation and high on the mysterious chemicals of energy drinks.

"I had a threesome."

"Haha, funny. Really, what happened?"

I gave her a slow nod letting her know I wasn't fucking around. Her big eyes got even bigger.

"You're serious. Shut up. Or no, wait. Don't shut up. Keep talking. Who with?"

I strummed my fingers on the library table. "Like I said, you can't tell a soul."

"I won't."

"I mean it."

"You can trust me. I didn't tell anyone you were gay in high school."

"I came out my freshman year."

"Well, I still didn't tell anyone." She grabbed my hand in both of hers, her eyes basically pleading with me. "Sebastian, I will not tell a soul. I promise. Please, I need this gossip or else I don't know if I can go on."

"Melodramatic much?" I inhaled a calming breath. I couldn't believe I was about to say this sentence aloud. "It was with Anton and Mr. Mathison, our old chemistry teacher."

Savannah stared at me unblinking.

"You okay?"

"I think I just had ten strokes at once."

I gave her a very brief rundown of what happened last weekend. As scared as I was about spilling the beans, it was a relief to share it with an objective third party. Yet it wasn't the sex part that Savannah got stuck on. Her face dissolved from giddy shock to something more heartfelt.

"So you and Anton finally hooked up?" I'd never heard her sound so sweet. Anyone who was close friends with me long enough usually found out about my crush on Anton, either by obvious context clues or me confessing my hidden feelings outright. Savannah had known about the crush for a few years, but to her credit, she never pushed me to act on it. She understood the complicated tightrope I walked.

"It was just the heat of the moment," I said.

"Are you sure about that?"

"We talked about it. Anton was just having fun. You know Anton."

"He loves to have fun," she said with a slight eye roll. "And he kissed you for fun."

"Heat of the moment," I reiterated, reaffirming this point for me.

"Was it good?"

I gave an exaggerated nod. There was no word that could describe how good it felt to taste Anton's lips. Only noises not appropriate for the library.

Savannah studied me as if I were on her final. "Sebastian had a fucking threesome. What was it like getting with Mr. Mathison?"

"That was also very good." Despite my feelings swirling for Anton, I wouldn't forget how drop-dead sexy Chase was on Saturday. He was adorably awkward at SpringFest, and then ravenous back at our apartment, then adorably awkward when he scrambled out the door. It was a thrilling kind of whiplash. I always appreciated a guy who could keep me on my toes.

"I'm debating whether or not I want details on that. I'll keep you posted." Savannah's face softened as it looked like a pang of pity flashed across her eyes. "How are you feeling about everything?"

I shrugged. "Good."

"Sebastian, you hooked up with the guy you've been pining over for years. You are not good."

That was the problem with friends; they had the power to read you.

"I told him I was cool with everything."

"Ugh, but you're not!" She slammed her head into her pile of books.

"Yes, I am. How do you know?"

"Because you're not the Cool Girl."

"I'm not a girl period." Trying to stay on Savannah's wavelength tonight was impossible. Med school was definitely breaking her brain.

"The Cool Girl is what every guy wants. She's a hot chick who he can bang for fun and not get attached. Have you really never read or watched *Gone Girl*? Ben Affleck goes full-frontal."

"I'll add it to the list." Savannah had recommended oodles of films to see over the years. I never watched one. I wasn't a movie person. My attention would go to my to-do list or ways I could be more productive.

"The point is, you're not a Cool Girl, Seb. I mean, *are* you cool with everything?"

I shrugged again, with less confidence this time. "I want to be."

I wished I could be as impulsive as Anton, wished I could be comfortable flying by the seat of my pants and believing things would work out. I wasn't built that way. Anton might've loathed his parents' boring relationship, but he didn't realize how much stability and security that kind of upbringing gave him. Some of us didn't have that luxury.

Damn it, Savannah was right. I wasn't a Cool Girl. I was seriously uncool.

"I have an idea," Savannah said. "You should go out with Anton, just the two of you, and try to create that spark."

My stomach twisted at the proposition. Red flags immediately sprouted.

"Yeah, it's fucking scary," she said, reading my face. "But what if this threesome made Anton see you as more than a friend? It's like a portal opened up." She spoke as if her brain was still catching up with her mouth. "What if your threesome was a portal to a relationship with Anton? The portal won't stay open forever. It's closing as we speak."

The farther I got away from Saturday, the more it would be a distant memory. And the more Anton would go back to seeing me as just a friend.

"You're right," I said, gobsmacked.

"Of course I'm right. I'm a doctor." Savannah tipped her head back and poured the final drops of her energy drink into her waiting mouth. "You're going to text Anton and invite him out for a drink tonight. Tonight, right? Tonight hasn't happened yet? Is it still afternoon? I'm so tired."

"It's still afternoon." I pointed out the window at the shining, sunny day.

"I trained myself not to look out the window. Too distracting and depressing. Anyway, invite him out for a drink. And when you're there, flirt with him, see if he responds, and then when you get back to your place...pounce."

She held up her hand like a tiger claw for emphasis.

"That will never work," I said. As if things would be that easy.

"If the portal is still open, it will."

I took out my phone. Savannah came around to my side of the table and watched over my shoulder as I texted Anton.

Sebastian: Hey, let's grab a drink tonight. I could use one.

I got her thumbs up before hitting send.

My phone buzzed with a response thirty seconds later.

Anton: Hell yes! Meet me at Remix at eight?

Sebastian: Sounds good.

"Ow! Did you just bite my shoulder?" I asked Savannah.

"Sorry. Heat of the moment."

I loved my friends, but they were weird.

"You are hooking up with Anton tonight. It's happening," she said with unearned confidence. "You better not be prudish. I expect your tongue to go wherever he wants."

"Gross."

"Prude." She stuck out her tongue, then wiggled it side-to-side. Mathias was either a very lucky man or a man in a lot of pain.

"We're just meeting for a drink, like we've done lots of times before." I wanted to brush off her idea, but I couldn't help thinking that she might be right about the portal. This could be my last chance before I was relegated to the permanent friendzone.

"Sebastian, one of us will be feeling the touch of another human being tonight, and sadly, it won't be me."

———

BECAUSE I COULDN'T HELP but get excited, I bought a new shirt for tonight, black and fitted. I couldn't go back to the apartment and change into something nicer or else Anton would suspect something. My heart pounded in my chest as I drove to Remix.

We had already kissed, and Anton seemed to like it. Usually, I wasn't one for risk-taking, but I took a leap with Anton once before. Maybe we'd both take one tonight.

Remix was a gay bar located at the end of an unassuming strip mall. On weekend nights, the place was packed, throngs of guys dancing to club music. On a Thursday evening, it was much calmer. One could actually walk around in there.

I took a deep breath before I opened the door.

The place was sparsely populated, a few guys dotting a few tables. In the corner by the back bar was Anton, his familiar face smiling at me.

And next to him was Chase, who gave me his signature awkward wave.

12

ANTON

When Sebastian suggested we go out for a drink tonight, my mind instantly thought of including Chase. Dare we try to recreate the magic of last weekend? I was game to try, even though Chase threw me for a fucking loop the other day with all his smart talk.

His words stuck in my head throughout the week. I wasn't used to feeling exposed like that. I didn't like it, but I also did?

What the actual fuck?

Fortunately, I got Chase to come out tonight. I was the guy who loved to have fun after all. If all went well, we would all fool around, and I would forget about how this science nerd got my heart all fizzy for a moment, like it was plopped into a can of La Croix.

My dick was half-hard just watching Sebastian approach. Some very dirty fantasies began to play in my head. As did some scenes that made my heart go fizzy again.

My heart really needed to take a chill pill.

"Hey." Sebastian gave me a half-wave. He stood just out of reach of our table for a few seconds.

"What's up, Dude?" I clapped him on the shoulder and brought him into a quick hug. "How's it going? How's Savannah?"

"Under a lot of academic pressure."

"To each their own." I took a swig from my beer bottle. I sure as hell dodged a bullet on the college stuff. "I was dealing with a ticked-off customer. Sourwood Fitness."

Sebastian nodded in understanding. "Is Maurice still complaining about the sounds coming from the machine?"

"I told him that's the hum of the motor keeping the drinks cool. He has *very* sensitive hearing."

I had a suspicion that Maurice loved to complain because in some way, it was his way of getting his money's worth.

"I'll deal with him tomorrow. First, I'm gonna order a drink." Sebastian turned to make a beeline to the bar. I blocked him with a firm hand on the chest.

"You remember Chase, right?" I pointed at Chase, who waved hello. Maybe it was just me, but I didn't think Sebastian had acknowledged him yet.

"Good to see you," Sebastian said, as if it were the lowest mandated form of conversation available. "I'm gonna get a drink."

And he was off, not to be stopped.

"You good, Chase?" I nodded at his mixed drink.

"Yes. It should take me about twenty to twenty-five minutes to finish my drink."

"I'm timing you. Once we hit minute twenty-six, I'm taking it for myself." I winked at him, then caught up to Sebastian.

Remix was fairly empty at the moment, making it easy for me to break into a light jog to meet up with Sebastian. Things didn't get going until Fridays, when this place became the center of gay Hudson Valley life. Guys liked to party, but most of them also had work in the morning.

I checked out his ass as he leaned over the bar to get the

bartender's attention, something I'd never done before in all our years sharing locker rooms and bathrooms. There was something about the three of us being in the same room together that got my mind surging with dirty thoughts.

And it was a really nice ass. One meant for quarter-bouncing.

"Hey. I'll cover this round." I took out my credit card.

"I already ordered." The bartender slid over a rum and Coke.

Huh. When Sebastian went for hard alcohol and sugar-filled beverages, that either meant he was looking to have a good time or that he was in a bad mood. Sadly, I was beginning to think it was the latter.

"Thanks." Sebastian left a tip on the bar and tasted his drink. "Hey," he said to me finally.

"You kinda just ran off."

"I wanted to get something to drink. I was thirsty." Sebastian made his way through his drink.

"I can see that. Is it cool that I invited Chase? I bumped into him a few days ago at South Rock when I was refilling the vending machines. We had a good conversation." A conversation that continued to reverberate in my head.

"You refilled the vending machines yourself? Don't we pay Alberto to do that?"

"I have a special place in my heart for South Rock. I wanted to make sure it was done right. Just because we're the boss, doesn't mean we can't still get our hands dirty."

"Well, the time you spent over there, you could've been prospecting or cold calling or networking for new business. But whatever. That's cool." Speaking of cool, I was getting an ice cold vibe from Sebastian. I thought inviting Chase to join us would be a fun surprise, but I realized that surprises weren't really his thing.

"Are you mad?"

"No," he said, obviously meaning yes.

"I didn't mean to spring him on you."

"You didn't."

Sebastian wasn't as go-with-the-flow as I was, but was inviting someone to meet up at a bar really such a big deal? Judging by the tension coming off him, the answer was yes.

"I can tell Chase we'll meet up with him another time."

Shit. What if Sebastian wanted to use tonight to talk business, and all I thought about was pleasure? Or, sensing the tension in the air, what if it was something more serious, and here I was letting my dick, uh, dictate tonight?

"You invited Chase just to hang?"

"Yeah. He's a cool guy. I'm learning that he has a really dry sense of humor." I glanced over at Chase, obliviously sipping on his drink. It took him a moment to catch my eyeline and wave back like a big, adorable dork. That smile of his was undeniably infectious. Who knew I had such a thing for nerds?

"You have no ulterior motives?" Sebastian asked, eyebrow cocked.

"I thought it would be good if we got to know each other better." Even before we got down-and-dirty last weekend, we all seemed to click at SpringFest. We had a good time together. And in the future, if we happened to fall into bed at the same time without clothes on, I would not object to those serendipitous circumstances.

"Okay," he said simply.

"Are you sure, Seb? Honestly, if you want it to be a bros night, I'm totally on board with that. Chase won't mind either." I searched his inscrutable eyes. They were *locked down*. "Was there something you wanted to talk about?"

"Uh, no. Just thought it'd be a good night to grab a beer. Or whatever." He sucked down half his rum and Coke, and that seemed to loosen him up slightly, like a knot slowly pulling apart. "It's always good to see friends."

Sebastian pushed past me, his shoulder bumping mine, en route to our table.

Maybe this would turn out to be an awesome night.

He gave Chase a hard pat on the back that made the science teacher audibly wince. "Hey, Teach. How's it going?"

Or maybe not.

13

SEBASTIAN

I was a moderately intelligent guy. I did well in school. I co-ran a business. I could squat 280 pounds. Why was it that Anton caused my brain to completely short-circuit?

Of course Anton invited Chase out tonight. He didn't want to hang out just us. He definitely didn't want to hear about my feelings for him. He had sex on the brain. He'd wanted to get the three of us together since the second Chase left our apartment last week.

How could I keep letting myself fall into these traps, thinking that we were going to have some breakthrough moment where we confess our feelings to each other?

He wanted Chase. Chase was the shiny new thing for Anton to play with. I was just a side offering to sweeten the deal. I was the plain baked potato they served with a sizzling sirloin steak.

"What are you drinking?" I held up Chase's glass and examined the contents. "Looks like Sprite?"

"Sprite and vodka."

"I didn't know that was a real drink." Chase grabbed for it, but I held it out of his reach.

It wasn't Chase's fault that he got roped into this, but that didn't stop my competitive side from unleashing itself. Unfortunately, my pathetic crush on Anton couldn't let me take it out on him.

I took a sip of Chase's drink and watched him recoil.

"All you do is combine Sprite and vodka. It's not rocket science," Anton said, taking the glass and handing it back to Chase.

"Technically, the alchemy of these two substances does share vague similarities with the combustants utilized to power rocket ships." Chase pushed his glasses up the bridge of his nose. "So it is a little like rocket science."

"How cool is that?" Anton softly rubbed his back, his hand getting dangerously close to ass territory. How many years had I longed for Anton to casually drift a hand down my back?

I slammed my drink on the table. "Chase, I have a question for you. Why does South Rock make students take science classes all four years of high school? I never understood that. Most of us will never use what we learned in your class in the real world. Seems kind of a waste, right?"

"It's not a waste, dude," Anton said. "Knowledge is power."

"Says the C-minus student," I shot back.

Anton was always the first one to make fun of his lackluster grades, but he froze up at my comment, a wounded puppy look flashing across his face for a second. Chase's eyes bugged open, reading the room. Just as I was about to apologize, Anton burst out laughing.

"I earned that C-minus fair and square, Dude." He toasted my drink, squashing at least some of the awkwardness around the table. His hand remained on Chase's back, refueling my anger.

"Chase, what do you think of the saying 'Those who can't do, teach?'" I asked.

"I would disagree," Chase said.

I snorted a laugh.

"What is your glass made of?" he asked.

"This?" I held up my drink. "Uh, glass? I don't fucking know."

"We've established that you are holding a glass. And again, we come to my original question. What is your glass made of?" A cunning smile curled onto Chase's lips.

"I don't know."

"You mix together sand, or silicone dioxide, soda ash, and limestone and heat them at a very high temperature to form a thick liquid. The soda ash lowers the sand's melting point, but if we left it at that, then the liquid would dissolve in water. We can't have glass dissolving when it hits water, or else your rum and Coke would dribble down your arm. That's where the limestone comes in. The calcium carbonate keeps the melted sand from dissolving, allowing it to harden from a liquid. There are multiple chemical reactions going on, raw materials working together in a tightly coordinated effort, all so you can enjoy a happy hour cocktail. Now, don't you think it's important for students to be taught the basic tenets of a discipline that's responsible for every single physical item in their world?"

Chase rested his face against his hand as he stared me down, bringing that Willy Wonka meme to life. It seemed I'd found the one nerd who knew how to push back. I wanted to squash him.

"Isn't it possible that team sports, like wrestling, are a bigger waste of time since the overwhelming majority of students don't go on to play those sports at a professional or Olympic level?"

"Hey now. Don't go dissing wrestling," Anton said, but he was becoming less of a factor in this discussion.

"Sports teaches kids discipline and teamwork as well as builds their confidence, and those skills seem more important than knowing what calcium carbonate is," I said with a dark chuckle. "But that's just my opinion."

"And opinions aren't facts," said Chase, with a backbone in his tone that I didn't expect from him.

"Two things can be true at once. You guys wanna play darts?" Anton pointed his thumb at the dartboard on the wall.

"There's only two sets of darts, though," Chase said.

"We can improvise, take turns."

"I want to play Chase." I narrowed my eyes at our former teacher. "If he's up for the challenge."

"I'm always up for a challenge," Chase shot back. I always took games way too seriously, and I had a feeling that Chase was built the same way.

"This'll be good. Chase versus Seb." Anton watched from the sidelines, apparently clueless as to the real competition going on.

"I'll let you go first." I handed Chase the darts. "Respecting my elders and all."

"Elder denotes a position of authority in several cultures, so I appreciate the compliment." Chase swiped the darts from my hand. He held the first dart right up to his eye, pointing toward the board. Back and forth his arm went, practicing his shot but not taking it.

"Sometime this year," I said.

"I'm sizing up the spatial obstacles of the game to better calibrate the velocity required to hit the board," Chase said.

Was all his technical speak a way to mentally fuck with me? I'd faced all sorts of opponents on the wrestling mat. He wasn't going to psych me out.

"I'm going to give each of you ten seconds to shoot. How's that?" Anton squeezed the dip between Chase's shoulder blades and let his hand drift down his back.

I cut between them. "You're distracting him, Anton."

"Anton is invoking Pareto's Principle. The task will be completed in the timeframe one is given," said Chase.

"What the hell does that mean?" I asked.

"It means I'm going right now." Chase sent his darts into the air, where all three hit two rungs above the bullseye. Not bad but not great. Chase seemed to have the same opinion.

"Seb, you're up." Anton gave me a light pat on the ass. I blocked out my reaction to his touch and focused on the game.

Usually, I was meticulous like Chase. But here, I used the element of surprise to psych him out. I fired off three darts in quick succession.

Where Chase's darts all clustered together, mine were all over the place. One hit just above the bullseye, one far above that, and the third hit the edge of the board.

"Fuck," I muttered under my breath.

"Hey, it's all good. You almost hit the bullseye," Anton said.

"Almost," Chase snarked. He pulled the darts off the board and motioned for me to step aside.

"Round two," Anton called out. He smoothed his thumb over my elbow. I tensed under his touch and stayed laser-focused on the game. I refused to lose to Chase. Not at darts, nor with Anton.

While I was distracted by Anton's touch, Chase usurped my strategy and flicked his three darts onto the board, quick jabs of his arm like he touched a hot stove. The third dart hit the bullseye.

"Damn!" Anton called out.

Chase remained quiet, a pleased grin as he stared at his shots.

"Your turn, Sebastian."

"You got this, Seb." Anton went to pat my ass again, which really pissed me off. Was he really trying to stay neutral, like a horny Switzerland? I threw his hand off me with lots of unnecessary force.

If I hadn't already ruined the mood tonight, seeing Anton slowly back away from me with his hands up did the trick.

Chase pulled the darts from the board and handed them over.

But instead of taking them, I bailed out of Remix altogether. What the fuck was wrong with me?

14

CHASE

Admittedly, I wasn't the sharpest when it came to understanding people. Molecular equations were a cinch. Human emotions were headscratchers.

I had expected tonight to go differently. Anton, Sebastian, and I would enjoy laughs, good conversation, and drinks. They were good guys. I found myself surprisingly comfortable with them.

But instead, I felt like one of those idiot children with neglectful parents who fell into the lion pit at zoos.

A warm gust of air hit me when I stepped out of Remix. I hadn't realized just how cold it was inside, the air conditioner likely set high to anticipate a swell of sweaty bodies later tonight.

The exterior of Remix was remarkably unassuming. Save for a small rainbow flag hanging outside the door and a beer sign in the window, the cars on the highway could rightfully assume the place was abandoned.

I found Sebastian around the corner, back against the wall, squatting a few inches off the ground. He looked remarkably sullen considering it was a friendly game with no money on the table. The stakes could not have been lower.

"Hi. I told Anton I forfeited, so you won." I tentatively approached.

"I think I forfeited first, technically." Sebastian leaned his head back and exhaled a lengthy sigh. The outdoor lights silhouetted him and showed off his cut jawline, something I shouldn't be focusing on at the moment, but my brain had other ideas. "What are you doing out here?"

"I wanted to apologize. Our social interactions seemed off tonight. I didn't mean for things to get antagonistic and competitive."

"Things weren't competitive. It was a friendly game."

"Sometimes I have trouble understanding sarcasm. Your comment definitely falls into sarcasm, but it sounds like you're being serious?"

As my friends would say, Sebastian had a bug up his ass from the second he walked into Remix. From the second he saw me. I wasn't always the best at reading the room, but the vibes going on tonight would throw off even astute social observers.

"Fine, things got a little competitive." Sebastian cracked a hairline grin, giving me the tiniest peek of his white teeth. He had a really nice smile. It was a shame he was kind of uptight and didn't smile more because he was absolutely beautiful when he did. "I can be a competitive person. It's the athlete in me."

"I can be, too, though I don't have an athletic bone in my body."

"I saw that." His forehead crinkled in confusion. It was another shame that he was always so self-possessed, because confusion was another attractive look on him. "You were shit-talking me."

"Just a little."

"It seemed off brand for you."

"I prefer buying off-brand products at the supermarket, so I take that as a compliment. Many of them are made in the same facility as name-brand products, but sold at a lower price point. It's one of the best kept secrets of consumerism."

Even I could tell I was veering too off-topic. But it let another sly grin escape Sebastian's lips. Maybe I should take back my previous statement. He was beautiful when he smiled, but possibly more beautiful when he was brooding, his lips pouting into a perfectly kissable shape.

I sat down next to him, kicking aside the stray cigarette butts on the gravel. I didn't like staring down at him. I wanted us to be eye level.

"How did a nerdy science teacher get so competitive?" he asked. "Too many science fairs?"

"No. Actually, can I share something with you?"

"Go for it."

"I think it stems from my dad walking out."

Sebastian jerked his head to face me, light cracking through his brick exterior. I remembered seeing his mom on back to school nights, the annual event where parents would visit their kids' teachers. For most kids, both of their parents showed up, but not Sebastian's. It was only his mother. And I'd gotten the sense that it wasn't because his dad worked late. I could tell.

"It happened when I was eight. He secretly started a family with another woman, and he decided to live with them. Before he left, he sat me down and tried to explain his rationale, which in retrospect was a pretty awful thing to explain to an eight-year-old. Deep down, I felt like I was in constant competition with this other family."

"Like maybe if you were the best son possible, he'd come back." Sebastian stared into the night sky. He didn't phrase it as a question.

"I signed up for soccer in the hopes of being a dynamic enough player to convince Dad to come back. He never came to one of my games," I said, the memory of an empty space in the bleachers haunting me as if it happened yesterday. "Which was probably for the best since my athletic skills were subpar, as previously mentioned."

"You probably weren't as terrible as you think."

"I kicked and missed the ball more times than I'd like to admit. And sometimes, I would hop to the ball like a bunny rabbit." I was born to be a weird kid.

"There's nothing you could've done to convince your dad to return. Guys like that are selfish. It's only about them." Sebastian kicked at the gravel. His hand squeezed my knee in support. "I'm sorry that happened to you."

"Things got messy, but they're better now. I have my life and my routine. It keeps me sane. I've learned to live without the mess."

"I try to stay away from the mess, too," Sebastian said, unclenched for the first time tonight. "It's difficult, though. It's so easy to get tangled up in feelings and crushes and shit."

"Life is much better when you focus on facts and avoid gray areas. But anyway, sometimes that competitive side of me rears its ugly head, like with playing darts. Or when fighting for someone's attention."

Was that what was happening inside? I didn't think Anton invited me tonight to compete with Sebastian, but why did it turn into that?

"I didn't mean to make things uncomfortable between you and Anton," I said.

Sebastian heaved out a sigh. "You didn't. That one was all me."

"You know why he invited me, right?"

"He wanted us all to hang out," Sebastian said.

"He wants us to have another threesome."

Sebastian's eyes went wide, surprised that I said the quiet part out loud.

"Was I not supposed to be blunt? Are threesomes one of those things that can't be talked about, only experienced?"

He burst out laughing, his face breaking into a humongous smile.

"That's what Anton is thinking, isn't it? He brings us to a bar, gets us to loosen up with alcohol, and then eventually has us make our way back to your apartment all through the not-to-subtle power of persuasion and flirting."

"You're ruining the magic, Chase."

"Doesn't the magic happen once we get back to your apartment?"

Sebastian doubled over laughing. I never understood why sexual matters couldn't be talked about. Wouldn't it make things easier if we were all on the same page?

"Frankly, I was blindsided when I came into Remix. I thought Anton and I were grabbing a happy hour drink," he said.

"He invited me to join. If I'd known…but now I get why you weren't happy to see me from the get-go."

"I wasn't unhappy to see you. I was surprised. I'm not the best with surprises."

"Same. Surprises are more for the surpriser than the surprised, which makes them inherently selfish acts."

"I've actually had that same thought. Great minds think alike." Sebastian's stormy eyes bore into me, sending a delightful chill up my back. "Can I ask you an honest question?"

"As opposed to a dishonest one?"

"True. Uh, did you want to…repeat last weekend?"

"Have another threesome. Yes. Yes, I would."

He reeled back in amused shock. "You don't mince words."

"I really enjoyed it. I liked being transgressive and wild. My life is usually none of those things." I kept thinking about what Anton said to me in school. Maybe I did have a wild side worth exploring.

"What happened to enjoying routine?"

"It's fun to step outside my routine now and then. I spend my weekends ordering pizza and putting together puzzles with Einstein. Well, I put together the puzzle and Einstein squeezes herself into the empty box."

"I'm assuming Einstein is a cat."

"A bossy one at that." I traced my finger in the gravel as a bit of nerves got stuck in my throat. "And to be frank, I liked spending time with you and Anton, even before the sexual stuff."

It was hard to describe and sounded implausible. We'd barely spent time together. One long afternoon. But I kept thinking back on it fondly, cherishing the easy chemistry we had. Anton's cockiness and Sebastian's seriousness and my quirkiness all combined in a dazzling feat of alchemy. It was rare for me to find people I clicked with. I wasn't someone with a million friends. Most people got sick of me pretty quickly. I was an acquired taste.

Sebastian was indecipherable at the moment. Conflicting thoughts seemed to be churning in his head.

"Seb, you're still here." Anton found us outside. He sat down in front of us, completing our circle. "Is everything okay?"

It was cute how much concern washed over Anton's face for his friend.

"Yeah. I just needed some air."

"That was a competitive game. You guys got really into it."

Sebastian and I shared a look of mutual understanding.

"What've you guys been talking about?"

"That you orchestrated this outing so that we could all have sex again," I said.

Anton's face dropped for a second before he broke out into an unashamed smile. "I mean, if that happened, that wouldn't be an uncool way to spend a Thursday night." He squatted down to our level, his thigh muscles bulging under his shorts. "Listen, we can all just grab another round of drinks and hang out for real. We'll shoot the shit, have a few laughs, no presh."

"I like that plan," I said.

"Bottom line: I like hanging with you guys." Anton shrugged.

"We could do that," Sebastian said, a mischievous eyebrow raised. "Or we could go back to our place again. We still have that case of hard seltzer in the fridge."

"This is true," Anton said, scratching his chin. "That's the more economical choice."

I laughed to myself. It seemed that some things would be left unspoken no matter how open we could be. I thought of it like one big game.

"Yes, I agree. I would rather relax in a living room than on those uncomfortable bar stools," I said.

"Totally! Our futon is far more comfortable," Anton said. He jumped up and extended a hand to Sebastian and me.

We took an Uber back to their apartment, and my body tingled with excitement the whole way there. Even though I had a feeling of what would happen, I couldn't stop myself from unraveling with anticipation.

15

ANTON

No lie: I was rock fucking hard the entire Uber ride home. The driver had a rule that if a passenger puked in his car, they had to pay a fifty dollar cleanup fee. But what was the fee if a passenger accidentally jizzed themselves?

I was in between two sexy, sweet guys and I was on the verge of potentially getting laid tonight. Sebastian, though, was still focused on work, judging by his phone screen.

"Dude, are you still checking emails?"

"Just want to make sure there are no fire alarms," he said.

"Do vending machines catch fire often?" Chase asked.

"It's what we call a customer emergency." I knocked his knee with mine. "The good thing about supplying vending machines to offices is that they're only used during work hours, so we don't really have to worry about a machine breaking down at three in the morning."

"That's not completely true. We have some machines at gyms and restaurants that are open late," Sebastian said. He put away his phone, finally off the clock.

"It's incredible that you've managed to start what seems to be a successful business right out of high school. Do you ever think about going to college, though? Just in case," Chase said.

"Just in case what? If Beverage Solutions goes under, then we'll start something else. College isn't for everyone. The only thing my older friends learned in college was how to do a keg stand and how to sneak out of someone's bed unnoticed."

"I learned neither of those things at college," Chase said. He turned to Sebastian. "What about you?"

Sebastian hesitated a moment, the uncertainty wafting off him threw me for a bit.

"You know, I like what we're building here with Beverage Solutions."

We'd talked about Sebastian possibly returning to school in the future. It was always a maybe just in case things went south with BS. The thought of Seb going off to college made me uncomfortable, like it would be a permanent break in our friendship. We'd promise to stay friends, but after a few months of hanging around intelligent college students, would Sebastian forget about me? It wasn't something I wanted to think about while we were en route to a potential threesome.

Fortunately, the Uber pulled up to our apartment building just in time. *College talk over. Let's talk about getting naked instead.*

I nearly bolted up the stairs to our place, taking the steps two at a time. Was I being a little too excited? Probably. But I badly wanted to relive the magic of last weekend and forget about the fizzy La Croix feelings bubbling inside me.

I had a taste, and I wanted more. Well, actually, Chase was the one who had the taste. *Unhhhh so hot.*

Our apartment was on the top floor. I waited at the door for Sebastian and Chase to catch up.

"Took you geezers long enough," I said as I held the door open for them.

———

WE BROKE open our hard seltzers, and in another favorable twist of the evening, we talked a little bit more. It was always a relief to enjoy the company of the person (or persons) you were fucking.

We tumbled into conversation, with Chase asking us more about Beverage Solutions and us asking him for gossip on South Rock High's sterling faculty. Was the teacher's lounge the place to be? ("No. It's sadly eventful.") Did Principal Aguilar really start dating a parent of one of his students? ("Correct. They grow cacti and apple trees together.") Does Mr. Z believe in conspiracy theories? ("Unfortunately, yes.")

I found that the best kind of flirting was actually good conversation. We talked and talked until I checked my phone and it was past ten. Time flew.

"Chase, you have to get up early for school, don't you?" Sebastian asked, hardwired to be a party pooper.

"I don't need much sleep. I'm at my best with six hours."

I nodded, impressed. I was always that guy who needed his sleep and could never get enough. Forcing high schoolers to start the school day at seven-thirty was cruel and unusual punishment.

"I could do another round," Chase said.

"Sweet." I slid into the kitchen *Risky Business*-style. I pulled three more hard seltzers from the fridge. I looked up and saw my reflection in the window. I had on a sloppy, contented grin. Whatever else happened tonight, I was having an awesome time chilling with these guys. I felt a kind of ease that usually evaded me on dates. I wasn't trying to sell myself. I was just being me.

"Here we go. El seltzers de los hard." That was the last remaining bit of Spanish I remembered from Mr. Shablanski's class. Chase and Sebastian had moved to the cabinet against the wall where Chase was admiring our wrestling trophies.

"It's nice you kept your trophies and that you display them," Chase said.

"It's nice...or a little corny?" Sebastian said, echoing complaints he'd said before. "Most athletes we know just put their high school trophies in a box to be rediscovered when their parents sell their childhood home in the future. Why must you display them, Anton?"

I looked on at my trophies with pride. "Because they're reminders of what I can accomplish with hard work and discipline. When I'm having a rough day with BS, I remember to not give up and that I'm more powerful than a bad day."

"That's kind of beautiful," Sebastian said.

"I have my moments."

"Is wrestling difficult?" Chase asked, a burp slipping past his lips. He seemed the slightest bit tipsy, the fun effects of alcohol taking over. "Isn't it merely knocking someone to the ground? Is there skill involved?"

"Is there skill involved?" I huffed out a laugh. Sebastian and I shared a look. "You want to take this one, Seb?"

"Wrestling is a difficult sport of executing complex, physically demanding moves to pin your opponent. It's not a street fight. There's a coordination to it."

"You have to stay within the regulation moves and outthink your opponent constantly," I said.

"I may need to see some of these moves in action in order to accurately gauge wrestling's degree of difficulty," said Chase. The way he spoke was unlike anyone I'd ever met. It was smart-sexy. I could barely keep up with him.

Sebastian and I moved the coffee table to the corner of the room, using the rug underneath as our mock mat. We got into opposite corners, hunched over, our wrestling training coming back to us.

"You both look like lions about to pounce," Chase observed.

"This is the starting position," I said. "Right now, I'm looking at Seb and sizing up my competition. Which foot is he landing on, which way is he tilted, is he right-handed or left-handed and how will that play into the moves he uses."

Sebastian, for his part, was really into the scenario, staring me down in full competition mode. "I'm doing the same to Anton. If I can see how he situates himself, I can take a guess at what moves he'll try first."

"Will you call go," I asked Chase, our unofficial ref.

"Uh, go?"

And we were off. Muscle memory came into play as Sebastian and I circled each other. His T-shirt clung to his chest, the dip between his pecs distracting me for a second, giving him the upper hand. Sebastian charged at me, throwing his arms around my waist and trying to pin me to the floor.

Trying being the operative word. I might've been thrown off by his hot bod, but I wasn't going down without a fight. We wrestled in our tight embrace, our legs out for balance, circling around the tight quarters, bumping into furniture. The friction of our chests rubbing against each other got me all discombobulated. I'd wrestled hundreds of guys in high school, and I never had this reaction. I prided myself on keeping my sexuality off the mat. I knew I was representing gay athletes, and one could not pop a boner during a meet. But the heat of Sebastian was intoxicating. Had my friend always been this manly and ravenous?

Sebastian grunted in my ear, and it set off mini fireworks as I remembered his grunting from last weekend. The way he threw his head back as he unloaded into Chase's pretty mouth.

And down I fucking went.

I stared up at the ceiling, pride wounded and head a blur.

"So with that round, I had to outthink him and get him off balance. Mind and strength."

You didn't outwit me, Seb. You unwittingly used your manly wiles to throw me off. Damn you and your sex appeal.

"We need a rematch," I said. "Best of three."

"You're on."

"I'm sorry, but what moves?" Chase asked. He stood over us, head cocked to the side. "All I saw were two semi-drunk guys in a bear grip trying to throw each other to the ground."

"We'll call out moves we're using," I said. That would help me stay present and not get lost in Sebastian's musky scent and manly grunting.

Sebastian and I returned to our starting places. I hunched over, heaving breath, refusing to lose again but also noticing the sparkle in his crystal blue eyes. Was that how he won championships? Hypnotizing opponents with his gaze?

"And go," Chase said half-heartedly.

I charged at Sebastian, but he sensed my move and ducked. I'd given myself away too easily. Shit. He pummeled me to the ground. Before he could pin me, I pushed out of his grip and threw him back. We circled each other, two animals on the hunt. Sebastian charged at me. I grabbed him back, my hands falling to his ass.

"That's an illegal move," he said between grunts that scrambled my circuits.

Extremely illegal. But man, what an ass.

"I'm trying to do a single leg takedown," I said with strained breath.

"You two are really getting into it," Chase observed.

Yeah, in more ways than one. Sebastian's hand grazed over the massive hard-on tenting my pants.

"Talk about an illegal move," I said, holding back a groan of delight at his touch.

Fortunately, my dick threw him off just long enough for me to pin him to the ground.

"Tie score," Chase said.

"Last round," Sebastian said, not as focused as he once was. He whipped off his shirt, revealing a chest I'd seen several times before, but never really appreciated. Sebastian was built wide, his arms two big corded strands of rope.

I took off my shirt. Then I kicked off my shoes and took off my pants.

"What are you doing?" Sebastian asked.

"I can't wrestle in my regular clothes. It's too constricting. Is this a problem for you?" My boner was outlined in my boxer briefs. I didn't care to hide it. Sebastian and Chase both checked me out. They liked what they saw.

I adjusted my junk in plain sight. I was proud of my equipment and wasn't afraid for others to know it. And I wasn't the first wrestler to adjust himself in his uniform.

"Round three, Seb? Unless you want to forfeit another game tonight."

"Not even close." Sebastian kicked his shoes across the floor. A twinge of need flickered in my gut at the sound of his belt unbuckling and then the clacking of it hitting the floor with the rest of his pants.

I'd checked out Sebastian last weekend when Chase was going down on him, but tonight, I got to see him in the light. We'd been friends and roommates, but it was the first time when I truly admired how flat-out gorgeous he was. And how much I wanted to run my tongue across his smooth olive skin.

Was that real or was that my horned-up brain playing tricks on me? I didn't have time to parse out the truth. I had a match to win.

Sebastian and I went to our corners. He was sprouting wood in his underwear, too, but we both ignored that for the moment. We wanted to win.

"Round three," Chase called from the sidelines. "And go!"

Off we went. Sebastian lunged at me with such force that I

almost hit the floor. I was on one foot, but I fought back, shoving my body against his, our sweaty chests causing enough friction to start a fire.

"Neither of us are giving up so easily," I narrated for Chase. "We're trying different moves but nothing is working so far."

Sebastian tried one move after another to throw me off, but I wouldn't give up. I wasn't losing. The touch of our bodies only made me stronger. Sebastian played dirty and grabbed my cock.

"You're just full of illegal moves tonight," I said with a smile.

I held firm and tried to flip him, grabbing onto his waist. I got him to bend forward, and sensing an opening, no pun intended, I jammed two fingers against his hole. He faltered and fell to the floor.

"Call it, Chase!" I said.

Chase counted to three. Anton, victor and champion.

"None of that was legal. You checked the oil," Sebastian said, frazzled, pupils blown wide.

"Checked the oil?" Chase asked.

"It's a very illegal wrestling move," I said. "Used to throw your opponent off guard."

I used an arm bar move to keep him pinned face down and shoved my index and middle finger against his ass's most sensitive point. Only a thin layer of underwear kept me from sliding into that valley of perfection. Sebastian bit back a moan.

"You asshole," he said, grunting to get out of my grip, which only made me want to keep going.

"You don't like getting your oil checked?" I glared at him, every fiber of me revved up with lust. I pushed harder against his hole, this close to ripping a hole in his underwear.

Sebastian raised his hips to give me better leverage, his cock straining against his boxers. I pressed deeper until I breached his opening and warmth enveloped the tips of my fingers.

"Do wrestlers actually use the checking the oil move?" Chase asked. There was a noticeable bulge in his pants.

"Sometimes," I said. I couldn't stop looking at Sebastian's face, awash in need. He'd never given me that look. "Did you want to try?"

Chase squatted down and pressed his fingers against Sebastian's bouncy ass tentatively.

"Shit," Sebastian gasped out as Chase rubbed his fingers in tight circles.

"How does that feel?" I asked Chase as I massaged his neck.

"Really good."

"Did you want to get your oil checked?"

He nodded yes, desire clouding his eyes.

"Good. Since you're an honorary wrestler, you should experience it for yourself. How about it, Seb?" I slapped Sebastian's ass to bring him out of his haze.

"Uh huh."

"Stand up," I ordered.

Chase looked down at us, so innocent in his button-down plaid shirt and pants, a touch of fear behind his thick glasses.

Sebastian and I stood up, our muscular bodies easily dwarfing his lithe frame. I undid his shirt and slid it off. Sebastian unbuckled Chase's belt, then pushed his pants to the floor. Chase rolled his head back and a sweet moan escaped his lips. I kissed along his shoulders. Sebastian met up and kissed Chase's back. Our lips got close but didn't touch.

"All wrestlers do this after each meet, to promote good sportsmanship," I said, my voice teasing. I reached behind Chase and stroked my fingers down Sebastian's side, savoring the curves of his abs.

"It's also a good way to stretch," said Sebastian. He reached forward and pinched my nipple, sending a jolt of lust up my chest.

My mouth skimmed Chase's neck, over his soft, stubbled chin, up to his pink, fat bottom lip. I pushed past his teeth, my tongue conquering him, Chase giving in to our heat. My hands grabbed at his back, then fell down Sebastian's chest. It was an abundance of riches.

Chase let out a hard gasp, his eyes bolting open.

He looked over his shoulder.

"And that's checking the oil," said Sebastian. His fingers were pressed against Chase's sensitive area, perhaps a little too firmly.

"It's very alerting," Chase said, catching his breath. His head fell back on Sebastian's shoulder as Sebastian continued to dig his fingers in. He pushed his ass into those greedy fingers.

Why were we still wearing underwear? I pushed Chase's to the floor. He was naked, pale, soft, all for us. He was prey ready to be attacked by two wrestling animals.

Sebastian gripped his arms around Chase's waist and threw him to the floor. I lifted Chase's legs over his head. He was very foldable, his knees coming to his chest. His hard cock dripped precome onto his stomach. His pink hole was up in the air.

I held out my middle and index fingers and slid them into Sebastian's mouth. Slicked up, I entered them into Chase's hole.

"Checking the oil," I whispered.

Chase croaked out a delicious moan. His composed demeanor fell in an instant. I slid my fingers in and out, while Sebastian dipped down and sucked his dick. We attacked him from both ends. He'd given us pleasure last weekend. It was our turn to return the favor.

An indecipherable string of pants and moans were falling from Chase's mouth. I lifted his hips for better leverage. He was practically upside down, ass and cock high in the air. I flicked my tongue over his opening, circling the pink rim and slipping inside while Sebastian disappeared his cock inside his hot mouth.

Chase was warm, pulsing under my touch.

"I really like wrestling," he said. "It's much more homoerotic than I thought."

"Mr. M., you ain't seen nothing yet."

I held out my fingers to Sebastian, silently commanding him to wet them. He took them in his mouth, coating them with fresh saliva. I re-entered Chase, stretching his tight hole.

"Does Teach like getting double-teamed by his students?" Sebastian uttered in a husky tone, his throat tight.

"Yes," Chase whispered. "More."

I fucked him with my tongue. His moans and his scent intoxicated me, as did watching Sebastian take him to his base. He dragged the flat of his tongue to Chase's balls. I met Sebastian for a sloppy kiss over Chase's most sensitive area. I pulled Sebastian closer, wanting to feel all of him.

"Anton," he said, barely above a whisper, as if my name came from the deepest part of him. It was scarily intimate.

Sebastian dipped his fingers inside Chase. I reached over and took Chase's cock in my mouth, pre-come hitting my tongue. Sharing was caring. We took turns fingering him, opening him up. Chase's body was tense and coiled. I could feel him tighten with need.

Chase hit his hand against the rug, the wrestler's signal that he was down for the count.

"Chase, you okay?" I asked.

Sebastian and I let him go, his body flopped to the ground. He heaved in deep breaths.

"That was intense," he said. "Oh my God."

Right back atcha. I had to catch my breath from everything swirling around. I rested my hand tenderly on his cheek, my other hand on Sebastian's leg. An unexpected sweetness broke through my rapacious desire. I looked at both of them with intensity but something deeper I couldn't explain. They were panting and vulnerable, and I had this urge to take care of them.

"My guys," I said to them. The term fit like a perfect pair of shoes. "How are my guys doing?"

Chase sat up, the whites of his eyes burning with delirium, a hand clinging to my chest. "I want you to fuck me, Anton."

16

SEBASTIAN

Anton ran to his room to grab lube and condoms, cock swinging between his legs. Chase was sweaty and catching his breath. I didn't blame him. I'd probably be a mess if I'd been rimmed and blown at the same time.

A thin layer of fog shrouded his glasses. I pushed my fingers under the lenses and wiped them off, revealing piercing eyes that were so heavy with lust Chase needed a spotter to lift them.

Locking eyes with him did something to me. It made my dick twitch. We were under a spell.

I want you, his eyes said. *And I will have you.*

Chase began to kiss down my chest. We were both on our knees on the rug where Anton and I had been wrestling. I arched my back, giving Chase my hot skin. He kept going south, his ass jutting into the air as his mouth got closer to my dick.

"Fuck." I pushed him the rest of the way down.

He took my cock in his mouth without stopping, right to the base, gagging on the thickness.

"Fuck, yeah. Suck that cock, Teach." I never called him Teach when I was a student, but the nickname was a turn on. What would it have been like for Anton and I to take him on his desk in his classroom, shoving tests and molecule models to the floor so we could have our way with him?

Chase greedily took my cock, stroking and sucking, his hungry blue eyes gazing up at me through the thick glasses. He didn't want a moment of rest. I leaned back and thrust into his mouth. My fingers combed through the blond strands of his sweaty hair and pushed him down.

"I could probably suck dick better than you," I said. I doubted that was true, but I wanted to bring out his fiery competitive side and make him work.

I humped into his mouth as we stared each other down.

"Stick out your tongue," I commanded.

I smacked my cock on his bright red tongue, the thwack sound making me even harder.

"You're so thick," he said, catching his breath.

"Damn right."

"Shit. And the party don't stop," Anton said when he returned to the living room.

"He's all ready for you, bud," I said. I moved my hand down Chase's smooth back and slapped his ass. Chase moaned against my cock in approval.

"He sucks good dick," Anton said. He knelt beside me, his musky scent driving me wild.

Chase took both our dicks in his mouth at once, our sensitive heads sliding against each other.

Anton wrapped his arm around my waist. Back at Remix, I wasn't having it, but here, I could let myself revel in his touch. Whatever anger I had had dissipated. The three of us were one cohesive unit.

I kissed him, because I could, because we were in the moment, and I couldn't get enough of his lips. I would worry about how this was lust, not love, for him tomorrow. Tonight, I chose to live in the present. He gently moved my cheek to slide his tongue deeper inside me, to fully stake his claim. I wanted him. I wanted him so bad. Even while I was having him, I wanted more.

My tongue swirled around his mouth as Chase's tongue swirled around our dicks. I moaned into Anton's lips.

"My guys," he uttered in a low tone, making every hair on my body stand on edge.

We were his.

Anton rubbed his cock along mine, sending shivers up my spine.

"Chase, you are so fucking incredible," he said as he rolled his condom on and coated his cock with lube.

"Please fuck me, Anton," he mewled.

Anton got behind Chase and lubed up his hole. Chase grabbed my thighs for support as Anton pushed his way inside. Taking Anton's dick seemed like no easy feat.

"How does that feel?" Anton asked, partly out of concern.

"You're bigger than most guys I've been with. I'm adjusting," Chase said, his technical voice back for a second.

"Tell me what you need. I don't want to hurt you." Anton kissed along his back and nuzzled into his neck, so tenderly, so caring. A twinge of jealousy hit me.

Chase hugged me tighter, clenching, his glasses digging into my abs.

"You okay?" I asked Chase, smoothing a hand over his hair.

"I'm good." He looked up at me with needy eyes, trepidation on his face as Anton slid deeper inside him.

"It's going to feel good. We'll make sure of it," I promised him. Tonight, here, we were on the same team.

"Don't stop, Anton. Please don't stop."

"You feel so fucking good, Chase," Anton said, his voice a low grumble.

Chase's pain quickly turned to pleasure as that hungry look

returned to his eyes. I fed him my dick, which he gladly took. It disappeared into his mouth, his moans making me rock hard and pushing me toward the edge.

Anton looked at me in bliss and disbelief. He couldn't believe this was happening, but he was enjoying the hell out of it. All that worrying and wondering about whether this was a good idea seemed so dumb in retrospect. This was easily the greatest sex either of us had had.

"Fuck yeah," he said. We bumped fists.

I loved the view. I got to stare at his chest and abs and the peak of his pubic hair as he pumped into Chase. And it seemed he was doing the same, drinking me in with delight.

"Hey, my eyes are up here," I said to him playfully.

"Yeah, I know," he answered with a smirk that drove me wild.

I leaned forward, being respectful not to mess up Chase's flow, and planted a soft kiss on Anton's lips. I'd never get bored kissing Anton. He met me hungrily, a heated kiss back.

"Shit," I gasped out. Chase took me to the base again. His mouth was freaking magic. Between Anton's sexiness and Chase's blow job prowess, I wasn't going to last long.

Anton pushed Chase's head down on my dick as he fucked him harder.

"Take him. Yeah, just like that," he commanded.

Chase sprung up, lips pink and swollen, face flushed. He'd been working hard tonight. Chase was competition, but he was also a good guy. We'd been through the same struggles. There was a connection there.

Anton pulled Chase to his chest and fucked him fast and hard. Chase groaned with agonizing delight. I grabbed his cock and mine and stroked them together, Chase's pre-come slicking us up.

Chase made unintelligible sounds, the kind of noises one made when words wouldn't suffice. His body was a firecracker of need, sizzling and crackling and bursting with color.

"Come for us, Chase," Anton said. "We want to make you feel good."

Chase was possessed, lolling his head around, his legs wobbling, chest shaking. Anton pretty much had to hold him up at this point.

"Oh my God, oh my God," Chase kept muttering. I stroked us harder, wanting desperately to bring us to climax.

Chase and I locked eyes, the heat and vulnerability spinning around like shapes in a kaleidoscope. My orgasm exploded out, pouring over my fist in unrelenting waves.

"Fuck," I cried out.

Chase rested his head on Anton's chest. His dick was red and hard, begging for release.

"You're so beautiful, Chase. You're so beautiful," Anton whispered into his ear. As I came back down to earth, the only person in the room post-orgasm, I couldn't help but feel another twinge of jealousy.

Chase cracked out a moan as he came, hot release hitting my thighs.

"I'm almost there, baby." Anton jackhammered into him. His baby. Before another twinge of jealousy could hit over that, I had the pleasure of watching Anton's O-face as he emptied himself inside Chase.

Anton heaved in heavy breaths. A silence took over the room, thick with sweat and heat.

I wiped off Chase's fogged-up glasses. He leaned forward to kiss me, and I couldn't explain what came over me, but at the last second, I gave him my cheek. He was still so in the heat of things, he didn't seem to care either way.

Anton didn't hesitate. He took Chase's chin and planted a wet, passionate kiss on his lips.

"Chase..." Anton choked on his words, overcome with emotion

that caught him, and us, off guard. His voice wobbled, something I'd never seen from him. Anton never got emotional.

He cleared his throat, and a second later, he was back to his sexy grinning self. "That was hot. You were definitely the MVP tonight."

Chase blushed. Anton stroked his cheek with the softest care. The jealous twinge kept rearing its ugly head, like it was pinching my neck. I tried pushing it away.

Anton put a hand on each of our asses. "I'm speechless."

"Is it customary for one to give a speech after sex?" Chase asked.

Anton and I busted out laughing, breaking the serious intimate moment, yet it felt intimate in its own way, the way good friends could laugh about anything.

Anton mussed up Chase's hair, and I joined in.

"You and Sebastian didn't waste any time while I was gone."

Chase and I shared a look. There was something guarded there, like maybe he did notice that I wouldn't kiss him.

"We're very efficient," Chase said.

"Let's hit the showers," Anton said, silencing the chaos in my head. At least, for now.

———

I WOKE up the next morning to a phone call from Craig. My hangover from hard seltzer and hot sex would have to wait. I immediately sprung into business mode when his number popped up on my phone. It was seven a.m., but it didn't matter. Business never waited.

"Craig, what's up?" I sat up in bed, wiping my eyes and at least acting like I'd had my morning coffee.

"I have some potentially good news for you."

Good news was always better than coffee. It was nature's stimulant.

"I like good news," I said. I jumped out of bed and paced in my bedroom.

"We received the renewal contract from our vending machine provider. Jim Hollis was livid. They want to jack up the prices twenty percent."

"Twenty percent?" I repeated in incredulity.

"They're saying it's inflation and higher costs on their end. We've worked with them for eight years. You don't just spring a cost increase like that when you send over an renewal."

"They didn't call you first to go over it?"

"Nope," Craig said, obviously pissed. I didn't blame him. That was bad business. Anton and I always delivered bad, or at least unpleasant, news face-to-face or via phone call. We'd never try to sneak it into an email or contract.

"That's kind of disrespectful. They were trying to sneak it in, it sounds like. Didn't they know Hollis was being more hawkish about spending?"

"They did, and it looks like they didn't care. Hollis got on the phone with them and chewed them out. We understand that costs go up. That's business. But they should've talked with us first. The owner apologized and agreed to come down on the increase, but it got Hollis spooked. He's having me vet and set up meetings with a few vendors that could be a viable alternative. I'd like to include Beverage Solutions on the list."

And here I thought my orgasm last night was the highlight of the week. I was wrong.

"I know our follow up call isn't until June, but we have to let our current vendor know if we're renewing by the end of the month."

"Yeah, absolutely. I totally get it. Time is of the essence. Anton and I are available to meet. When were you thinking?"

"Today's Friday, and Hollis is big on no weekend meetings. So let's schedule for next week. We're having all vendors give presentations next week, and we're going to bring back the top two contenders sometime after that."

We loved competition. It only made us work harder.

"Works for me." I pulled up our calendar. I was in boxers, still high on last night, but that would wait.

Craig and I found a time late next week to meet with Jim Hollis, the head honcho. Despite him urgently wanting to talk, his next available appointment wasn't until Wednesday afternoon. Such was the life of a busy CEO. It worked for us.

In less than a week, we'd be meeting with the decision maker for our biggest potential sale, one that could launch us to the next level. If we signed Hollis Property Management, that would give us credibility with bigger clients. I smiled at my bedroom wall in a daze, thinking about how Anton and I started this crazy venture in his parents' garage. We were inspired by a podcast we listened to and thought we could sell vending machines. Even after the spark of inspiration faded, and we were left with the day-to-day grind of running a business, Anton remained determined, undeterred by reality. He'd put his hand on my shoulders and bore into me with those bottomless wells of brown eyes.

I know this is crazy, but we can do this, Seb. You and me. We're gonna take over the world.

We hadn't taken over the world just yet, but maybe we were a bit closer than yesterday.

I jumped out of bed and walked across the hall to his bedroom.

"Anton, you're never going to believe what hap–"

My breath whooshed from my body. Anton lay on his bed spooning Chase, both fast asleep.

They looked peaceful, like a couple.

In that moment, I forgot about Hollis and business and everything else in my life. It was as if someone drove a spike through my heart.

Anton stirred awake, his eyelashes fluttering open. He took his thick, strong hand off Chase's waist—a hand that I had wanted badly to cradle me.

"Hey," he said creakily. "What happened?"

But I lost the ability to speak. We'd been more intimate than ever last night, but now I felt farther away from him than I had in my life.

"Seb." His grogginess vanished as he must've seen whatever the hell my face was doing.

"Sorry. I–yeah." I shut the door and darted into the kitchen, for coffee, for the fire escape, for any escape.

"Shit," I said to myself. I opened the fridge door, not sure what I was looking for, but it was another wall to hide behind. Maybe reciprocal love would never be in the cards for me. I didn't have it with my dad, and I didn't have it here.

I pulled out a container of Greek Yogurt. Anton was waiting on the other side of the fridge door.

"Seb." He pushed the door closed and blocked my way out of the kitchen. "It's not what it looks like."

How could it not look like he and Chase had slept together? Actually slept. The kind of sleeping one did with a partner.

"Whatever. I don't care," I said with as much nonchalance dudebro attitude as I could muster under the circumstances.

"Yes, you do," he said firmly. I hated how much he could read me. It wasn't fair. "After last night, you went to your bedroom and crashed. Chase and I couldn't sleep, so we watched some TV. He offered to sleep on the futon, but we couldn't get it to open. You know how fucking janky it is."

We'd gotten it free off Craigslist. It wasn't until after we walked it eight blocks, then up three flights of stairs to our apartment that we realized it had trouble opening into a bed. We'd gotten what we paid for.

"He's too tall to lay on the futon as is. He tried, but I could tell he was very uncomfortable. So I invited him to crash on my bed."

"I don't need a play-by-play, Anton."

"I thought about going to get you, but you were fast asleep. You've always had the gift of being a deep sleeper, Seb."

"I said it was cool."

He came closer and rubbed a hand on my arm. I flinched reactively, even though I wanted him to keep going.

"I don't want you to feel left out. This wasn't a move against you."

"I know that." I gripped the counter to steady myself. *Stop falling in love with him.* There was only one ending with Anton: a broken heart.

"Seriously, Seb. I wished you were in bed with us. I'm sorry for not waking you and having you join."

I wanted to keep telling him it was fine, but he knew. He knew me well enough to know it wasn't fine and that I felt hurt. As he did in his garage years ago, he bore into me with those bottomless wells for eyes.

"Please don't be upset." He stroked his hand up and down my arm. "It won't happen again. Not without you." He kissed my cheek softly. "We're a trio. The Three Amigos, but with sex."

I looked up at him and wanted to believe.

"God, you were so fucking hot last night, Seb. I'd never seen you like that. I want more."

Just when I thought he was going to lean forward and kiss me for real, out of the corner of my eye, I spotted Chase in the doorway. And the moment came to a halting crash of a stop.

"Morning," I said, pushing past Anton. "We have coffee, yogurt, toast. Help yourself."

"Thanks. I think it's best that I get going. I have school," Chase said.

"You sure you don't have time for a quick breakfast?" Anton asked. The hopeful note in his voice crushed me.

I hated that my jealousy was like a cloak I could never take off. I hated that I was forever waiting for the moment when I would be ditched. Fuck my dad and the permanent damage he etched into my heart.

"He has school," I said to Anton. "His students are waiting for him. Don't let us stop you."

Chase nodded, seeming a little dinged by the remark. He waved to both of us. "Farewell, then. Until we meet again."

"We're definitely meeting again," Anton said.

His resolve was both a turn on and a pit of dread in my stomach. I had to face the ugly truth. I wasn't built to be in a relationship, and definitely not a threesome. When the afterglow faded, jealousy would inevitably remain.

17

CHASE

"It's in your best interest as my friends to know that I had another threesome."

I said this to my friends three days after the aforementioned sexual encounter while standing on an alteration platform with a seamstress measuring my inseam. She didn't flinch. She was Italian and ninety years old. She had likely heard worse.

Everett bolted from his dressing room and put his hand over his chest.

"What are you doing?" I asked.

"I'm silently giving you the Pledge of Allegiance."

"That isn't patriotic."

We were getting fitted for suits for Pop's big day. Usually, I wasn't one for the pomp and circumstance of weddings, but I did look good in this suit.

"What do we think?" Julian exited his dressing room in a gray suit that matched ours. He was on the heavier side, but he wore it well. He knew how to dress himself.

"J, you look awesome!" Amos said.

"I agree. You wear clothes very well," I said.

"You look fabulous and Chase had another threesome with his students," Everett said, picking at a stray string on his matching gray suit.

"Former students," I said.

"Once a student, always a student. What did you teach them this time? How to handle their test tubes?" Everett was having way too much fun.

I should have had a lesson on that with my students. Over a dozen test tubes had been dropped and shattered this year alone. Taxpayer dollars tossed in the garbage.

"Was it good the second time around?" Julian asked, checking himself out in the three-panel mirror.

A smile flitted on my face. "Better, actually. More interactive."

The seamstress at my feet continued on with her business, undisturbed and thoroughly uninterested in our conversation. Still, it seemed inappropriate to get into details in front of someone just trying to do their job.

"It was wonderful. Very easy," I said. "I thought there'd be more difficulty coordinating who did what, but we fell into place seamlessly. It was an easier experience than some of my one-on-one sexual encounters."

It reminded me of two pieces locking together in one of my Friday night jigsaw puzzles. There was no effort needed to force pieces together. Either they fit or they didn't. We seemed to fit.

"Was it hot?" Amos asked. "I mean, I can only imagine that a threesome has to be inherently steamy because of all the extra limbs."

Here, I could not tell a lie. My face turned red as I thought back. "Yes. Yes, it was."

I loved how Anton could be both rough and tender in handling me, and how Sebastian was cautious and strong. I gave them some choice details from the night, like going down on both guys and having Anton fuck me.

But there were some details that I kept to myself. Like the swoon in my heart when Anton called us "my guys" and when Sebastian promised it would feel good. (It did!) Was it just the effect of an extremely intense orgasm, or was the connection I felt something real? While I didn't have much experience with threesomes, I suspected swooning wasn't a typical reaction. My friends would likely criticize me for not understanding the assignment.

Speaking of my friends, I had seemingly done the impossible: rendered them speechless.

"Where are all the witty comments? This silence is not indicative of past reactions to similar stories. It's mildly disturbing."

"We're impressed. Chase, if you were a character in *A Midsummer Night's Dream*, you'd be Bottom," Everett said.

"If you were a 2000s sitcom, you'd be *Malcolm in the Middle*," said Amos.

"If you were a toy, you'd be one of those Chinese finger traps," said Julian.

Ah, that was more like it.

"Do you think this will be a regular thing?" Julian asked.

"It better," said the seamstress, sending us all for a loop. She stood up, rubbing at her lower back but showing no sign of slowing down. "That should be it. All of you, hang your pants and jackets carefully on your hangers. Leave them on the hooks in your dressing rooms. Don't touch any of the pins."

She pointed at each of us. It would be her first, last, and only warning. We would not disobey.

The four of us went into our dressing rooms. I delicately moved my feet up and out of the pant legs, then delicately hung the pants on the hanger, which I delicately placed on the hook. It was as if I was walking through a field of landmines.

"You are living the dream, Chase. A recurring threesome," said Amos from his dressing room.

I wish I could feel as ecstatic about the arrangement as my

friends were, but the tense moment from the morning made me concerned that it was two-and-done.

"To be perfectly frank, I don't know if it'll happen again," I said. "I thought we had a good time, but I got a sense that Sebastian seemed displeased."

"Displeased? Did he not finish?" Everett asked.

"Oh, he did. He had a good time, but he seemed like he didn't." Typically, I wasn't at a loss for words. I was in exception territory. "When we met up at a bar, he seemed not to want me there, but then we still had sex. And he was very much engaged. And then we showered together, where he was also very engaged. And then the morning after, he went back to acting upset that I was there. Is there such a thing as a split personality that only comes out during sex?"

"Sex can be a sort of truth serum," Amos said.

"Truth serum?" I asked, intrigued. "Go on."

"It can be a place where you shuck your inhibitions and let your true self out. You can act differently than you would normally and say things you might've been too afraid to say."

"Because the chemicals flooding our nervous system overpower our brain's ability to regulate our actions?" I asked, even more intrigued.

"When you fuck, your prefrontal cortex basically goes rogue," Everett said with his usual directness.

"Interesting." I sat on the tiny stool in my dressing room and stared at myself in the long mirror. Perhaps this flood of chemicals was skewing my feelings on Anton and Sebastian. I liked spending time with them, not just for sex, and I liked the way I felt in their arms, not just for sex. I wanted to spend more with them, not just for sex, even though our relationship was supposed to be just for sex. It was all very confusing.

I left the dressing room in my comfortable clothes but carrying a feeling of discomfort over the strange dynamic developing between Anton, Sebastian, and me.

My friends and I walked out of the store into the warm, sunny afternoon of downtown Sourwood. People were out and about, enjoying the weather. The decorative flower beds at street corners were in full bloom.

"Threesome Rule Number One." Amos held up a finger, returning my attention to Sebastian's odd behavior. "Never get in the middle of drama for the sake of sex."

"Do you have an actual list of rules for threesomes? Did you compile this yourself or source it from somewhere?" I asked.

"I've never been in one, but I have gotten in the middle of awkward situations. Same rules apply, just with less clothing. It sounds like you might be a wedge between Anton and Sebastian. They're close friends, right?" he asked.

"And business partners." It was starting to make sense. Sebastian and Anton were under a lot of pressure to land a large client. Sebastian was probably worried about that and frustrated that Anton just wanted to fool around. "I wonder if our gatherings are distracting them from their vending machine business."

"It could be. Maybe they're feeling weird about having sex with the same guy. What if they think you have a preference for one over the other," Julian said.

We walked down the street and stopped at a gazebo that in the fall would be overflowing with pumpkins.

"Do you?" Amos asked.

"No. I like them equally, in different ways. Anton is fun and charming. Sebastian is more reserved. I think we're more alike."

"It sounds like they're dealing with their own drama. Drama can be a boner killer," Everett said. Drama equated to mess, which I did not want in my life. "Are you sure you want to get in the middle of that for the sake of fun sex?"

It was a fair question. My gut was only giving me one inconvenient answer.

"Yes," I said. Even though I didn't want to deal with any mess, an unusually loud voice in the depths of my heart compelled me to keep seeing them. "I don't want to stop," I said with a resolve that took me aback.

"You don't want to come between friends. Unless the position calls for it." Everett bit back a smirk. "You know what I mean, though. Maybe it's best to back off for a bit, let them figure their shit out."

"True." Everett had a point, which my brain agreed with, but my heart begged to ignore.

"It all sounds delicate, so it might be best to give things time." Julian sat back on the gazebo bench. He, too, made a valid point, which I, too, wanted to ignore.

"You're right," I said. "But it also might be worth trying to be a peacemaker."

In other words, forge deeper into the mess like a soldier advancing into enemy territory. This made zero sense, yet I could not stop the words from tumbling out of my traitorous mouth.

"You're choosing to get further in between these two? That is incredibly illogical," Everett said. "I'm totally here for it, but that's because I'm a messy bitch who craves drama. But you're... not."

The logic pieced itself together in my head. "In most experiments, the reason molecules don't link together is because of an inactive chemical. There may need to be more of this chemical added or subtracted in order to get the balance just right. Perhaps one could look at Sebastian as this inactive element. We are still getting the balance right, and as the person in this arrangement with the most scientific background, it seems incumbent on me to go forth and get things as they should be."

I rubbed my hands, which were sweaty all of a sudden, on my

thighs. Logic, rationalization—what was the difference? A few extra big words?

I knew logically that this wasn't worth the mess. I could step back, enjoy the times we had, and move on with my orderly life. Yet that damn loud voice wouldn't shut the fuck up. I couldn't avoid feeling the rush of warmth that hit me when I was in their arms, when they were grunting my name, when they were running their lips along my skin, when their beam of intensity made me feel seen.

Before my friends could push back on my faulty logic, and my chemical explanation that was riddled with falsehoods, Julian's grandmother Judy powerwalked by in a bright pink jumpsuit. Shopping bags dangled from her fingers. She was elderly, but the very definition of "with it."

"Grandma!" Julian called out to her to get her attention. She came up to the gazebo.

"Grandma Judy! Be still my beating heart," Everett said. "I didn't know it was pink jumpsuit day. Ugh, you should've told me so we could coordinate."

Even though she was Julian's grandmother, she was like a grandmother to all of us. Always there to dispense sage advice or brutally honest remarks. She once told me that I seemed destined to have a threesome because it was in my aura, whatever that meant.

"Julian! And the boys!" She blew us kisses. "Why are you here and not spending time with your gorgeous men?"

"We were getting fitted for our suits for Hutch's dad's wedding," Amos said. "Are you coming?"

"I just RSVP'd. There better be an open bar."

Grandma Judy and Pop had gotten to be friends by going to the same physical therapist. It seemed most old people knew each other through repeated run-ins at the doctor.

"I can't wait to see you boys in your suits. I have to go. I'm meeting my husband for dinner. Seriously, go find your men. You have the rest of your lives to chit chat with each other. Might as well use your bodies while you're still flexible."

"Grandma..." Julian muttered, face turning beet red.

"What did I say?" she turned to me, the lone single member of the group. "And Chase, have you taken my advice and had any threesomes yet?"

Grandma Judy had once remarked that I had the face and personality of someone meant for threesomes, as if I were Luke Skywalker fulfilling his destiny of restoring order to the galaxy.

Usually, I demurred from her question. But this time, I had good news to share. "Actually, I've had two."

18

SEBASTIAN

What did you call a roller coaster that only went down? That was how the last few days had been for me, guaranteeing that I would never visit another amusement park again.

Things started on a high after that amazing night with Chase and Anton. Then, I lost my cool after seeing them in bed. Then, Anton and I lost a client who was going with a competitor. And now this.

I turned the card around in my hands, Elmo's happy, smiling face a dash of salt in a wound that refused to close. Some people had the worst timing.

I wished for a day I could live like Anton, letting things roll off my back, never letting things get to me and demolish my focus. Anton liked to tell me how smart I was, but sometimes, I wished I could turn my brain off.

It was impossible trying to do any work, but I tried. The hustle never quit. I took my laptop to a picnic table at Renegade Park, which was right on the river. I managed to get some admin work done while the sun attempted to elevate my mood.

Chase texted that morning and said he needed to return something to me. We hadn't spoken since I pretty much pushed him out of our apartment. This would be interesting.

"Hello." Chase waved at me as he approached. And then he handed me a travel-size tube of toothpaste.

"Um. Hi." I took the toothpaste and examined it. "Thank you?"

"I used some of your toothpaste the other morning, and I wanted to replenish your supply as a thank you."

Once a weird kid, always a weird kid. It was kinda cute how earnest Chase was about toothpaste.

"Okay...I guess this will come in handy when I travel." An amused smile broke through my sullen mood, the first of the day. "You didn't have to do that. Really, truly. I've never heard of someone replenishing toothpaste they used."

"There's a first for everything." Was it just me, or did Chase seem nervous? He had the tightness of someone trying not to crack on the witness stand.

I examined the tube once more. "Thanks, Chase."

"Great." He turned to leave, but did a kind of dance move, pivoting back and forth on his heel before spinning back around.

"Sebastian, I didn't come here to bring you toothpaste. That was a Trojan Horse to something else I wanted to discuss."

"I figured."

"Would you mind if I joined you?" He slid onto the empty picnic bench across from me. His crystal blue eyes were opened super wide, and I got lost in their ocean pull for a moment.

"I feel like social protocol requires that I apologize, but to be perfectly honest, I'm not entirely sure what I'm apologizing for. I can see that I'm causing tension within your relationship with Anton, and that's the last thing I want to do. I am the element bringing instability to your dynamic. Yet it seems like we all get along when we're in the thick of...it. But once it's over, you get tense again. I'm honestly a little confused."

There wasn't much to be confused about. I was hopelessly in

love with my best friend who only wanted to kiss me when there was a third guy bouncing between us. And I wanted to like that third guy, but it hurt my heart to stand by and watch him get dicked by the man of my dreams.

"We're good, Chase." It wasn't fair to drag him into my perpetual heartache.

"Are you sure? Because as I just finished explaining, it doesn't seem that way. Would you like to discuss anything? My door is always open."

"You used to say that in class."

"I still do. None of my students ever take me up on it. But contrary to the whispers in the halls, I can be a good listener."

I was tempted to take the bait. "I have some shit I need to work out with Anton. This is new for us..."

"Of course. You're friends and business partners and suddenly you're involved sexually. It's a lot to process."

"Exactly. I just want to make sure the business doesn't suffer," I said, thankful Chase gave me an easy out. Blame it all on the business. I held up the toothpaste one last time. "Are you sure you don't want this?"

"To be brutally honest, I don't use Colgate. Only Crest."

"Fair enough."

"You and Anton should think about switching. It's the superior brand, per all available data."

I smiled to myself. Was it strange that I found his weirdness cute? I knew there was a wild, horny guy lurking under the quirky demeanor.

"I'll keep that in mind." I opened my backpack to toss the toothpaste in.

"Is that Elmo?" Chase pointed at the card, which had slipped out. I turned as red as the *Sesame Street* mainstay, like some secret had been exposed.

"Is that for a nephew?"

"Uh, no," I said, fumbling for an answer.

"The envelope's been opened, which means...someone bought you an Elmo card? As a joke, right?" Chase asked.

If fucking only. A purposeful joke would've been less cruel.

"My dad sent it. It's a birthday card."

"Oh. Happy birthday."

"My birthday was seven months ago." I flicked the card into the backpack and zipped it shut. "And I'm about twelve years too old for Elmo shit. Elmo's the last thing he remembers about me from before he left."

We shared a look, remembering the sad truth we had in common and how it would forever mark us.

"My sob story isn't as bad as yours. He didn't leave us for another family. He wanted to be an actor and live out his dreams in California. My mom and I were holding him back." I rolled my eyes. I used to think maturity came with age. Dad proved me wrong.

The unique sense of anger mixed with hurt that came with abandonment churned in my gut. It was a constant back-and-forth of wanting to lash out for what he did and wanting to cry because no matter what any parent, relative, or therapist told you, you always felt it was because of you. The pain never left. No scar tissue was strong enough to let that part of us heal.

"I'm sorry," Chase said softly. Unlike most people who said that when they heard about my dad, it wasn't a hollow refrain.

"You know what it's like. Maybe that's why I can be a competitive asshole, too."

"You didn't say anything outside Remix."

"It's not something I like to talk about. I don't want it to define me. Most people don't get it anyway. They try to empathize by saying they lost a relative when they were young, but it's not the same."

"It's not the same at all! I hated when people said that. It was in no way an equal comparison. We didn't lose our dads. They left. Having a relative pass on shares no similarities with a relative who is still very much alive and choosing not to be part of your life."

"You don't have to convince me, Chase. I didn't feel like bringing it up at the bar. And I was still pissed at you for crashing my evening with Anton."

"I didn't crash anything. I was invited. There is a concrete difference. But I'm sorry all the same." He reached out and rubbed a thumb over my hand.

"He was fucking seven months late sending a card with a twenty inside. You were there the day I was fucking born. You were the second person to hold me. You honestly don't remember that day? You can't even be bothered to make a fucking calendar reminder for yourself?" I ground my fists into my forehead, willing myself to find that calm and control I so craved. "Sorry. See, this is why it's not worth talking about. I wish he'd stopped sending me cards altogether. It only hurts when I receive them."

"He'd probably be relieved if you asked him to." Chase bit his lip. "Sorry."

"Don't be. You're not wrong. He doesn't need to send me a card. He gave the best gift any son could want: abandonment issues and a drive for perfectionism that masks an inability to connect with others." I silently thanked my old therapist for helping me come to that realization.

"What a coincidence. My dad got that for me, too." Chase cracked a smile. Was he just sarcastic? Stranger things have happened. "It was all so *messy*, and I told myself I wouldn't add to the mess. I studied hard, focused on schoolwork. I gravitated to science because it was based in facts, not feelings. Molecules can't break your heart unless they're cancerous."

"And didn't it feel like we had to be even stronger and more put together because we were gay? Gay guys already have this internal drive to be the perfect sons because of shame, and now we had to be even more perfect in order to lift our families' spirits."

"I'd never thought of it that way, but you're right." Chase stared out on the water.

I really knew how to bring the mood down, although oddly enough, this conversation with Chase was cheering me up in a way I couldn't explain.

"Hey, we're here. We're doing awesome." I rubbed my knee against his, sending a burst of electricity up my leg.

"You know what was most frustrating?" Chase said. "My dad promised he'd teach me how to throw a baseball, but he left the weekend we were supposed to go to the baseball diamond. Knowing how to throw is something I wish I'd known, even though I never use it. Perhaps that's why I was never interested in sports."

"I can show you."

"Didn't you wrestle?"

"I did Little League for years as well as basketball and hockey."

"My Lord, you did a lot of sports. That seems redundant."

"I wanted to stay busy, not think about my dad being across the country duhhhhh." I brushed a lock of blonde hair from his eyes. It felt like silk in between my fingers.

I had him stand up, then handed him a sheet of paper crumpled into a ball. "Let's play catch."

I jogged a few paces away and got into catcher position. "Aim for my hand. Pull your arm back and release."

"Are we actually going to have a game of catch? It seems the time has passed."

"If I can still receive Elmo cards, then you can still play catch." I felt alive, lighter than I had all week.

Chase hurled the ball into the air. Because of its low weight, it was unable to gather much acceleration and fell to the grass between us.

"That's my bad. I'm too far away." I got closer and tossed the ball back.

Chase pulled my arm back and flung the ball directly at me, landing it square on my chest.

"Good one!" I shook out my hand. "Damn, you got some speed on that one."

"Every scientific law contradicts that."

I threw the ball to him underhand. "Good catch!" I exclaimed.

We tossed the ball back and forth in the glow of the waning afternoon sun. It was dumb and simple and just a crumpled piece of paper. Even still, I couldn't help but feel a swell in my heart at Chase's first father-son game of catch. His dad was an idiot for walking out on a son like him.

Sadly, the game couldn't last forever. I had work to do, and Chase had a cat at home who needed to be fed.

"Thanks for the catch," Chase said. Our fingers touched when he handed over the paper ball. Another spark of electricity traveled through me.

"Anytime. Thanks for the talk. I enjoy talking with you."

"As do I."

I raised my hand to high-five him goodbye, but instead, Chase leaned forward and pressed his lips on mine in a sweet kiss that had me instantly aching for more.

He seemed just as surprised as me at what happened.

"Bye." Chase gave me the high-five that had been left hanging and walked away.

We were both guys who overthought things, but in that moment, nothing felt more right.

19

ANTON

I liked to jump rope to clear my mind. The repetition of the rope swooshing in front of my face was like a brain cleanser. My favorite spot to do it was on the roof of our apartment building, where I could look out on Sourwood and the river, finding a sense of calm above the hustle-bustle of daily life.

I had a lot on my mind today. It wasn't something I was used to. My mind was an airport, busy with planes coming and going all day. I chose to find peace and let life unfold as it did. Whatever happened, good or bad, I would figure out a way through.

Yet the past few days had been a mindfuck. We had a presentation with Hollis coming up, the most make-or-break meeting of our entrepreneurial lives, and Sebastian and I found ourselves in a weird place again. Just when we needed the lines of communication to be open, I couldn't help but sense a wall between us.

And I wasn't sure why.

I explained to Sebastian why I invited Chase into my bed and apologized for not including him. The threesome was supposed to be a fun experience, but it was making things thorny.

For him, and for me, too. Whenever I thought back on that fun night of sex, I thought less about how hot it was and more about the sweet faces of Chase and Sebastian. I thought about how they were *my guys*, even though I didn't know what that meant.

They were making me feel warm and fuzzy, not hot and bothered. Big problem. Because warm and fuzzy feelings led to trouble. They led to someone getting hurt, and that someone would probably be me. In our trio, I was the odd man out. Could I keep up with Chase and Sebastian outside the bedroom, or would they find me dull?

I jumped faster, my fists curling tighter around the ends of the rope. My speed got so fast that I stumbled over the rope and nearly tumbled over the building railing.

Yikes.

I whipped off my sweat-drenched shirt and used the few dry spots to wipe my face. No matter how hard I exercised and how many endorphins I pumped, I couldn't find resolution.

When I got back to the apartment, Sebastian was sitting on the futon, reading an article on his phone. He was full-on chilling while I was a neurotic mess. How dare he full-on chill and seem at ease.

"Hey," I said.

"Hey." He looked up. "Jumping rope on the roof?"

"Yep."

"Nice. Looks like you got into it."

"I did," I said defiantly, ready to start a fight without knowing why. Ugh, I hated being confused. Why couldn't sex just stay sex?

"I'm gonna hop in the shower."

"Good call. You smell."

"What's that supposed to mean?"

"It means…you smell." Sebastian could barely meet my eyes. He went back to reading his phone. Sebastian could be so put together, which really pissed me off right now. He was coming off as reserved and cold.

Who the hell did he think he was—some British dude?

I summoned all my years of Little League pitching practice and threw my sopping wet T-shirt in his face.

"What the fuck!" He threw it on the floor, avoiding the rug. I kicked it onto the rug and mashed it into the fibers to spite him. "What the fuck was that for, Anton?"

"Because you're being British!" I spat out before realizing that Sebastian wasn't privy to the conversation happening in my head.

"Dude, have you been taking performance enhancing drugs again, because I told you that shit messes with your head."

"You're the shit messing with my head!" I ripped the phone from his hands. His iPhone was new and important to our business, so I lightly tossed it on the futon. "We have a huge meeting coming up, and we can't even talk about it because you're being weird and frosty like that guy in that movie about the blonde chick who everyone calls fat but is actually a normal size."

"*Bridget Jones's Diary*?" Sebastian crinkled his forehead in confusion, which I found adorable, even though it was totally not the right time to fawn over his fucking forehead. "That movie that we watched with Savannah?"

"Yeah. You're the Draco guy!"

"Mr. Darcy?"

"Yeah!" I pointed an accusatory finger at him. "Darcy!" I caught my breath and realized that I might not have been making perfect sense. "Something's been up with you ever since we started hanging out with Chase, but then when I bring it up, you say everything's fine. Like, what the fuck was up with being pissed in the kitchen the other morning? Since then, all we've had are hella awkward exchanges. It's all just *weird*, and I don't understand what's gotten into you when we're on the cusp of landing the biggest client in Beverage Solutions history."

I stomped into the kitchen and pulled off a few sheets of paper towels for my sweaty hair. Sebastian charged in while I was mid-rubbing my head.

"You really have no idea why I've been weird?" he asked, kinda curious but also kinda glaring at me.

"No!"

"So every time that you've been flirty and touchy with Chase, I get weird, and you have no idea why? You have no idea why I've never been fully supportive when you describe your latest hookups?"

"You have high standards for me?"

"Let's go back to Bridget Jones and her motherfucking diary, shall we? Why, does it turn out, has Mr. Darcy been weird around Bridget for the whole movie?"

I replayed movie highlights in my head, especially remembering when Savannah swooned at the line Darcy says about liking Bridget just as she is.

"Because he's actually...in love with her?"

Like the faulty switch in our bathroom, the light bulb suddenly went off in my head. Oh shit.

Sebastian stared at me, letting it sink in. Just beyond his tense glare was something more sensitive and wounded peeking through.

"You like me?" I asked.

"I'm in love with you, you fucking dipshit."

It was as if *Bridget Jones's Diary* had the twist ending of *The Sixth Sense*. That was why Sebastian was acting weird. He wanted me all to himself. This whole time, he loved me.

How had I been so blind as to not realize his feelings? Maybe I was forcing myself not to think about them because they led to an uncomfortable gray area in our friendship.

What happened when the high of hooking up faded away? Would he still be in love with his not-so-bright friend? Could I keep up with him?

I pushed those fears aside for now and stared at Sebastian's intensely beautiful face. I couldn't imagine my life without him. He wasn't just a part of my life. He was the key that made the whole thing turn. The feelings that had been brewing inside me didn't just come out of nowhere.

"When we kissed during the threesomes, those kisses meant something to me. What did they mean for you?" he asked, almost like a dare.

They were so fucking hot. I couldn't stop thinking about his mouth on mine. "They were amazing. I wanted to keep kissing you even after we were done, but I didn't want to make it weird. I, like, haven't been able to stop thinking of kissing you."

Sebastian knew me better than anyone in this world. I wanted to be close with him. Was this what it felt like to be in love? Was love just the constant wanting of someone, and when you have them, it only makes you want them more?

All this thinking was hurting my head. *Just go with it*, I told myself.

I pulled him to me, my sweaty chest imprinting on his T-shirt.

"Seb, let's make it weird."

Our lips met in a heated kiss filled with tenderness and years of history. We were more than friends. We were fused together.

And yet...it was off in some way.

It reminded me of baking cookies with my mom as a little kid and forgetting to put in the salt. Cookie recipes only required a tiny amount of salt, but even so, we noticed the difference when we bit into them hours later.

Fuck, was this me overthinking again? I was kissing my best friend, and it was amazing, but also...it needed salt? I told myself that it would be less weird the more we did it.

I pushed Sebastian backwards, out of the kitchen and against the wall, rattling the pictures hung behind him. He pressed his chest against me, squeezed my ass with his greedy palms.

I used every maneuver in the Anton Makeout Handbook. (not a real thing, but maybe that was an unexplored business idea?) My tongue swept into his mouth as I cradled his chin and moaned against his lips. Sebastian bit my bottom lip in a rush of heat.

His taste drove me wild. The smacking sound of our lips was like a brilliant symphony.

And yet...salt.

WHERE WAS THE FUCKING SALT? WHY DID SALT NEED TO BE IN COOKIES? MAKE IT MAKE SENSE.

Sebastian was wearing a ratty old South Rock wrestling T-shirt. He had a million of them. He wouldn't miss this one. I tore it open, revealing his bronzed, delicious chest. He threw his head back and gasped my name.

I kissed down his chest, flicking a tongue on his nipple.

Not all cookies needed salt, did they? Was it some scientific requirement for baked goods? Ugh, this was why I stayed away from complex carbohydrates.

"Come here." I grabbed the remnants of his shirt and yanked him flush against me, mashing our mouths together in a heated kiss. Then I shoved him onto the futon and lay on top of him, thrusting my hips.

There was heat, for sure. But I felt myself working overtime to make up for something that was lacking that I couldn't put a finger on.

Who needed salt? It only made you bloated and led to high blood pressure.

Sebastian pulled back and caught his breath. "Anton."

"You okay, Seb?"

Confusion flickered across his face. My kiss really did a number on him, and maybe not in a good way.

"What is it?" I asked.

"Does something feel off to you?" He squirmed under me. A relief I couldn't describe washed over me at the admission.

"Honestly? Kinda."

Sebastian sat up and wiggled out from under me. "It feels like something is missing."

"Salt!" I shouted.

He raised an eyebrow. "Buddy, seriously, lay off the PEDs."

I wished there was a way for friends to read each other's minds. It would save us tons of time from having to explain things. Friend telepathy. I filed the idea away as another future business prospect.

"I mean I agree. I love kissing you. I want to keep kissing you. I'm so stoked that we're doing this finally. But something is missing."

"Chase," Sebastian said. He seemed as surprised as I was. "I wish Chase were here."

"Fuck. Me, too." The thought of him kissing us, his silky body between us, revved my engine more than anything in the past few minutes.

CHASE IS THE SALT.

"Wait. I thought you didn't like Chase," I said.

"We hung out earlier today."

"Cool," I said, a twinge of jealousy hitting me.

"We cleared the air, and he's a good guy. He amplifies my feelings for you, and I think I have feelings for him, too. When the three of us are together, it's..."

"Magic." The word slipped from my lips. It was apt, though. There was magic between us. It was a special kind of heat mixed with something deeper.

"We both like Chase?" Sebastian asked, as confused as I was.

"Huh. How about that?" It opened up all new questions for us. My heart expanded with warmth thinking about being with Sebastian and Chase. I wanted more warm and fuzzy and hot and bothered. With them, I could have both. Sebastian's ripped physique in one arm, Chase's smooth, soft features in the other.

My guys.

I wanted to have fun and explore with Chase and Sebastian, just as long as it didn't get serious. They only wanted Bedroom Anton, not Relationship Anton.

"How about that?" Sebastian chuckled to himself. We shared a bewildered gaze between us as he flicked on the TV.

"*Schitt's Creek*?" he asked.

20

CHASE

Statistically, Fridays were the busiest day on the group chat. My friends were restless after a week of teaching, counting down the minutes until the weekend like our students. We'd share funny things from the week and discuss weekend plans. While I chastised them for texting during the school day, I secretly enjoyed the cellular commotion.

Yet here we were, Friday afternoon, and tumbleweeds were blowing through our group chat. Not even Everett chimed in to complain about something.

Chase: Is this thing on?

Amos: Busy day! My students are giving final presentations, and they're all shockingly good.

Everett: Chase! Your campaign for Teacher of the Year is picking up steam. I took a broad vote in my theater arts class, and a majority are voting for you.

Amos: Doesn't your class only have ten students?

Everett: Eleven! And every vote counts. Kids are coming around to you.

Chase: If only they came around to studying harder for my tests.

Amos: Same.

Julian: Same.

Everett: I don't believe in tests.

Chase: What's going on tonight?

Amos: Hutch and I are going out to dinner to celebrate the one year anniversary of his promposal.

Chase: Was that an event that typically required an annual celebration?

Amos: I like milestones!

Everett: Raleigh and I are going to see the new *Fast and Furious* movie. I hear in this one, Vin Diesel drives in reverse at such high speed he accidentally travels back in time and races against Ben Hur's souped-up chariot. My suspension of disbelief will be working overtime.

Chase: Julian?

Julian: Seamus has a baseball game, and I'll be watching in the stands. Next Friday, though!

Amos: Sorry, Chase.

Chase: No worries! I get to have a Puzzles and Pizza night with Einstein.

I coined Puzzles and Pizza Night back when I was in high school. Since my social life was quiet, mostly by choice, I spent most Fridays ordering myself a pizza and putting together a puzzle. I knew the phone numbers for all local pizza establishments by heart, and not to brag, but they knew me by name, too.

A casual observer might have seen this and deemed it dispiriting, or even pathetic. But I never did. I loved Puzzles and Pizza night! I didn't have to share my pizza with anyone, didn't have to peel off unwanted toppings that edged onto my half of the pie, didn't have to make smalltalk or drive around aimlessly or stand out in the cold pumping a keg or whatever cool kids did.

After school, I did my grocery shopping for the week. Supermarkets had the lowest foot traffic on Friday evenings. When I got home, I put away the groceries and collapsed on the couch, saving up my energy for a very difficult puzzle. Einstein, my fat, compact kitty, tiptoed onto my chest. She gave me a look wondering if this was okay, even though she'd rest there anyway.

Einstein had a lush shading of fur that was a mix of brown and gray. Her expressive, oversized eyes could turn the most cold-hearted person into a pile of mashed potatoes. She was gorgeous, and she knew it. It was going to be me and Einstein versus one thousand pieces of Van Gogh's *Starry Night*.

I shut my eyes for a minute, but under my eyelids, I kept seeing Anton and Sebastian. They were probably busy tonight with parties or meeting up with friends. What would it be like to have their hulking bodies in my small apartment? What would it sound like to have their laughter and merriment bounce off my sparsely adorned walls?

I pulled out my phone. Einstein jumped up from her reclining position in a panic. Why did cats always panic when their humans made the slightest move? We could learn a lot thanks to science, but cats would always remain a mystery.

"I'm just getting my phone," I told her, putting a calm hand on her back. "You don't need to move."

She kept eyeing me, like something was off. And perhaps it was.

Chase: Hello! What fun plans do you guys have tonight?

For the record, I was content to enjoy a Puzzles and Pizza night alone, for all of the aforementioned reasons. I was merely curious what Anton and Sebastian were up to. They seemed like gentlemen with exciting, enthralling lives.

Einstein wasn't having this bullshit.

"There is no crime for texting someone," I pleaded to my four-legged judge, jury, and executioner.

If cats could roll their eyes, Einstein would have as she returned to resting on my chest.

My phone buzzed a few seconds later. I held it over Einstein and read the message from Anton.

Anton: Seb and I were doing some admin work to end the week, then we were probably going to grab a bite to eat. You?

Sebastian: Correction. I'm doing most of the admin work. Anton is reading about old wrestlers on Wikipedia.

Anton: It gets really dark, man.

I chuckled at the exchange, imagining them squabbling in person.

Chase: I'm having a Puzzles and Pizza night with myself.

Sebastian: I can't remember the last time I did a puzzle. Maybe elementary school?

Anton: Where did you order pizza from?

Chase: CJ Pizza.

Anton: Soooooo good.

Sebastian: Did you get the cheesy bread, too?

Chase: Negative. Cheesy bread is pizza without the sauce. It's mildly preposterous that it would be a separate item on the menu. It would be analogous to someone ordering a side of chicken wings with their chicken tenders.

Anton: Mmmm. Chicken tenders with a side of chicken wings. That sounds tasty. Why have I never done that before? They're two completely different foods.

Chase: They're both chicken.

Anton: One is breaded and boneless. One is glazed and has bones.

Sebastian: You're splitting hairs, dude.

Anton: Chicken don't have hairs. They have feathers. BOOM! You just got science'd, bro.

Anton: How does it feel to be owned?

Anton: Ow.

Anton: Seb just smacked me upside the head IRL.

Sebastian: Fully deserved.

Einstein was unenthused about all the laughing I was doing, my chest vibrating up and down. She came to this spot to rest, not for an earthquake drill.

Anton: Sounds like you have a nice night planned for yourself, Chase. Have fun!

I did. Puzzles and Pizza night never disappointed. Yet why did I feel a sense of deflation that made my chest sink? (Another thing Einstein didn't approve of.) I had my thumbs summon their texting courage.

Chase: Did you guys want to join me?

Chase: I haven't ordered the pizza yet nor started the puzzle.

Sebastian: I'm down!

Anton: Totally!

Humans are wired to be social creatures. Thus, I was biologically compelled to invite them over. The excitement spreading through me at being in their presence was a natural response, yes? I've enjoyed countless Puzzles and Pizza nights solo. It would be an interesting experiment to include outside elements and see how those variables impact the enjoyment of the evening. In the name of science, and not in the name of my swelling dick, I *had* to invite Anton and Sebastian to come over.

The warmth filling my heart and tightening my pants were completely incidental.

Chase: I'll go ahead and order a pizza.

Anton: Just one?

Chase: I only have two slices usually, so we could all split one?

Sebastian: Oh, Chase. We're going to need a LOT more pizza.

AN HOUR LATER, the three of us were eating pizza and drinking beer in my living room. I held court on the couch, while the guys stretched out on the floor. Three pizza boxes were sprawled out next to them. Anton and Sebastian had unusually large appetites, but they did have more muscles that required more fuel.

We talked about our day. They gave me the rundown on a very important meeting they had coming up, and I shared about what was going on at South Rock. I went deep on an article I read about greenhouse gasses, bringing down the mood for a moment. Sebastian, and especially Anton, were fascinated, giving me their rapt attention.

Typically, I started on the puzzle as soon as the pizza was delivered. But this was nice, too. Sitting around and chatting. Chilling, if you will. It was remarkably easy to talk with them. A part of me worried that I would be forever an outsider since Anton and Sebastian were close friends and business partners. Yet I felt nothing but ease around them.

While my feelings for the guys were complicated, Einstein had no qualms declaring her crush on Anton. She bashed her face against his palm and seconds later curled herself onto his lap.

"Anton, you're a cat whisperer," Sebastian noted.

"The ladies love me." Anton held his plate above Einstein's head so he could eat in peace. Sadly, that was not going to happen. She batted at his plate. "Can she eat pizza?"

"No. She doesn't like pizza, but that won't stop her from wanting it. She can likely smell the fat of the cheese," I said. Einstein was curious whenever I got pizza, but this was next level.

"Lady, have you tried playing hard to get?" Anton asked her. In a compelling show of her flexibility, Einstein batted a piece of crust off his plate and ran with it in her mouth.

"She'll be fine," I told him. "She'll quickly realize she doesn't want it."

"She just wants to be included." Sebastian was also a cat whisperer. He was tender with her, scratching under her chin and between her eyes. I was impressed that Einstein wasn't swatting him away.

I grabbed her box of cat treats from behind the couch and put a few in Anton and Sebastian's hands. She didn't know where to go first. She ran back and forth, her stomach swinging as she moved. She was in heaven.

She reminded me of myself.

"Your cat is much nicer than my aunt's cat, Link," Anton said. "Whenever I come over, he hides under her bed. I've only seen him once, when I camped outside his litter box on Thanksgiving. How is Einstein with your friends?" Anton massaged my foot hanging off the couch, while one of his feet rubbed up and down Sebastian's leg. Like everything else, it all felt very easy.

"She tolerates everyone," I said. "Loves no one."

"She loves you," Sebastian said.

"I'm not sure about that. Do cats love? Or does she realize that she's completely dependent on me for food, water, and shelter?" I was equally confused about love as my cat.

"Love via Stockholm Syndrome." Anton flashed his winning smile.

Cats could be very withholding, but that's what I liked about them. They weren't furry balls of slobbering love like dogs. They made you work for it.

Meanwhile, I was turning into a cat myself because the more Anton circled his fingers around the soft skin of my ankle, the more I wanted to purr in his lap. I reached down a hand and ran the tips of my fingers over Sebastian's head.

"So where's this puzzle?" Anton asked. "And do we have to do it?"

"Yes. Or else we can't call this a Puzzles and Pizza night. It would just be a pizza night, which anyone can have," I said.

"*Starry Night*," Sebastian read the puzzle box cover. "One thousand pieces. Looks challenging. You finish this in a night?"

"Never. It takes me a few days to complete a puzzle, but I get a good start on Fridays."

Anton eyed the box. "We can get it done tonight."

"That is highly doubtful. It's a very difficult puzzle, and I'm only one person," I said.

"What about us?" Sebastian asked.

"You haven't done puzzles in years, you said. You're both novices essentially."

"Is that a challenge?" Anton asked. He glanced at Sebastian. "Seb, I think Chase thinks that we can't do this puzzle."

"Chase does think that." Sebastian smiled back at him. "Do we ever back down from a challenge, Anton?"

"We do not." Anton grabbed the box and stood up. "Let's puzzle this bitch."

21

ANTON

When Chase invited us over to eat some pizza and do a puzzle, I thought that was code for eat some pizza and have some sex.

And it could've been. We were all pretty comfortable in the living room, but as Sebastian said, I never backed down from a challenge.

And *Starry Night* was proving to be a challenging fucker. Van Gogh came to play.

The plan was to do the puzzle for a little bit, to keep up the spirit of Puzzles and Pizza night, but it turned out that puzzles were more addictive than opioids.

The night wore on, but we couldn't stop. We were on a mission. The three of us sat around the kitchen table, listening to music, and working on the puzzle in near silence. The quiet was punctuated by my routine cursing when two pieces didn't fit and my routine whoops and hollers when I got two together.

Who knew Puzzles and Pizza night could be legit fun?

"Here's a window piece for the town section." I pushed it over to Sebastian.

"I think that's part of the sun," Chase said.

"Shit."

"Don't give up. This isn't an easy puzzle." Chase rubbed my back.

"I never give up," I declared with all the seriousness of a locker room pep talk.

Sebastian snickered to himself. Yeah, I was getting into it. I played to win, no matter the game. We were going to finish this puzzle tonight.

"Girl, don't you even dare." I narrowed my eyes at Einstein, who hopped on the table, my warning meaning nothing to her. She locked eyes with me as she lounged across my puzzle section.

"Einstein. Off!" Chase said.

She stretched out her legs, pushing into the piles of pieces, not a care in the world. Chase grabbed her and moved to the floor. Two seconds later, she was back.

"Einstein is a chaos agent," Sebastian declared.

Chase grabbed her again and put her in the bedroom. "Say goodnight, Einstein."

She gave us the saddest eyes on the planet before disappearing into his room.

I stood up and stretched my back.

"What are you doing?" Sebastian asked as I went into a round of pushups.

"I'm getting the blood flowing."

"You are cracked out."

But he got on the floor and joined me, too. We kept going to see who'd stop first.

"This is Puzzles and Pizza night. Not Puzzles and Pushups," Chase said, standing over us.

"Regaining our strength," I said through strained breath. I hopped to my feet, letting Sebastian have the win this time. "What do you do for exercise?"

"Um, nothing?"

"Chase, you might be naturally slim," I put my hands around his waist, loving how easily he fit there. "But you still need to exercise. You should come with us to the gym tomorrow."

"You're going to the gym tomorrow? On a Saturday?"

"Yeah. Why not?" Sebastian looked at him cock-eyed. "Fitness doesn't take weekends off."

"Come with us! We'll get you in shape." I rubbed a hand over his chest and arms. "Get you nice and jacked."

"I don't need nor want to be jacked. I like my body as is. Though I suppose some resistance training with weights can help improve bone density."

We hunkered back down to the puzzle. Even though we were all super focused, there were still opportunities for touching here and there. I had a hard time keeping my hands to myself. But it wasn't about getting us closer to the bedroom. I just wanted to feel their heat, inhale their natural scents, and comfort them.

Was I the odd man out, though? I tried keeping up while Chase was talking about that article on greenhouse gasses. For years, I thought that greenhouses were emitting toxic chemicals into the air. I didn't realize the greenhouse part was just a metaphor for our thinning atmosphere. And what happened to protecting the ozone layer? How was that going? I kept my opinions and questions to myself so I didn't make myself look like a total idiot.

We made more progress, and when I looked up, two hours had passed. It was almost midnight. My eyes were heavy, weighted with the desire to sleep. Puzzling took a lot out of us.

"I don't think this puzzle is going to happen tonight," Sebastian said. We were maybe a third finished.

I had never spent a Friday night doing a puzzle—and enjoying it. My Friday nights were spent going out on the town, living it up, making memories. Chase was turning me into a nerd, and I didn't hate it.

"We've made remarkable headway," Chase said. "I've never gotten this far on the first night. I guess that means you'll have to come back to help me finish."

"That sounds nice," I said, kissing his arm and rubbing the back of Sebastian's neck.

That really does sound nice.

Since when did I want nice, though? This arrangement was supposed to be about hot sex and exploration. Pizza and Penetration.

I was about to suggest that we take ourselves to the bedroom to end tonight with a bang, but instead, a yawn ripped out of me. I was exhausted. Puzzling officially kicked my ass.

"Give me a minute." I went to the couch and flopped onto the comfy cushions. I leaned my head back and willed myself not to fall asleep. The week rapidly caught up to me.

The coziness of Chase's apartment swaddled me, not letting me go. I would find my third wind and bang the brains out of both of them. We would turn this apartment into a fuckfest.

When I opened my eyes, an episode of *Schitt's Creek* was playing on the TV and a quilt was draped over us. Chase and Sebastian sat on either side of me, their arms meeting behind my head, fingers drawing circles in my hair. God, I had never felt more relaxed. I could stay like this forever.

"I think you fell asleep," Sebastian said.

"I just rested my eyes for a minute." Fuck. That was something my dad said to my mom when she caught him falling asleep at his computer.

"I made popcorn." Chase passed me the bowl of microwave popcorn, its buttery aroma impossible to resist.

I dug my hand into the puffed up snack. We could finish this episode, then we'd go to the bedroom and fuck. Because that was why we were here tonight, wasn't it? Although, could fucking even match the high I was feeling right now?

I rested my head against Chase's shoulder while Sebastian continued to massage his fingers through my hair.

Einstein leapt up and curled herself into a cat loaf on my lap, her sleepy but determined eyes signaling she wasn't moving anytime soon.

It was all...no other word for it...nice.

22

SEBASTIAN

I woke up sandwiched. I generally tried to avoid sandwiches because of all the excess carbs, but this was one I could get behind.

Chase was cradled in my arms, while I was the little spoon for Anton. The three of us lay in a row in Chase's bed after a whirl-wind night of...puzzles and pizza.

It wasn't sex, but it was just as incredible.

The warmth of Chase and the weight of Anton pressed against me. I was in a cocoon of cuddles. A man could get used to this.

I nuzzled my cheek into Chase's hair, the flutter of his fruity shampoo filling my nose. Anton's cadenced breath hit my ear, sending the best kind of shivers down my back. His morning wood ground into my ass, and I, in turn, ground mine into Chase's.

The three of us. Was this actually a thing? Anton only wanted to explore and keep things hot. Cuddling on the couch was neither of those things. For now, I wasn't thinking of any of that. I turned my planner brain off and luxuriated in this moment.

"Good morning," I whispered to Anton, whose morning wood was threatening to rip a hole in my boxers.

"Mmm hmmm." Anton wasn't a morning person, as much as he wanted to be. He preached about seizing the day, but getting him out of bed was a herculean effort.

"Are you trying to take my temperature?" I asked of his insistent cock.

"Are you trying to take mine?" Chase asked.

I moved my hips back.

"I didn't ask you to stop." Chase turned his head and flashed me a sleepy grin.

I canvassed my hand across his chest, then dipped it under his shirt, skimming his soft, creamy skin. Chase responded by jutting his ass against my cock. The little nerd was all mine. Or ours. He'd gotten two jocks to spend their Friday night doing a puzzle and loving it.

"Hey hey hey, what's going on over there?" Anton asked, his voice raspy with the last vestiges of sleep. "Do I need to send you two to the principal?"

"We are outside of school grounds, so Principal Aguilar's jurisdiction doesn't apply." Chase set him straight.

"Welp, if you can't beat 'em," Anton pulled down my boxers and squeezed my ass. "Join 'em."

I let out a moan as he slapped his cock against my crack. I had always been a top. Part of being a control freak. But I was very tempted to explore bottoming.

I gripped Chase closer the more Anton played with me, sinking my fingers into his flesh, palming his erection and pushing him back against my rock hard staff.

"My guys," Anton purred. "Fuck, I love watching you play with each other."

I spun Chase around, and we instantly began making out. I pulled down his boxers, tangling our cocks together. Anton tugged off my shirt and grabbed my ass. Chase tasted so freaking good, our tongues lapping over one another, wild for each other and for Anton. I wanted Anton salivating over us.

"Yes, that's so hot," Anton said, his dick thrusting against me.

Chase jerked both our cocks in his hand. His eyes were two blue lasers burning bright.

"Chase," I breathed out, wanting him, connected to him, sinking deeper and deeper into this moment.

He slid down and took me in his mouth, bolts of heat shooting through my chest. I made him take all of me. I could tell Chase liked things a little rough, and I was happy to oblige. He winked at me as he sucked, a teasing smile on his lips. As if I wasn't already turned on.

I threw my head back against the pillows and came face-to-face with Anton's meaty cock. He smiled down at me, as if to say "get to it."

He didn't need to ask me twice. Or once.

I'd dreamed about sucking Anton, and reality surpassed every fantasy. He was wet, salty, manly, mine. His thick cock entered my mouth, the bitter taste of pre-come hitting my tongue. I probably could've started slow and worked my way up, but I was already at an eight out of ten by the time his cock was in my face. I sucked him fast and hard, matching the orgasm building in my balls. He threw his head back.

"My guys," he muttered. He leaned down and spanked Chase's ass. Chase got on all fours to give him a better angle, which also helped him deep throat me with ease.

I was on fire at both ends, heat raging inside me, a deep well of need that could never be extinguished.

"Hold up," Anton said. He pulled out of my mouth.

"Huh?" I asked, catching my breath.

He pointed to the corner of the bed where Einstein watched us with casual disdain.

"Ignore her. She doesn't care," Chase said.

"Are you sure?" Anton asked.

Einstein folded herself into a bread loaf shape. She blinked at us, then stared at the wall.

"She could care less. She just likes that spot on the bed," Chase assured us.

Einstein licked her paw, really digging between her nails, as if this were all a regular morning for her.

"See?"

"She won't try to crawl on us, right?" I asked, imagining worst case scenarios of claws going where they shouldn't.

"Not at all. She can tell we're engaged in activity. She only likes to rest on people when we're perfectly still."

"So she's just going to sit there while we..." I scratched my head.

"Most likely, unless she gets bored of the bed. She prefers to rotate around the apartment throughout the day," Chase said.

I supposed that was one way to be an ally.

"Einstein, you're a nasty-ass freak, and I'm here for it," said Anton.

She continued licking her paw, giving him no mind at all. Cats did the cold shoulder thing better than any human ever could.

Chase moved up and licked Anton's shaft. "As we were."

"Don't need to tell me twice." Anton winked at us and gently pushed my head back to blow job position.

Chase and I made out with Anton's cock between us, our tongues sliding around him like we were strippers on a pole. Anton fingered Chase, who remained on all fours for the best access.

"Fuck. Just like that," Anton creaked out in his deep, rumbly voice.

Chase took his balls, while I sucked his cock, both of us working to serve and please him. We were his guys, after all.

Anton gave both of us a firm tap on the shoulder.

"Coming," he said through strained breath.

Hot come flooded over our twisted tongues as he emitted a loud, ferocious grunt.

"Holy shit. Holy shit," he said as he came back to earth, his chest heaving with breath. "That was so intense."

His eyes glowed in reverence as he looked down at Chase and me, our mouths crested with his seed.

"You two, finish each other off," he commanded.

Chase seemed as excited as I was at being ordered by Anton. We both liked a sense of control, and there was a thrill in giving it over to someone we trusted. We got into the sixty-nine position. I sucked Chase's long, leaking dick while I fucked into his mouth.

We amped up the speed and heat. I grabbed his ass, shoving his cock deeper down my throat. His tongue snaked past my balls and flicked over my hole. Every piece of me crackled with lust.

I emptied myself into his mouth at the same time his salty come surged into mine. I was spent beyond belief.

Anton leaned down and kissed both of us, getting a taste of each.

"A man could get used to waking up like this," he said.

I agreed.

Einstein was neutral on the whole thing.

———

I SUGGESTED we go out to breakfast, but Chase had other ideas.

"I have in my possession what I consider one of the top three best pancake recipes." Chase unclipped a faded index card from a CJ Pizza magnet on his fridge. "I have eaten many pancakes in my life, so I consider myself an apt judge of pancake recipe quality."

"Sold!" I said. Anton and I hunched over his small IKEA

kitchen table, which was built for slender Europeans, not hulking American guys.

"Yeah," Anton said, not paying attention. His mind was focused on the puzzle. We had three sections of *Starry Night* built out, and he was determined to connect them. It was in his nature to be a uniter.

My stomach rumbled with impatience. "How long do they take to make?"

"Thirteen minutes to prep the ingredients, and eight minutes for the first batch to cook."

Anton looked up and pulled out his phone. "I'm going to time you, Mr. M. I expect a pancake on this table in twenty-one minutes."

"If there's no pancake in that time, then we'll have no choice but to go out for breakfast, per the expectations set." I gave a playful smile to Chase.

"Seriously. If you deliver a pancake in twenty-one minutes and thirty seconds, then it goes in the trash. We take our carbohydrates very seriously." Anton leaned back and crossed his arms.

Chase seemed to enjoy our brand of shittalking.

"When does the timer start? It should start when all the ingredients are on the counter, as is comparable to the setup on cooking competition shows."

"Okay, then. Get your ingredients ready." I tapped the nonexistent watch on my wrist. "Time's a ticking. I'd hate to see these pancakes wind up in the trash."

"Is there anything we can help with?" Anton asked.

"There's fruit in the fridge. Perhaps you can cut up a fruit salad in between puzzling," Chase said.

"That we can do." I pulled blueberries, strawberries, and peaches from the fridge, while Anton grabbed a bowl and cutting board—and Chase's ass. I gave it a squeeze, too. For someone who had never done a squat in his life, it was a very nice ass.

"Okay, Chase. You got this." I rubbed his shoulders as if he were about to go into the boxing ring.

We took our seats. Anton dramatically lowered his finger on the timer button.

Putting together the fruit salad was easy. We dumped blueberries and strawberries into the bowl. I cut up the peaches into slices. The main event was happening by the stove, and we couldn't look away.

Chase worked with precise diligence, his face dead serious as he measured and mixed ingredients with care. There was no winging it here. He used a knife to slice off runoff from a measuring cup to get exact amounts. He studied batter consistency with the gravity of heart surgery. He acted as if he were tasked with cooking the world's best batch of pancakes. Anton and I would've been happy no matter how they turned out.

Anton's expression of sweet awe, that someone would care this much about our breakfast, matched mine.

"We've hit the thirteen minute mark!" he exclaimed. "The question is...will the first batch of pancakes make it into the pan on time? Sebastian, what do you think?" Anton had filled in as announcer at a few South Rock football games, despite having no experience. Just lots of confidence. He still had the golden touch.

"Well, Anton, Chase has been hitting required milestones so far on his pancaking journey. But will this be the end of the road?" I asked, attempting an announcer voice myself. "Wait a minute. Wait a minute. What's this? It looks like he's..."

Chase poured the first cup of batter onto the sizzling pan.

"He's doing it!" I yelled.

"Out of the frying pan and into the fire? No, more like into the frying pan to create some fire pancakes," Anton said. "And boom! Another pour of pancake batter onto the pan. In all my years of pancake broadcasting, I've never seen a pour like this. I don't know about you, Sebastian, but it's bringing a tear to my eye."

"It was a spectacular pour. Yet will the frying pan be friend or foe? We have to let chemistry take its course now. Can these pancakes heat up enough without getting burned?"

Despite our idiotic broadcasting, Chase didn't flinch. He was fully in the zone. His level of concentration was something to behold. I could tell Anton wasn't having it. He saw another challenge.

He stood up and waltzed to the stove. "I'm going on the field for a closer look."

Chase gave a terse nod.

"Chase Mathison, the country's preeminent pancake maker isn't letting the increased attention diminish his skills. But what happens when other stimuli enter the picture?" Anton kissed the spot where his neck meets his shoulder. "Will this disrupt the all-important pancake flip?" He kissed across his neck, nuzzling into the back of his head. "We can't eat half-pancake, half-batter."

"That won't happen," Chase said through stifled breath, his composed demeanor breaking by the second.

"You won't let that happen." The announcer voice was gone, replaced with something more tantalizing. Anton grabbed the spatula and thwacked Chase on the ass. The jolting cry that escaped from his lips made my dick stand at attention.

"I'm going to need my spatula soon," he said.

"Sure thing." Anton whacked him on the ass again, then handed the spatula back to him. He took it with a shaky hand and flipped the pancakes.

I grabbed an extra wooden spoon. "Do you need this, Chase?" I pressed the handle end against his ass, as close to his hole as I could get over his pajama pants. "To scrape up the extra batter?"

I circled the end around his clothed sensitive area.

Chase closed his eyes. "You guys are really asking for burnt pancakes."

"Are we?" Anton nibbled at his ear lobe, while I smacked his ass with the spoon.

"Is he going to make this batch in time?" I asked.

Anton reached under his shirt and flicked his nipples. Chase stifled a moan.

"We should be careful around an open flame," he said. He did have a point.

"Will these be the best pancakes of our lives, Seb?" Anton gave his nipples a harder squeeze. He held Chase back from falling forward. Anton eyed me. That was a close one. We took it down a notch.

We pulled Chase back from the stove and continued torturing him with our hands and tongues. Chase reached for his spatula, his fingers clawing the edge. He broke free from our clutches just in time to remove the pancakes from the frying pan. Golden brown discs slid onto a plate. His kitchen smelled like the world's best diner.

Chase calmly put the pancakes on the kitchen table. "Breakfast is served."

He then proceeded to go over the freezer door and fan the cold air against his face.

When he joined us by the table, he flashed the sweetest smile. He was exceedingly proud of his pancakes and that he got to make them for us, that was obvious.

No guy had ever made me breakfast. Chase was special. What was happening between us was something special.

But I knew that any relationship, no matter how special it seemed, even the one between father and son, could be ripped away at any moment. As great as this morning was, in the back of my mind, I knew things could change in a heartbeat. An extra minute on the frying pan, an extra ounce of flour in the recipe, and the pancakes would be inedible.

Still, I didn't let that thought echo too loudly in my head. We had a delicious breakfast all laid out for us.

"Let's eat!" Anton said.

Chase blocked both of us from sitting down. He had a hand on each of our chests.

"Not so fast. You're not the only ones who get to have fun at breakfast." He sunk to his knees, pulling down our boxers to the floor with him.

23

——————

ANTON

Two Weeks Later

[Chase edit: Actually, if we're being precise, it was sixteen days later.]

The past two weeks have been perfection.

Ever since Puzzles and Pizza night, the three of us have clicked on a spectacular level.

We've had mindblowing, galaxy shattering fun in the bedroom, Sebastian and I passing Chase back and forth like a joint, Sebastian and Chase worshiping my dick. Why had I never thought to have threesomes on the regular before? There were so many positions, or permutations as Chase liked to say. No matter the permutation, they all ended with the three of us spent and glowing, wrapped in each other's sweaty arms.

I saw myself not as part of a threesome, but a grand protector. I would do anything for my guys. I wanted to take care of them and use my strength to keep them safe. From what? I wasn't sure. We were in a very peaceful suburb. But still, they knew that I always had their back.

Even outside the bedroom, we had fun. Chase popped by our office after school a few times. Once, he pretended to be a prospect for cold call practice. (Although I've never had a prospect go down on me during a call. That was a fun first.) We surprised him at school during his lunch period. Though no way in hell was I eating South Rock cafeteria food; we did take out. We've enjoyed more puzzles and pizza nights together, taking on 1500 and 2000-piece puzzles.

Sebastian and I were also getting closer, the walls that had surrounded him were crumbling down now that our feelings were out in the open. I was seeing a whole new side of him, and I wasn't just talking about his fine ass. I got to see the vulnerable, tender, unsure of himself sides that he usually hid under his stern demeanor. That he let me see these parts of him only made me care for him more. Chase was the special sauce. He was also a fun onion to unlayer.

Was unlayer a word? Chase said that language was always evolving, so I took it as a yes.

The other times we got sweaty together was at the gym, where we dragged a reluctant Chase. He might've been naturally slender and flexible, but everybody needed exercise.

"You got this," I said to my favorite science teacher.

Currently, he was tackling his first time doing a bench press. I stood over him, hands under the barbell ready to hand off. Sebastian was one bench over doing an incline press.

"Chase, stop looking at my junk," I told him.

"Stop putting it in my face then."

"I'm spotting you. You're about to lift forty-five pounds over yourself. Get in the zone. Boom-boom can come later."

And it would. Chase and Sebastian were sweaty and grunting.

It was a hell of an aphrodisiac. I had to make sure my own barbell didn't thwack Chase in the face.

"Let's go. You got this. Let's aim for five clean ones," I said. This was the first time he was benching with the barbell, after I assured him I wouldn't let it slip and choke his airways.

I helped him lift the bar. Chase exhaled a huge breath as he pushed it high, then lowered it to his chest.

"Elbows in." I repositioned his stance for maximum chest tearage.

Chase launched the barbell up, then down, in smooth, controlled movements. He could probably handle more, but he wanted to take things slow lest he pull a muscle. It was only in the bedroom where he liked taking on more than he could handle.

"Good. Nice, Chase. Are you feeling it?"

"Yes," he grunted out.

"Those look really clean, man," Sebastian said after finishing his set.

I tapped Chase's pecs. "You feeling it there? Each time."

"Yes."

I pressed down to feel them flex. No, this wasn't a sly move to touch Chase; that was just a bonus. I wanted to make sure he wasn't using his shoulder and potentially causing damage.

"If you keep touching me there, I'm going to get ticklish."

I grabbed the bar and racked it. "The fact that you can talk in complete sentences tells me you aren't benching enough. I'm adding ten to each side."

His eyes jutted open. "While I love and admire your bodies, I don't have a compelling need to be quote-unquote jacked."

"We're not going for jacked. Let's aim for toned and see where we fall." I touched Chase's pec. For my own selfish curiosity. Chase flexed his chest for me, daring me not to get hard.

Sebastian cleared his throat between us. "This is a family gym."

"Right, right." I clapped my hands and added ten pounds of weight to each side of the bar. "Let's do squats while your chest cools off," I told Chase.

Chase already had a rocking ass. Squats would only help.

Sebastian joined us, and the three of us did squats in a line. We probably looked like totally ridiculous gym bros, but who cared what other people thought?

Before he returned to his last set of incline presses, I gave Sebastian the look that he was familiar with by this point. It asked him *Are you okay? Is this cool?*

I never wanted him or Chase to feel like third wheels. I never wanted Sebastian to feel like I didn't take his feelings one hundred percent seriously. Yeah, we were having fun, but I wasn't going to lose this relationship.

He nodded back at me. We were good.

After a little more bench pressing and a little dash of arm curls, we wrapped up our workouts with a quick treadmill run. Chase didn't try keeping up with Sebastian and my crazy speed competition. He enjoyed a leisurely cool down walk.

"How are you feeling about the big meeting?" Chase asked.

In a truce, Sebastian and I lowered the speeds on our treadmill so we could answer him without huffing and puffing.

"I feel great," I said. "There's no way Hollis will say no."

Sebastian and I crushed the initial presentation to Jim Hollis and his VPs and were selected to the final round. We were smooth, personable, and persuasive. I didn't let the fact that I was in a conference room surrounded by MBAs and Ivy League graduates intimidate me. They might know more than me about EBITDA and country clubs, but I knew vending machines.

"There are plenty of potential reasons why he could say no." The endorphins of our workout hadn't made their way to Sebastian's head yet.

"We're a no-brainer. We have the best product, great reviews, competitive pricing, and charm out our b-holes." I increased the speed a tad, just to show him.

"You don't know what Hollis is thinking. Let's not get our hopes too high."

"I agree with Sebastian. You want to take a measured approach, lest you come off too cocky," said Chase. It was two-against-one, and not in the fun way.

"But you also want to be confident because if Hollis smells weakness or shakiness, he won't invest a dime with us," I said.

Chase tipped his head, as if it were a literal scale weighing both sides. "He has a point."

"Booyah!" I pumped my fist.

"I'm cautiously optimistic," said Sebastian.

"Seb, you're cautiously optimistic about crossing the street."

"Well, to be fair, you never know when a car could come around the bend." Chase shrugged.

I hopped off the treadmill and whipped both of their cautiously optimistic asses with my towel.

We went into the locker room and grabbed our gym bags, then left. We preferred to shower at home...for obvious reasons.

———

TWO DAYS LATER, it was time for the final meeting with Hollis. Fuck cautiously. I was full-on optimistic. Chase made us his world-famous pancakes, yet I was so nervous, I only had four.

I had to be careful with my diet. Apparently, the way to my heart was through Chase's pancakes.

"I was looking at your numbers again, and I think you can shave five percent off cost and still come out ahead. If I'm reading these correctly." Chase handed us printouts of our profit and loss statements and Powerpoint deck that he'd reviewed. We'd asked him to look it over since he was the smartest person we knew.

"I think you might be right," Sebastian said, eyes widening at the sheet of numbers. "We can keep this in our back pocket. We need to sell him on us versus Main Street Vendors. If we do that, he'll love the numbers."

"People buy from people," I said, the most common piece of advice in sales. It wasn't as astute as Chase's cost analysis, but if Hollis liked us, he would rationalize the data.

Main Street Vendors was a soulless, corporate entity with a deviously ironic name that got big by eating up smaller competitors. Their leadership was based in Los Angeles. They didn't know the first thing about Main Street.

"Good luck! It's very odd seeing you dressed up," Chase said. "I've only seen you in shorts."

"You can't stop looking at our legs," I said.

"This is true. You guys are going to kill it. Kill it in a good way, like a hunter slaughtering a moose in order to feed his family." He wore the cutest fucking apron that said "Cooking with Chemistry."

"Thanks, Chasey." I stood up and without thinking planted a good-bye kiss on Chase's lips, as if I were a husband going off to work and Chase would have a pot roast ready when we came home. He seemed a tad surprised at the gesture, too.

Sebastian kissed Chase, too, and straightened his glasses.

It was all very domestic. And impossibly sweet.

I got into my sales mindset and pushed whatever I was thinking to the back of my head. We had an account to win.

―――――

SEBASTIAN and I turned on the charm for Hollis. Fortunately, he wrestled in college, so we had a very easy in. He was a real man's man. The kind of guy with a natural barrel chest who ate steak on the regular. Fuck cholesterol. A cowboy hat hung on a hook behind his door, which wasn't something one normally saw in upstate New York.

The meeting went great. Sebastian and I were on fire. Hitting him with charm and numbers. We didn't make a compelling argument for BS. Nobody liked arguing except lawyers. Instead, we had a compelling conversation, learning about his pain points and how BS could fix them. Hollis was frustrated with his current vendor, lots of little paper cuts that were adding up. Sebastian and I kept bringing up those pain points throughout the conversation.

I closed with my final line. "Hollis, with our bespoke services and cost savings, Beverage Solutions can alleviate the hassle you're having with your current vendor. We will work hard for you day and night. What can we do to win your business?"

"I like you boys. You're young. You got spunk. And unlike Lou Grant, I love spunk!"

I didn't know who the heck Lou Grant was, but I nodded along and made a mental note to Google later.

"Do you see yourselves doing this business long term, or do I have to worry about you getting bored and moving onto the next thing?"

It was a fair question. People our age switched majors and careers on the regular. He didn't want to be left with vending machines and nobody to service them.

"Hollis, that's a great question, and I understand where you're coming from," said Sebastian. "We are in this for the long haul. We love what we do, working with customers. We're not going anywhere."

An inappropriate flutter of butterflies hit my stomach when Seb said that. Was he really invested in doing this long-term, or was he just saying that to satisfy Hollis?

"I love your passion and enthusiasm. You have that fire that I had when I was your age."

"That you still have," I said.

Hollis teepeed his fingers together, giving us a quizzical look. "Do you have serious girlfriends?"

Usually, I was good at sensing where a prospect's head was at and what questions he might have. This was a first, and it threw me for a loop.

I locked eyes with the cowboy hat and in a split second made a choice not to correct him. "We do not."

Sebastian didn't jump in and object.

"I know it's not only any of my business, but I like working with people who have families. It gives them a sense of commitment that single fellas might not have. No offense. I know how it is. I was a single fella once."

"We are very committed to Beverage Solutions. I turned down a scholarship to give this business my full attention," Sebastian said.

"We've taken out loans. We have over twenty clients. We mean business, Hollis." I cracked my most confident smile.

"You are very motivated individuals, I'll give you that. But as I said, I'm in this for the long haul. What's tying you down? What's stopping you from picking up and backpacking across Europe for six months?"

I was about to say that I don't even have a passport, but that probably would only convince him less. I was used to handling objections to our company, not objections to my life.

"What's tying any of us down?" Sebastian asked, his voice getting barbed. "People pick up and leave families, too."

I wanted to reach over and squeeze his hand in support.

"That's true. I like working with people who have roots—family, real estate. We're a family company here. My wife and I started this together when we had two little rugrats at home. They were my why, pushing me to work harder. I'm not saying no. I like your product, and I believe in your passion. I'm going to think about it. I have to look out for this company, for my customers. I'd be signing a substantial amount with you. I don't want to be in a position where the vending machines are down, and we can't get in touch with you."

"You would have both of our cell phone numbers. Call us twenty-four seven," I said, then clamped my mouth shut before I sounded desperate.

"Why don't we touch base in a week?"

Touch base was the fuck off of business jargon. He might as well have kicked us in the balls. Still, I made Hollis set a time and date on the calendar, even though he would likely blow us off.

Were we being rejected for being single?

"What the fuckity fuck?" I asked as soon as Sebastian and I got into the elevator.

"That was interesting. I wish Craig would've warned us that Hollis was big into families." Sebastian watched the floors tick by.

"It's a shame we're *single fellas*," I said in Hollis's voice. The man was born and bred New Yorker yet had the slightest Texas twang. It had to be fake.

"Are we?" Sebastian glanced my way, but had trouble meeting my eyes. "Are we single?"

Shit. I knew what he was getting at, and it caused my throat to tighten. If three people hung out enough and had sex enough and cuddled enough, did that make them a real couple? Were we still exploring?

The elevator suddenly got very stuffy, the walls closing in around us. I couldn't think about this along with stressing about Hollis.

The doors dinged open to the lobby. I beelined outside, where I inhaled fresh, much-needed open air.

"Fuck his family values," I said. I wanted to put this meeting in the rearview mirror and bathe in hot sin. "If we're young, single fellas, let's be young, single fellas."

I pulled out my phone. My fingers hit the keypad with fierce determination. I wouldn't let myself be rattled by this bullshit probe into my personal life—or Sebastian's question about our situation.

"I'm texting Chase to come over as soon as school is out. We're going to fuck his brains out."

I slapped Sebastian's ass hard, and looked behind me, secretly hoping that Hollis or any of his family-minded employees saw that.

24

CHASE

"Look at all these kids with their hopes and their dreams and their futures." Everett shook his head, wondering when the inevitable cynicism of adulthood would sink in.

The four of us hung out on the roof of South Rock at a secret spot that had been a smoker's lounge for teachers and students up until the 1970s.

Today, the seniors picked up their yearbooks and graduation caps and gowns. In a few days, they would be graduating. End-of-year excitement permeated the halls. Kids walked around sans books and backpacks. They knocked on teachers' doors by choice to say goodbye. South Rock went from being a place of education to one of celebration.

From our perch high up, we watched kids congregate on the front lawn, signing yearbooks and enjoying one last hang before they left these hallowed halls forever. That was one the best and worst parts of being a teacher: watching the passage of time.

Amos said it was best to relax on the roof to avoid the mad rush of fevered seniors, but really, we didn't want to get choked up in front of our graduating students.

"They grow up so fast." Amos looked out on a group of kids trying on their caps. "Soon, they'll be off to college, getting jobs, having families of their own."

"In no time, they'll be having sex with their former chemistry teacher," Everett said.

My friends cracked up, breaking the sentimental moment we were sharing. I felt myself turn red.

"How is naked wrestling practice?" Amos asked.

"You've been less forthcoming on details. We want to hear all about the wild times." Everett elbowed me in the ribs.

"Only if you want to share," Julian said.

While I had gotten used to my friends making jest of my current sexual situation, their comments had recently begun to cause an unfortunate pit to form in my stomach. Whatever was happening with Anton and Sebastian felt less and less like something that deserved to be a punchline.

"I'd prefer not to, actually." I straightened up.

Usually, I didn't mind sharing details of sexual escapades with my friends. We all traded stories over the years and had a good laugh about awkward experiences or unforgettable nights. Something stopped me from turning this into an anecdote.

"It's not all sex. They came over the other night, and no clothes were shed. It was actually scandalous because we had a Puzzles and Pizza night...on a weekday."

"Tell me more," Everett deadpanned. I knew he was being sarcastic, and yet I went on.

"Well, we puzzled for about an hour, until Einstein skittered off the finished part when she heard the silverware drawer open. She took the pieces with her. The look on Anton's face..." I broke out in laughter, remembering the moment. "He and Einstein are in a love/hate relationship. After that, we turned on this 2000s playlist and had an impromptu sing-along. Every time Sebastian was about to carry a tune, Anton would throw him offkey. It should have been annoying, and yet it came off charming. I tried rapping to *Lose Yourself*, but the only line I remembered was when Eminem regurgitated his mother's homemade pasta dish onto his clothing."

The guys could be incredibly silly when they wanted to. Anton always knew how to keep things light, yet then he could turn around and be intimate and sweet. I found myself smiling from the inside out in their presence, the kind of smiles reserved for the top of a roller coaster or stumbling upon a used book store.

"Wow." Julian had a hand on his heart. "Who knew three-ways could be so wholesome?"

"We're not having sex every waking minute we see each other. That would be exhausting and potentially cause dehydration."

"It sounds sweet. Are you sure this is casual?" Amos asked.

"As opposed to what?" I wondered.

"Something more serious?" Amos studied me for a moment. "Because it seems serious."

Being a history teacher, objective facts weren't his forte. The only fact of history was that it was written by the victors seeking to puff up their reputations. However, he had a keen interest in emotional truth.

"Are you guys like...together?" Everett pounded his fists together to demonstrate, but even in that rudimentary example, there were only two fists.

"As in a couple?" I shook my head no. "That's impossible. Couples are defined as two people. Three people can't be romantic."

"Throuples are a thing," Everett said.

"Just because you make a portmanteau doesn't make it real. Attraction and relationships are based on two people uniting. Those are the rules upon which society has been based for millennia. It's as close to scientific fact as there is."

"And society has never shown a proclivity for making bullshit heteronormative rules before," Amos said with his own heaping of sarcasm. "Three people are allowed to be attracted to each other. You are allowed to love two people at the same time."

"Love? Who said anything about love?" Heat hit the back of my neck.

"Just saying. It's not outside the realm of possibility."

Amos said his declarative sentences without hesitation, but they still didn't make complete sense. There was a leap in logic there. Could a person love two people equally? Sure, history had evidence of polygamous relationships, but it was about men controlling multiple women, not an equitable distribution of romantic feelings.

"Chase in a throuple? I did not have that on my bingo card, but then again, I don't play bingo." Everett shrugged and messed a hand through my hair.

"I am not in a throuple," I said definitively. "I liked to avoid the mess of relationships, and that was with one person. Three people? That's mess cubed."

I shook my head, reiterating my previous protestation.

———

WE HAD a half day at school, so once the seniors got their yearbooks and caps, we were allowed to go. Another school year for the record books.

When I got in my car, I turned my phone off silent. It blew up with messages from Anton and Sebastian.

Anton: What are you up to? Do you have a half day? We want to see you.

Sebastian: Hang out.

Anton: We want to blow off some steam. With you.

Anton: No clothes allowed.

Anton: You there?

Sebastian: Do they have a full day today? Man, South Rock has gone downhill since we were there.

Anton: Play hooky, Mr. M. We won't tell.

I could feel my heart race and throat go dry as I read their messages. It was merely a physiological response to my sexual attraction for them. Sexual attraction. Not romantic.

Chase: I just got done with school. Apologies for missing your previous messages. I keep my phone on silent.

Sebastian: You are probably the only person in that school who does.

Sebastian: Still down to come over?

Chase: Sure. Did you want to order Chinese takeout?

Anton: Later. Let's earn it first.

Anton was being more forward than usual. My heart kept racing, making it difficult to pay attention to navigating the parking lot. I stuck to a slow speed and weaved around clusters of students taking their sweet time getting to their cars.

Chase: What did you have in store?

I drove around the big grassy circle at the front of the school with a flagpole and students exchanging yearbooks on benches. As a good driver, I refrained from peering at my phone.

But then it buzzed with a text. I was going slow enough and knew this parking lot like the back of my hand.

I opened my phone. Anton had sent a close-up picture of his and Sebastian's dicks, both hard and touching. Their cocks were so powerful that they sent my car rolling onto the curb.

I slammed on the brakes, coming within a few inches of mowing over the flagpole and a commemorative bench. Principal Aguilar peered into my passenger window.

"Mr. Mathison, are you all right?"

"Yep! I think I need to get my tires rotated." I sped off before he could ask anymore questions or glimpse the boner tenting my pants.

Twelve minutes later, I was buzzing Anton and Sebastian's apartment. Thirty seconds after that, they came to the door, Anton picked me up, threw me over his shoulder, and carried me upstairs.

"Hi, sweetheart. How was your day?" he asked in a faux Sitcom Dad voice and gave my ass a hard slap.

I took it as a rhetorical question.

Once inside the apartment, he pushed me against the wall and smashed his lips into mine in a surge of heat.

"We missed you," he said. I couldn't tell if this was a line to increase arousal or if it was genuine. Perhaps a bit of both.

"How did your big meeting go?" I asked.

"No talk about work," he said firmly. "We want to have hot, dirty sex with you."

He pushed me into Sebastian's waiting arms.

"Hiya, Teach." Sebastian wrapped his muscley bear arms around me and kissed down my neck. He held me in place as Anton unbuttoned my shirt.

"You feel so good, Teach." Sebastian's tongue found my ear, while his fingers tweaked my nipples, unlocking a treasure trove of lust I'd locked away for the school day. Even after all the sex we'd been having, their hands and mouths still felt like fire on my skin.

Anton rubbed his crotch against me, like we were barely more than animals in heat. He unbuckled my belt. Cold air hit my naked body as my pants dropped.

"Fuck, you're hard," Anton said.

"I have two jocks kissing and rubbing against me. It's simple friction," I said in between moans.

Anton cracked a smile that had the smallest bit of danger hidden in his lips. He and Sebastian had big plans for my little body, but I trusted them. They would never hurt me. They would only make me feel good.

I pulled Anton's dress shirt from his khakis. It was weird seeing him and Sebastian dressed up. Anton yanked open his shirt, buttons going everywhere.

"That was a nice shirt," I said.

"Fuck it." Anton tossed it to the floor. Our chests pressed together as he hugged his arms around Sebastian and me, pulling us tight, smooshing me between two virile, hungry men.

I reached between Sebastian and me and felt his erection through his pants.

"You want that dick?" he purred in my ear. "You have to raise your hand."

I raised my hand, unsure if we were segueing into role playing.

"I was joking." Sebastian's breath danced on my neck as he laughed.

Anton unzipped and dropped his pants. Fortunately, he didn't rip them off. Good quality, well-fitted pants were hard to come by.

"Seb, take your fucking clothes off," he commanded.

While Sebastian undressed, Anton and I stroked each other. His pupils were pitch black and wide open. He was a tornado of lust, and I was the poor Kansas cornfield in his path. Yet underneath the heat was a layer of care, silently making sure I was okay. He always found moments to be tender, making my heart sing. I planted sweet kisses along his jaw.

"You're magnificent, Anton." I tried to convey with every syllable how deeply I felt this simple statement.

A flash of fear hit him before he launched his tongue into my mouth.

Our kisses were a battle of lust. We couldn't jerk each other fast enough. I was a moany, leaking mess.

That was kicked into overdrive once I felt Sebastian's tongue sweep across my dick. A primal groan gusted from me and Anton. He looked down, in pleased surprise.

"Damn, Seb. How long have you been wanting to do that?"

"Shut up, Anton. You love it." Sebastian took his thick cock all the way into his mouth, silencing Anton.

"Oh fuck." Anton threw his head back, a blissed-out smile on his lips. He wrapped his hand around my neck and pulled me in for a kiss while Sebastian swapped his dick for mine. His mouth was wet and hot, tongue swirling around my shaft. He fit the head of Anton's dick in there, too, our cocks rolling over one another, a new sensation that lit me up like South Rock's non-denominational holiday display.

"This is...very good," I said.

Sebastian popped up, that hyperextended smirk stretching ear to ear. He kissed me softly, stroked my cheek, sending a flutter to my heart. My heart fluttered again as I watched him kiss Anton, their friendship perfectly unfolding into something more, something I was maybe a part of.

"Seb." Anton rested a hand on his roommate's chest, their eyes locking in a heady gaze that transcended the pheromones and heat filling the space. He pulled me close to join them.

"My guys. You're my fucking guys," he practically growled.

And they were my guys, my dopey sweet jocks.

"Enough sentimental shit," Anton said.

"I know what to do." I got on my knees, face to face with their meaty cocks.

"Actually, I have an idea," Anton said. He motioned something to Sebastian I couldn't see.

In a whoosh of movement, they each hooked an arm under me and picked me up to standing. Then their hands went to my back and stomach, and in another whoosh, I was upside down. Once again, face to face with cocks.

I wrapped my legs around Anton's neck and went to town

sucking his cock. It turned out that this angle gave me better leverage, making deep throating a breeze. Anton grunted his approval above me. I let out a guttural moan when I felt a tongue in my hole that I assumed was Sebastian's. My mind was a blur of need. Now I was the tornado coming to rain hell on the Kansas cornfield.

In another whoosh of movement, Anton passed me off to Sebastian. My legs went around his neck, and his cock surged into my mouth, bitter pre-come hitting my tongue. Anton spread my cheeks wide and swirled his tongue inside my opening. I loved the feeling of being passed between them, weightless in their strong, protective arms.

Anton slapped my ass cheeks as he darted his tongue in and out, nearly mimicking the real thing. Sebastian's salty, warm cock hit the back of my throat. I felt his muscles flex, holding me up, his arms wrapped around my waist.

They put me down, and we all had to catch our breaths. They were in better shape than I was, but I could tell from their red faces and panting breaths that we'd all had some kind of workout.

"I don't know how pornstars can do that for hours on end," Anton said. He rubbed his shoulder. "I was starting to cramp."

White spots dotted my vision as blood rushed from my head. I stumbled onto the futon and sat down.

"Chasey, do you need water?" Anton asked. I didn't know when he started using that nickname, but I liked being claimed.

We all had a quick drink, the water giving me a second wind. I slumped on the futon. I forgot that I'd been on my feet for half of today at school.

"Here. Lay back, Chasey." I rested my head on a pillow on Anton's lap. His fingers made delicate laps in my sweaty hair. He straightened my glasses. "I want to watch Seb fuck you until you come."

I nodded yes, yes to all of that. Yes to being here, entangled in these two. My heart couldn't stop beating, tapping me on the proverbial back to remind me it was here, in the middle of all this, feeling feelings.

I lifted my legs. We'd ditched condoms by our second week together after getting tested. We plowed the savings into purchasing higher-quality lubricant.

Sebastian slicked up my hole with lube. His face softened with a dash of nerves mixed with a dash of bravado.

"Are you nervous?" I asked.

"I want this to be good for you," he said.

"It will be," Anton assured him. I nodded in agreement.

"I want you inside me, Sebastian."

And inside me he slid, his thick cock spreading me wide. I threw my head back at the slight wince of pain, but there was Anton, nuzzling my cheek, letting me know it was all okay. We were safe.

Sebastian thrust into me with boarish heat, his arms flexing above me.

"So fucking hot." Under the pillow, Anton stroked himself while keeping his eyes flicking between me and Sebastian.

I couldn't take my eyes off the man fucking me. He lived his life reserved and orderly, but now, in heat and want, he shucked off his guard. He showed me all of him. Eyes whole and open. That was the thing about jocks, what I secretly loved about them. How their masculine facade could be paper thin for the right people. I reached up, and our hands met and fingers locked. Anton kissed along the ridge where our knuckles met.

"Please don't stop. Please don't stop fucking me." The orgasm raced through me, blinding me, setting off every light in my body. I was begging, wanting resolution but never wanting him to stop.

"So fucking hot. My fucking guys," Anton said in a low mutter.

It was everything. It was the physical, the heart, everything I was feeling tumbled out of me, emotions refused to hang tight until I reached physical climax.

"I want you. I want you both. I want to be with you. I think... I'm falling in..." I lost control of my breathing as I shot waves of come across my chest. I didn't know if I'd even finished my sentence. Sebastian pulled out and added more to the glorious mess covering me.

I turned and pushed the pillow to the floor. I was still high on my orgasm as I took Anton in my mouth. It only took a few sloppy sucks before he emptied himself down my throat.

"That was fucking unreal," Anton said as he caught his breath.

He and Sebastian got off the futon and let me stretch out. I lounged, dizzy headed, like Kate Winslet posing for Leonardo DiCaprio in *Titanic*. *Draw me like one of your French girls, indeed.* Everett made us watch that movie endless times during a bad dating lull pre-Raleigh, to the point where I felt bad for the owner of the car the characters fucked in. Not only did strangers desecrate his beautiful automobile, but then he didn't even get a chance to drive it in America.

Anton brought us cups of water. Sebastian pulled towels from the linen closet and passed them out. I wrapped myself in one, and he the other. Now I understood why old people kept plastic on their sofas. Easy cleanup.

I packed myself into the corner of the futon. Had they heard what I said right before I came? My prefrontal cortex had officially gone rogue. With any luck, my confession would be chalked up to the high of orgasm and discarded, even though a part of me hoped that they would say those words back.

"Dude, that was amazing," Anton said, pulling on his underwear and laying back. "You are amazing, Chasey."

"Damn." Sebastian sipped his water.

We rested for a long moment, the hum of cars outside the only sound in the apartment, until Anton finally broke the silence.

"What did you want to do tonight? There's a new mini golf

course that opened up by the river. I'll bet Chase uses mathematical precision to get holes in one every time."

I should've told them that my math skills weren't as strong as my chemistry knowledge, that despite math and science being similar, there were major differences in these disciplines. But I couldn't talk.

Neither of them made mention of what I'd said. I had uttered something illogical and ridiculous, and it had been fortunately swept away.

Never to be spoken of again.

Good.

I found myself agitated, though, not relieved. It made no sense. It was the exact opposite reaction I should have been feeling. Mess was clouding my vision.

"I'm not sure if you'd heard over the sounds of moaning and panting before, but I have very strong feelings for both of you."

There. Now there was no doubt they heard it this time.

"Really?" Something began to shift on Sebastian's face, like one of those puzzles where you moved pieces around on a grid to form the picture.

"I...I think so. While I began our arrangement under the guise of having lots of hot sex, I think it's turned into more than that." I was trying to make sense of it in real time, too.

"It's the orgasm talking," Anton said. He flashed me his trademark charming smile, yet there was that look of fear again, flashing across his eyes. "I've said crazy things in the heat of sex. Isn't it scientifically proven that when a guy is close to finishing, his brain circuits go haywire?"

"I don't think haywire is an accurate scientific definition."

"But you know what I mean. We were in a heightened state. Don't worry, Chasey. I know what you mean." Anton rubbed a hand through my hair, ignoring the fact that he didn't know what I meant, or didn't want to know. "I care about you two a lot. I like spending time with you. It's magic. Let's just keep things status quo."

He kissed me on the lips, but his touch suddenly gave me a chill. Sebastian remained mum, closing in on himself.

"Yeah," I said, unsure what I was agreeing to. I just wanted the mess to go away.

25

SEBASTIAN

"Savannah, this is a public park."

Savannah met me at Renegade Park for lunch and immediately stripped off her T-shirt to sunbathe in a barely-there bikini top.

"I'm not breaking any indecency laws." She rested on her elbows and inched down her heart-shaped sunglasses frames. "They're just boobs, Sebastian."

"People don't really come to Renegade Park for sunbathing. There's a playground and a nature center."

"There's also a view of the water, and when there's water, there's good sun to be had." She swished her hair behind her, a young woman utterly carefree. I was a tad jealous that she got to experience summer vacation. Her college was finished for the year. No more libraries. No more endless studying. No more notebooks. Just boobs and water.

I rolled out my towel next to her. Large rocks abutted the river. Over the years, people had graffitied them with drawings and initials. Some kids liked to climb them, while Savannah saw a perfect sunbathing opportunity.

The sun shone through the clouds, warming my skin. I put on a hat and sunscreen.

"Seb, take off your shirt. Live a little."

Live a little with skin cancer later in life was what she actually meant.

"I didn't see you put on any sunscreen," I said to my fair-skinned friend.

"It's all good. I took an edible before we met up."

Apparently, Savannah left her functioning brain back at the library. I took initiative and sprayed sunscreen over her legs and arms. She didn't object. I was happy to see her relaxing after a year of academic hell.

"Sometimes I wonder why I'm even studying to be a doctor. Why am I putting myself through all of that shit? I'm totally a feminist, but a part of me wants to marry rich."

"You're dating a law student, so that could happen."

"Bitch, please. Mathias wants to be a public defender." Savannah rolled her eyes, but deep down, his big heart was what she loved most about him. "Although maybe, I can pull a Sebastian and introduce another man into the relationship, a sugar daddy for Mat and me."

My face burned red, no summer sun required.

"I told you that in confidence."

"I haven't told anyone." She raised her gazelle-like legs, letting them soak in the sunshine. "I'm just saying maybe you're onto something. It doesn't have to be another man. I could bring in another woman. Mat would love that. I might, too, actually."

"Have I brought out your bisexual side?"

"I'm carpet curious."

"I'm glad you're so open-minded," I sneered. "Though be careful, because shit can get complicated with three people."

Maybe it was just one person in particular who was stubbornly choosing to complicate things.

"How's it going with all that?" she asked, taking a break from her suntan and her high to be a concerned friend.

"Things were going great. Really great, actually. We get along shockingly well. It doesn't feel weird." We were three puzzle pieces meant to interlock. "But Chase blurted out that he has feelings. Strong feelings."

"For you or Anton?"

"Both of us."

"I love that." Savannah made an aww face. "Do you feel that way? I mean, we all know that you're madly in love with Anton, but what about Chase? Oh, and did you get around to asking him why he gave me a B on my end-of-year experiment write-up?"

"No, Savannah. Your grades haven't come up in conversation."

"It was definitely A-level material." Savannah took her grades as seriously as her free time. "Sorry, you were saying..."

I mulled it over in my head. Ever since Chase confessed his feelings, I'd been thinking about him, and us, and what we were doing. I was a guy who liked a plan. I didn't jump into anything without knowing where I wanted to go. This was the first time in my life when I pulled an Anton and let myself get carried away, and it was fantastic.

"I think I'm falling for Chase, too. But I still love Anton. Chase is thoughtful and listens. He indulges my Type-A side. Anton sets me free."

I loved two men equally and differently. Was it that simple?

"I see no problem here."

"Anton isn't having it. He pretty much shut down when it came up." Typical Anton. How dare a guy have actual feelings for him. This was part of why I'd kept my feelings hidden for so long. Whether or not they would be reciprocated, he would only let things go so far.

"Who says it's up for him to decide? It's two against one."

"This isn't kids deciding what video game to play at someone's house. You can't force people into a relationship. What if we actually start dating, and then Anton gets cold feet, or Chase gets cold feet? And then they're gone."

"They won't be gone. Anton won't leave like that. You two have a business together."

"He could dissolve it." We were on the verge of Hollis slipping through our fingers because we didn't have anything tying us down to Beverage Solutions. Anton could peace out, we'd split up clients, and that would be that. I'd already watched a father walk out. I couldn't bear watching my best friend do the same.

"Do you think Chase would leave you guys?"

"He could. He could get freaked out and bounce." Chase was fragile like I was. He'd had a parent leave, and he didn't want the thorny parts of a relationship. He was like a cat. One loud noise could cause him to skitter under the bed.

"You think these guys would do that to you?"

"Anyone can leave, Savannah."

"Bullshit." She sat up and whipped off her sunglasses. "Listen to me, Sebastian: Good people stay. Your dad? Not a good person. He is the minority. You have good people in your life. We stick around, whether you want us to or not. You and I have had our share of disagreements and flat-out arguments. But I didn't bail, and neither did you. Your dad isn't representative of all men. You've done a good job of only surrounding yourself with non-assholes. Anton and Chase care about you." She squeezed my hand in her soft palm. "Good people stay."

THE NEXT DAY, I met Chase at Bark to the Future, the local pet store in downtown Sourwood, where he was scouring the cat toy aisle.

"You look very deep in thought," I said.

"Einstein's taste keeps getting more and more particular. I used to be able to give her a bottle cap, and she'd spend a week playing with it." He selected a banana-shaped, velvety catnip holder. "What did you want to talk about?"

"Did you mean what you said?"

"That it's mildly insulting that this pet store chose a dog-centric name that excludes cat owners?"

"No. The other thing." I met his eyes, refusing to let him deflect. The objective, quizzical side of Chase slipped for a second, revealing a worried, wounded man.

"I'm going to purchase this before I forget. It's so small, I could put it in my pocket by accident and get arrested for shoplifting."

I followed Chase to the register, where the acne-faced kid rang him up.

"Have a barktastic day!" the kid said upon handing over the receipt.

"I'm a cat owner. I will have a meownificent day, but I appreciate the sentiment."

I gave the confused kid a goodbye head nod and followed Chase onto the sidewalk. We walked in silence. The aloof side of him was shut off. Vibrant thoughts illuminated his face. Oh, how I would love to be inside that head for a day. I was sure it'd get confusing, but it would be quite a ride.

In the middle of downtown was a small park with a gazebo where the annual Christmas tree would be raised in a few months. Kids chased each other while mothers and fathers checked their phones nearby. Chase led us into the empty gazebo away from the hubbub.

"Did you mean what you said? About having strong feelings about us?" I found myself nervous at hearing his answer. Whether he said yes or no, everything was on the verge of changing.

"I...might have uttered something while in a very heightened, emotional, compromised state." He could barely look at me. He was just as nervous.

But he didn't brush me off. He didn't ditch me. Chase was here, having this awkward conversation. Good people stay.

"I caught Anton by surprise. And he's supposed to be the one of us that likes surprises." Chase squirmed on the bench. "Has he said anything to you?"

"Nope, but that's Anton."

I shuffled closer to him on the bench.

"When we were sophomores, Anton wore the same hoodie for a month straight. It started to smell. Be thankful he wasn't in your class then. My locker was next to his. It wasn't pretty. He said that he kept wearing it because it was comfortable. But I knew that was the hoodie his grandfather gave him the Christmas before. It was a corny, touristy hoodie from Rockefeller Center that Anton rolled his eyes at when he got it. He wanted an XBox. One month later, his grandfather died of a sudden heart attack. But Anton would never, ever admit that that was why he wouldn't stop wearing the dam hoodie. It was just comfortable, according to him."

"It's obvious that he's lying and that the hoodie was a representation of his grief over losing his grandfather, as well as guilt for not being grateful for the hoodie."

"Ding ding ding. That is correct. Everyone knew that, but Anton wouldn't let himself admit it. He's not the best with that kind of stuff."

"I'm assuming his emotional investment in our arrangement also falls under that quote-unquote 'kind of stuff,' too."

"You are correct." Anton was a great guy, but there were times when he used his charisma as a shield, shutting people out rather than welcoming them in. "I know that Anton cares about us, and he loves being with us. He's just very anti-relationship."

"Why? Humans are wired for it?"

"Not Anton."

Chase scoffed. "You mean to tell me Anton is the exception to the approximately 109 billion of humans that have lived?"

"He does think very highly of himself. And it's actually 117 billion humans."

"You actually looked this up?"

I shrugged. "I have a thing for numbers. Any kind of numbers."

He laughed over our shared nerdiness. People couldn't believe I was such a numbers guy. The chiseled physique threw them off.

"Anton isn't one for the parts of a relationship that aren't sex," I explained.

"He seems to love it. He's a master cuddler. He's the most excited of the three of us when it's time to watch a movie on the couch. He bought me a new spatula for flipping pancakes because my old one was getting rusty. None of those scream sex."

Maybe Chase had a point, and I hadn't been looking hard enough.

"Anton says he doesn't like things to get boring."

"Huh. I find comfort in boredom," Chase said, giving me a little breakthrough myself. Such a simple sentence could contain multitudes. "What about you?"

"I do." For the first time, I let myself feel what I wanted to without restriction. I interlocked our fingers in a tight grip. "I'm falling in love with you, Chase."

We gazed into each other's eyes, and we were thinking the same thing.

"All that's missing is Anton," he said.

We sat in silence for a moment, unsure where to go next. Chase eventually shrugged his shoulders.

"Oh well. It's for the best," he said.

"What are you talking about?"

"It's for the best that Anton doesn't want this to go any further, whatever his reason. We enjoyed each other's company socially and physically. We created memories that will last a lifetime. And perhaps that's about as good as something like this can be. This was a highly illogical setup from the get go." Chase stood up and patted my hand. "As students love to write in yearbooks, thank you for the memories. Have a great summer."

He turned to walk away. I couldn't believe he was actually walking away. A big light up sign inside of me that read *What the Fuck* blinked in my head.

I jumped off the bench. "Are you seriously leaving?"

"Yes."

"You're walking away, just like that?"

"I would, but you're blocking my exit." Chase's objective stare was back on his face, but I wouldn't forget what was lurking underneath.

"You're done? You're seriously done?"

"What other options do we have, Sebastian? This doesn't work without Anton. We don't have Anton. Hence, it doesn't work. Maybe we can be friends in the future, but for now, it's best that we go our separate ways and find a way back to our normal lives before things get even messier."

"I don't want to go back to my normal life! My normal life was pining for my friend. It was feeling this gaping hole of loneliness. It was thinking that I was permanently fucked up because the first man in my life bailed on me. This weird, illogical thing that the three of us have is worth fighting for."

Newfound surge of life filled my lungs. Dammit, I loved these guys. I wasn't letting them go so easily.

I jabbed my finger into Chase's chest. "Now you listen to me. I don't care that you were my teacher. I don't care what people walking down the street will say. I'm not giving up. You may use your stuffy overly formal language, but I've seen you at your most vulnerable, Chase Mathison, and you are scared, *terrified* of this uncharted emotional territory. Guess what? I am, too. But I'm not going to hide. I'm not going to run. Fuck, I've been doing that forever. We both have." I pushed Chase against the edge of the gazebo. His glasses went askew on his face. "I'm not letting myself get dumped by not one, but two boyfriends."

I crashed my lips onto his like I was a race car driver with a death wish. Fuck, he tasted so good, his natural Chase scent lingering on my tongue. I pulled him against me, wanting to feel his heartbeat against my chest.

"I love you," he said in a breathy exhale, his bottled up emotions proudly uncorked.

"Me, too."

"And I love Anton."

"Me, too."

"I don't want to get hurt."

"Me, too."

Chase sighed. "So what are we going to do?"

A bright smile overtook my face. "We're going to win over the man of our dreams."

26

ANTON

I went over to my parents' house for our weekly dinner. Dad had decided to grill. The man knew his way around a barbecue as well as he did around an economic forum. It was a lovely late afternoon, one of those rare New York summer days with high sun and low humidity, the days that tricked you into believing it'd be like this all summer long.

Our pool sparkled in the waning sunlight. We had never used our pool as much as we should have. It was mostly a nice back-drop for cocktail parties.

I shucked corn-on-the-cob while my parents discussed the latest current events. Potential recession on the horizon (Dad) and a new novel that received a rave in the *Times* (Mom). No mention of the nail-biter of a Yankees game last night. (Me) Their chatter was white noise that allowed me to zone out.

My mind kept flipping back to Chase admitting he had feel-ings for me and Sebastian. Hell, the guy practically said he was falling in love with us. The fun times were getting serious; I was never good at serious. I was the fun, casual guy. What if my serious relationship side was paper thin? What if he and Seb realized that

I wasn't at their level? It felt like no matter what, I was bound to lose them.

Dad was looking at me, waiting for me to say something.

"What?"

"Have you noticed anything on your end with your business?" Dad asked me mid-burger flip.

"What? Yeah, uh, I mean, business has been good." I wanted Mom and Dad to know that I was taking my business seriously. This was not helping. "What was the question?"

"Have you seen any impacts that could foreshadow an upcoming recession? As someone who works with offices, have you heard of any layoffs?"

I shook my head no. One day, when my head wasn't filled with thoughts of two hot guys, I would be able to have a real conversation with my folks.

"How's the business going?" Mom asked.

"We're on the verge of landing our biggest client yet," I said, choosing to be optimistic about Hollis, even though we were pretty much dead in the water. He hadn't canceled the placeholder meeting we put on his calendar yet, which was a tiny sign of life.

"Congratulations!" Dad raised his burger flipper in the air, reminding me of Chase and his pancake spatula. It was for the best that we leave things behind now, before anyone got seriously hurt (Me. All me.)

The doorbell rang, which saved me from further questions about business. I dropped my corn and raced to the front door.

My guys.

Any feelings I'd tried to push down about Chase and Sebastian came hurtling to the front of my mind. My heart did an Olympic-style flip.

"Is it okay that we stopped by? I know you guys have your family dinner," Sebastian said.

"Sebastian!" Dad made a touchdown shape with his arms.

"Good to see you." Sebastian was a class act who shook Dad's hand and kissed Mom on the cheek. He could talk with Dad about numbers, and engage with Mom about a book he'd just read. Sometimes, I wondered if my parents loved him more than me. I wouldn't blame them. Seb's the best.

"Mom, Dad. This is our friend Chase." Something got caught in my throat. Maybe it was calling him my friend. Chase winced slightly at the label.

"Come join us! We've got plenty of food," Mom said.

Sebastian and Chase's eyes darted to me, a weight between us.

"Stay for dinner," I said.

We all sat down at our outdoor patio table. What should've been an awkward meal turned into something nice, where the conversation was flowing. Like everything else with Chase and Seb, it was magic. Did this count as my boyfriends meeting the parents? Although, they weren't technically my boyfriends, were they? We left things in a weird, gray area. A gray area filled with hot sex, but a gray area nonetheless.

My phone buzzed with a text in the middle of Chase regaling my parents about an article he'd read about nuclear power.

Sebastian: Can we talk somewhere private?

I glanced across the table at Seb, the crinkle of his forehead underlining his ask. He and Chase hadn't come here for grub. I became paralyzed, afraid to leave the table, grateful for the first time ever that Mom and Dad told long, involved stories.

"It's a nice night out. You should take a dip in the pool," Mom said to us after we cleared our plates and hit that post-meal lull.

"Unfortunately, we didn't bring our bathing suits," Chase said.

"You can borrow Anton's," she said.

All eyes went on me. I cleared my throat. "Yeah. I've got plenty. I'll, uh, take you back to my room."

Usually, I would be excited to bring two boys back to my room.

This time, nerves bounced around like my stomach was a blow-up house.

I clicked the bedroom door shut behind us. My parents kept my room intact and neater than I ever did. I pulled open the bottom drawer of my dresser and tossed each of them a swimsuit.

Sebastian and I had borrowed each other's clothes for years. My bathing suit was a little baggy on Chase, which was its own kind of adorable. I turned away from them to change.

"Anton?" Sebastian cocked his head at me.

I busied myself with tying my bathing suit. My jaw tensed.

"Why so serious?" I turned around and whipped on my sunglasses as if I was about to say a snarky catchphrase in a summer blockbuster.

"Because I'm in love with you," Chase said. "We both are."

And there it was. The L word. The big, fat, serious, L word. The word that changed everything. But hearing it also made my heart beat with fresh verve.

How could a word bring both fear and exhilaration?

"I meant what I said the other day. It wasn't said in the heat of passion. It was said from the bottom of my heart." Chase's eyes went wide like a lost puppy.

"I love you, too, Anton. And I know you feel the same about us. We're not going to let you run," said Sebastian.

I sat on the bed. My heart kept beating wildly, enjoying this turn of events.

"We have a good thing going. Why do you want to ruin it?" I asked.

"How does this ruin anything? Love has proven over the entire human existence to strengthen relationships," Chase said.

"Or make it hurt more when those relationships break apart," I retorted. A quick pang of hurt ripped through me as I flashed to a world where Sebastian and Chase weren't in my life.

"We're not going anywhere," Sebastian said. "I've loved you for a long time, Anton. You know that. None of us expected this to turn into something serious. But it has. It's wonderful. I've never been happier doing a puzzle and eating pizza with you guys."

Fuck. Those were good times. Just thinking about puzzles and pizza made a coziness full up my chest. It was home.

But I remembered where relationships lead.

"Things are on fire now, but what happens if you get bored?" I rubbed my forehead.

"We won't," Sebastian said.

"How do you know?" I asked. His confidence unnerved me. Sebastian was the guy who ran the numbers and triple-checked things. How could he be so sure? "What happens when you get bored of me?"

He and Chase traded a look of skepticism. "What?" they asked at the same time.

I couldn't hold it in any longer. "What happens when things stop being new and exciting? When I'm just a guy you're dating and it's not just sex? What if..." I pushed past the lump in my throat. Being this exposed was so not my thing. "What if I'm not enough for you?"

Chase squinted in confusion, another cute look on him. "I'm trying to deduce where you would have thought that, but I'm coming up empty."

"See! That! You and Sebastian are brilliant, intelligent people. You use words like deduce in casual convo. I'm just a slick sales guy who knows how to close the deal but then hands off the account to customer success to nurture."

"My lack of sales knowledge makes your metaphor hard to follow."

Sebastian stepped forward. "Who says you aren't intelligent, Anton? You're one of the smartest guys I know."

"Chase said that to me, too, but how can that be true? I'm a C-minus student. I don't read scholarly articles like my parents. I can't analyze numbers like you, Seb, or go deep on topics like you can, Chase. I'm the fun guy. I'm not the serious guy. Dudes want to fuck the fun guy, not date him, not make a life with him. One day, you're going to realize that I can't measure up to this dream guy image that's in your head."

Jesus, I just about word vomited every deep, dark feeling that'd ever been in my head. I'd been less exposed streaking in public that one time Bobby Diller dared me. Charming, cool guys could be just as insecure as neurotic headcases. Who woulda thunk it?

I couldn't stay here, in this room, in this enclosed space with my guys and my feelings, letting the silence grow into a chasm. I reverted to what I knew best: being the fun guy.

"Let's swim before the sun goes down," I said. "Last one in the pool is a rotten egg!"

I charged out my bedroom door and raced into the water.

———

THE LAST GASPS of sun sprinkled itself across the sky. Flecks of amber and red illuminated the pool. I made Chase and Sebastian go down our water slide after me to break the tension between us.

It would not break.

"Nothing beats a water slide, right?" I said, smoothing my hair back.

"Is that what you think?" Sebastian asked.

"I don't think I'm alone in being a fan of water slides."

"I'm not talking about the fucking water slide, Anton!" His eyes rivaled the sunset with their blaze of fire. "You had the confidence to start a business straight out of high school. You can talk for hours on end about sales and entrepreneurship. You have an incredible ability to read people. You're loyal and you're kind and you're caring. How fucking dare you think you're not good enough." He moved toward me, swishing through the water like a shark. "I haven't been in love with you all these years because you're the 'fun guy.'"

"While I've been in love with you for less time, I echo Sebastian's points. You're simply wonderful," Chase said, right behind him, a sweet smile overtaking his face. "For the record, I've spent ample time around so-called smart people, people who've published articles and conducted extensive scientific research. And they're all, well...boring as shit."

Emotions clogged my throat. I wanted to believe them, but I was still scared. I'd never been in a relationship. I'd never attempted anything serious. Would I be good at it?

Changing everything could be great...or a huge, flaming disaster.

"How about a little game of water basketball?" I pointed to the basketball hoop and tossed the ball between my hands. I had to stay in motion.

I passed the ball to Sebastian. "Two against one. You need all the extra help you can get, Seb," I said, egging him on.

Sebastian couldn't turn down a challenge.

"What are we playing for?" he asked.

"Just a friendly game." I bopped in the pool.

"Let's make things interesting. A game isn't as fun when there aren't stakes attached," Chase mused.

"What are you boys thinking?"

"If we win, then you have to be our boyfriend," Sebastian said. "First to five."

He threw the ball at me before I had a chance to object.

"Okay," I said. "And if I win, then we keep the status quo."

"Deal," said Sebastian, with Chase nodding behind him.

And we were off. I was on fire from the jump, intercepting a pass to Chase and sinking an easy basket. For points two and three, I weaved around Chase to dunk and then scored a lucky break half-court shot. The universe was on my side. Yet each point

I won didn't make me feel more victorious. It felt like a door closing, darkness rolling in off the hills.

The victory was short-lived.

After a quick huddle, Sebastian and Chase brought more passion and force to their game, as if they were playing for their lives. Chase, who until this point had zero basketball skills, nailed a clean shot and then a dunk. For the tying point, I waved my hands in front of Chase who used his height to leap above me and pass to Seb for a dunk.

It was three-three, but I wasn't giving up that easily. As I faced Sebastian down, I was held in place by the intensity of his eyes. The want, the hurt, the years of longing. I got a glimpse behind the thick curtain.

I turned my back to him in an attempt to weave around to the basket. He pushed against me hard, really making me work for it.

I squeezed past him and hurled the ball at the basket before sinking underwater. I let myself hang there for a moment, a quick respite from the grueling game. I could win this. Yet the thrill of potential victory wasn't there.

When I came back to the surface, Chase informed me that I'd clinched the lead. Four-three.

This time, Chase was in charge of blocking me. Like Sebastian, he stared me down with a naked intensity, a glimpse behind his own rigid wall. The aloof Chase was gone, and all I wanted to do was protect him and bring that sweet Chase back.

Fortunately, I was more agile in the water than Chase. He wasn't as fast as I was, so I darted around him with ease. But when I went to shoot, Chase punched the ball out of my hands with such force I thought my hand was going to fly off with it. Dang. Darts wasn't a fluke. Chase really was just as competitive as Seb and me.

Sebastian scooped up the floating ball and easily shot it into the basket.

"Tie score," Chase said.

"Game point," I said.

For the final point, Chase and Sebastian met me at the half-court line, both staring me down. The win was in my sights. But what was I winning?

Lighten up, dudes, I wanted to say. *It's just a game.*

Only it wasn't. They were fighting for me.

I'd never had someone fight for me.

I cared about my guys deeply. I thought about them all the time. Home was having them in my arms. Why wasn't I fighting for us? Was I really going to let these guys slip through my fingers out of fear? Since when did I give into fear?

"Ready?" I asked.

They nodded, and off we went.

Sebastian charged past me. I didn't block him or reach for the ball. In fact, I didn't move at all. I turned around and watched him pass to Chase, who delivered the ball to the basket in a glorious lay up.

My guys.

I love my guys.

Sebastian and Chase didn't whoop and holler with victory. They looked at me, knowing that no matter the outcome, it was up to me.

I put a hand on each of their shoulders. "Looks like we won."

27

CHASE

It was the last week of school, and I couldn't stop smiling. Not just because I was about to have my summer free. But because I was twenty-four hours into my first real relationship. After our water basketball game, we went back to my place and made love, then slept in each other's arms. This morning, I made pancakes for us. I supposed nothing much had changed, except that none of us were going anywhere.

During homeroom, some of my students kept looking at me, wondering why their usually stern, stoic teacher was grinning like he was high.

I turned my back to the students and wiped down my marker-board while the morning announcements blared through the loudspeaker. Principal Aguilar came on at the end.

"Good morning, students. I can't believe we're wrapping up another school year. The time really flies! I have the results for the Teacher of the Year poll, voted on by you. The winning teacher will address our seniors at graduation later this week. I can't believe our seniors are graduating. I'm getting a little choked up. Anyway..."

Students glanced my way, putting an uncomfortable spotlight on me. I hadn't much cared about the award, but in that moment, it began to feel real.

"And our winner for Teacher of the Year is…"

Seconds passed by like hours.

"Mrs. Gonzalez!" he announced, sending a gust of wind out of my body. "Congratulations! And congratulations to all of our students who participated in voting. Let's have a great week, Huskies!"

The loudspeaker turned off, leaving the room in silence. Now I had a room of students looking at me with pity. I couldn't let us get offtrack.

"Congratulations to Mrs. Gonzalez," I said. I watched the clock, waiting for the bell to ring. This was homeroom, not an actual class, so I couldn't jump into a lesson.

"I voted for you," said a student.

"Me, too," said another.

Other students nodded as well. I'd thought I had a so-so reputation at South Rock. I wasn't a fun teacher. I didn't try to be cool. But perhaps I had managed to garner a little bit of respect.

Once the bell rang, the class emptied out. I checked my buzzing phone.

Everett: Fuck Mrs. Gonzalez!

Julian: She's actually a very nice woman.

Everett: Oh, she's lovely. She always leaves a birthday card in my cubby. But also, fuck her. Chase was robbed!

Amos: You were so close. I could feel it.

Chase: It's okay. The award has absolutely no bearing on my job.

Everett: It's going to happen for you next year, Chase. You're going to have goodwill from this year to carry you. It's like when Nicole Kidman lost the Oscar for *Moulin Rouge!* and because of that, she won it the next year for *The Hours*. We're going to do a year-round campaign for you.

Chase: That really isn't necessary.

Amos: I'm with Everett. Chase. Teacher of the Year. It's going to happen.

Julian: I'm with them. You deserve it.

There was no stopping my friends, especially when it came to looking out for one of us.

Chase: Okay. Let's make it happen next year :)

————

"I HAVE BOYFRIENDS. I HAVE BOYFRIENDS." No matter how I said it, this statement of fact sounded like retro cat-centric internet slang. *I can has cheezburger. I has boyfriends.*

I was practicing how to introduce my new social situation to my friends over some creamy cherry goat cheese vanilla ice cream that Amos had made. The recipe used four different kinds of dairy, which would wreak havoc on my stomach later.

Everett and Raleigh had found someone selling a brand-new ice cream maker on Facebook Marketplace and bought it before realizing that they had neither the time nor patience to make ice cream. Everett would rather buy a carton at the store, and Raleigh said something about abs being made in the kitchen then lifted up his shirt. They gifted it to Amos and Hutch for a one-year anniversary gift.

We relaxed on Amos's balcony, another beautiful summer evening stretching out before us.

"This is my boyfriend Sebastian. And my other boyfriend Anton," Julian said.

"I'm dating...people," Amos said between bites. "You're right, Chase. There is no practical way to say this."

"I'm having threesomes on the regular. And how are you?" Everett said. "How about that one? It'll shut people up."

I rolled my eyes, even though yet again, Everett's bluntness was probably the best call.

"I'll take these all under consideration." I sprayed another dollop of whipped cream on my sundae, adding more dairy into the mix.

"No matter what, you'll have to rip the band-aid off," said Julian. "People might not know what to make of it, but that's their problem. All that matters is that you're happy."

A smile took over my face. I was. I was brilliantly happy in a way I'd never been before. It'd only been two weeks since Anton, Sebastian, and I made it official with a victorious water basketball game. It was two of the best weeks of my life. Waking up cuddled by both men, laughing together over breakfast, feeling part of a new family. Ever since my dad skipped town, I'd gotten used to holding people at arm's length. But finally, I let two guys in and held them tight. There was no mess, only warmth. As Sebastian once said to me, good people stay.

"I've thoroughly enjoyed watching the three of you find your true love over this past year. I assumed it wasn't for me. I thought I was a noble gas, but I actually like being an element with multiple valence electrons."

"I have no idea what you just said, but I'm sure it was sweet," Amos said.

"Not as sweet as this ice cream. This is incredible." Julian scooped the last bits of it onto his spoon.

"What are you guys doing?" Hutch called from the sliding door, his voice high with accusation. Raleigh and Seamus peeked their heads in behind him.

Raleigh held up delivery bags. "We're back with the takeout."

"I thought we were going to have dinner first, then ice cream, as has been done by civilizations for thousands of years," Hutch said, his accusatory stare aimed at his boyfriend.

"Dessert as we know it is a fairly new phenomenon," Amos said.

"Stop! It's summer vacation. You're not allowed to talk about school stuff. No learning allowed," Everett said, a rule he held firm on.

"You regale us with musical theater trivia all year long," Julian said.

"Well, my subject is fun. It's not history."

"History is fun!" Amos exclaimed.

"Stop changing the subject!" Hutch kissed his boyfriend quiet. "We were all going to have the ice cream after dinner. That was the plan."

"I wasn't. Gotta protect these bad boys." Raleigh pulled up his shirt yet again. Did he think he was the only person on this planet with abdominal muscles?

"Dude, I will pay you five bucks to keep your shirt on for an entire day," Seamus said. He turned to Julian. "How is it, Jules?"

"Heavenly."

Seamus swiped a finger through the melted ice cream at the bottom of Julian's dish, then licked his digit clean. "Dang, that's good."

"Where are you going?" Hutch asked as Seamus went back into the condo.

"I'm not waiting for dessert. I'm having some now."

Hutch shook his head at Amos. "Look what you started."

"Don't freak out. There's plenty left for you guys."

"I'm not having any," Raleigh said, about to lift his shirt before thinking better of it.

"I'm having his portion," Everett said. "How amazing was this ice cream maker, though?"

"What a find!" said Hutch.

Raleigh sat on the arm of Everett's chair. "We were buying an old end table from this guy, and we saw it in the corner. He'd gotten it as an engagement gift, but then his fiance called off the wedding. He sold it to us for ten bucks."

"Originally, he wanted twenty, but we got him to come down and throw in a set of measuring cups from Crate & Barrel," Everett said.

"You were incredible, Ev," Raleigh purred. "The way you negotiated him down. As if we were going to accept fifteen. It was hot."

"Not as hot as when you casually mentioned that he should include the measuring cups," Everett purred back.

"No secondhand shopping sex on my balcony," Amos said.

And I thought *I* was the oddest friend in our friend group. Raleigh and Everett were gunning for my crown.

Hutch and Seamus came back with a bowl of ice cream. Their moans of delight matched our initial reaction.

"Hutch, I need to talk to you about Pop's wedding," I said. "I would like an extra invitation."

"He has a plus two," Amos said.

"Oh right. You've got a boyfriend," Hutch said.

I held up two fingers. "Boyfriends."

"Threesomes galore," Everett added, something I should've been embarrassed by, but no lies were told.

"Is it too late to add another guest to the list?" I asked.

"I'll have to check. We're already close to capacity, and it's a cramped space as it is," Hutch said. "Do you think Sebastian *or* Anton could go with you?"

"Not both?" I asked for clarification.

Hutch squirmed in his seat. He didn't like to be the bearer of bad news.

"I would prefer not to. We are a package deal."

Hutch pressed his lips together as he deliberated. "Would other people start asking for another plus one?"

"Hutch, are you discriminating against a throuple?" Everett asked. "Chase has two boyfriends and thus deserves two plus ones."

Not only were my friends accepting of this arrangement, they firmly had my back.

"Let's call Pop," Amos said, putting his phone on the table.

"He's at work," Hutch said.

"It's his lunch break." Amos dialed, and two rings later, Pop picked up.

"Amos! What's going on? To what do I owe this midday call?" Hutch's dad was always in the best spirits. Even last year, as he dealt with one health issue after another, he would greet us with warm smiles. It was as if he'd known all of us for years, and not a few months.

"Hey, Pop. Question: can we squeeze one more guest into the wedding? Chase needs an extra invite." Amos looked at me, silently asking for permission to bring up my boyfriend situation.

"HI, Pop. This is Chase. I'm dating two men."

"Do they know about each other?" Pop asked.

"They do. We're all together. One cohesive unit." I hunched over the phone, biting my lip, wondering if Pop was hip enough to understand.

"Oh, like those polyurethane relationships?" he asked, after a pause.

"Polyamorous," I clarified. "And yes."

"Pop, I know things are tight, but it would mean a lot to Chase to be able to bring both of his boyfriends," Amos said. "It'd mean a lot to Hutch and me to support our friend."

Hutch's eyes popped open at being roped into this. I understood his main concern was making sure Pop's wedding went off without a hitch.

"Uh, yeah, Pop," Hutch said. "Is this cool?"

"Absolutely! If Chase has two boyfriends, he will need two

invites. I'm with it, boys. And as luck would have it, your uncle Milton has gallstones, so he won't be able to come."

"Shucks," Hutch said, then wiped his brow with relief for our eyes only. "Thanks for being cool about this, Pop."

"Of course! And if worst case scenario, we're a little tight in the reception, we'll survive. I'm still getting married. I'll be eating the first slice of cake. If you boys have to fight for scraps, that's your problem."

Amos put the phone on mute. "He's kidding. There will be plenty of food and cake." He took us off mute. "Thanks, Pop!"

"Thank you, Pop. I really appreciate it. I can't wait for you to meet Anton and Sebastian!" I sat back and let good vibes wash over me. If a sixty-something guy could be cool with my relationship, then there was hope that other people would be accepting.

And as a bonus, I'd get to see Anton and Sebastian in suits. Delightful.

———

It usually took me a few weeks to fully shake off the school year and start enjoying my summer. Fourth of July was the turning point, a big holiday to usher us into the heart of the season.

Anton invited us over to his parents' house for a barbecue. They weren't fazed in the slightest over the fact his son was dating two guys. It helped that they worked on a college campus where many of their students were in unique relationships, and also that they really, really liked Sebastian and me.

I helped Anton on the grill, making sure he was hitting the right temperature to get the burgers cooked without getting dry.

"How are you such a good cook?" Anton asked, slipping his hands around my waist and kissing my neck.

"It's science. Knowing which ingredients complement each other, the ideal temperature to cook meat. All of it."

"I don't think so. I just think you're a genius." Anton continued kissing my neck, sending goosebumps up my head. I'd gone through most of my life sure that I was better off alone. I almost missed out on these moments, on the touch of another person.

Or people.

Sebastian was an excellent cuddler, too. Sometimes, I wondered if he and Anton were in competition with each other about who could be the better boyfriend. Too bad for them, there would always be a tie.

Sebastian emerged from the pool like a model, water rivulets traveling down his abs, his wet bathing suit clinging to his tree trunk thighs. It was hard not to stare. Seb planted a kiss on Anton, then on me.

"Seb, Chase is changing the game on these burgers," Anton said, giving my ass a light tap.

"He cooks us breakfast. He grills us dinner. Anton, we need to reciprocate," Sebastian said.

"That's not necessary. There is no barter system with relationships where each partner must deliver an equal amount of culinary skill," I said.

"We gotta make this up to him," Anton said, ignoring my point. "Chasey, we're cooking you a nice dinner this Friday."

"Really nice." Sebastian raised his eyebrows.

"Cloth napkin nice," added Anton.

Sebastian turned to him. "Do we have cloth napkins?"

"Shit. We don't. But we'll get those fancy paper napkins." Anton pecked me on the lips. "A fancy paper napkin dinner. With caviar."

"I don't like caviar. I tried it at a faculty event once, and found it tasted like stale dirt."

"Caviar looks gross, man," Sebastian said. He slapped Anton's shoulder. "Steak dinner!"

"Steak fucking dinner with fancy fucking paper napkins."

Anton ground his fist into his hand, the scenarios swirling in his eyes. "Get ready. You're going to think you died and went to Michelin heaven."

"I'm happy to help. This is a relationship of equals. I prefer to pull my weight," I said.

"Nope. You can't help. We want to do this for you. And if we have to tie you to the chair, then so be it." A Cheshire cat smile slinked onto Anton's lips.

While I had never met every person on the planet, I had to believe I was one of the luckiest people on earth. Or at least in the top 0.01%.

Later that night, after delicious burgers and corn on the cob, we all returned to the pool to watch the South Rock High fireworks celebration that would be lighting up the sky. The high school hosted the fireworks celebration with people gathering on blankets on the football field. That was what my friends and I had done in years past. Here we were, all with our own relationships, happier. It was a true marker of time.

For the fireworks extravaganza, Anton, Sebastian, and I squeezed onto a raft. The extra weight sunk the raft into the water, but we made it work. I was sandwiched between them, feeling secure and protected and loved.

"You ready, Chasey?" Anton asked. In seconds, his beautiful face was lit in silhouette from the wild colors of the fireworks. Flickers and flashes took over the clear night sky. I glanced at Anton, then Sebastian, their features aglow against the patriotic backdrop.

Who knew mess could bring such order to my life? It was chaos theory come to life, but it was easier to call it love.

I took his hand and Sebastian's hand and squeezed them tight as fireworks tore through the sky. There was no other place I'd rather be.

SEBASTIAN

I looked at Anton. He looked at me.

"You ready to do this?"

"Hell yeah," he said.

The elevator doors dinged open. We strolled down the hall of Hollis Management, armed with confidence and decked out in our nicest suits. We took a breath when we reached the corner office at the end.

Anton gingerly knocked on the door.

"Come in," Hollis called from the other side.

My friend—my boyfriend—gave me a tight nod. This was it. Go time. No looking back. Despite his boatloads of confidence, he could still be nervous when nobody was looking.

"Hollis, good morning. How are you?" Anton flashed him his million-dollar grin.

Hollis wore a blue polo and plaid shorts, which meant he likely was leaving early to hit the golf course. Even the top dog could enjoy his summer Friday.

We shook hands. Hollis had a firm grip, which I reciprocated. My muscles weren't just for show.

"Thank you for meeting with us again," I said.

"I appreciated your follow up." He laughed to himself. "Very clever."

Hollis handed over a picture of himself next to the singing telegram we'd hired, dressed up as one of his favorite actors that he'd mentioned in an old magazine interview I dug up.

"You boys sure do your research."

"We felt there was more to this conversation," Anton said. "We know you're in a bind with your current contract, and we wanted to make sure you had all the facts before making a final decision that you'd be locked into for years."

Anton and I took our seats.

"Listen, boys. I appreciate your passion and drive. I did before, and I still do. But my concerns remain the same." Hollis leaned back in your chair and teepeed his fingers together. Did people learn how to do that hand motion in business school?

"We understand. We're young, and young people change their minds all the time. Every time I try to arrange a party with our buddies, it becomes a march of the flakes." Anton let out a chuckle. "But the thing is, we do have attachments and roots."

Hollis leaned forward in his chair and raised a curious, bushy eyebrow. His chair squeaked in response.

Usually, Anton was the smooth talker, but I jumped in before he could. I wanted to be the one who said this.

"Anton and I are in a relationship with each other, and a third guy. Chase. We love each other very much." I glanced at my friend and boyfriend who responded with a nod that told me he wasn't going anywhere. "Our relationship is real and serious."

To his credit, Hollis maintained a stone face. Whatever shock he was experiencing, he kept to himself.

"We're also looking into leasing bigger office space for Beverage Solutions in the future." Anton handed over a letter from the bank approving a business loan.

"I didn't know you two were...you were athletes, right?" Hollis stumbled over his words.

"Yes," I said without correcting his stereotypes. Gay guys can play sports.

"Although our other boyfriend Chase has zero athletic ability. It's cute," Anton said.

"Uh huh. This is a funny joke, gentlemen. It's not business appropriate, though. You're going to scare off clients with your sense of humor."

"It's not a joke. We are in a very modern relationship, but it's real, and we love each other." I reached out, and Anton squeezed my hand.

"I see. You and your third person? Chuck?"

"Chase," Anton hissed out.

Hollis shook his head, more confused than disdainful. "Your generation...y'all love to do things your way. Doesn't make it the right way."

I was tired of trying to play into some image that Hollis or anyone else wanted for us. If people wanted to leave, then that was their problem because we're awesome.

"If you decide not to work with us, that's your choice," I continued. "And if you want to stick with your current vendor, who is overcharging you and increasing customer dissatisfaction which will lead to greater turnover in your buildings, that's also your choice. Or if you want to go with Main Street Vendors, where you're just going to be another mid-level customer to them who will get ignored in favor of servicing their enterprise clients, that's also your choice. You've done a remarkable job of building your company into a formidable business. Your kind of success is what Anton and I are trying to create. We don't know much about office real estate, but we do know vending machines, and we know that if you're going to continue with your status quo, all because of issues you have with our personal lives, you're only going to wind up hurting your customers and your bottom line."

"But hey, you do you," Anton said. "We've gone over the numbers. You know we're the better choice. You don't want to let fear dictate this decision for you."

I took out a copy of the contract we proposed and placed it on his desk. "The deal we offered expires at the close of business today. None of us want to drag this out, so if you're not interested, we don't want to waste anymore of your time. As we said before, we would love to work with Hollis Management."

"We're hungry. We're smart. And we will work hard for you and your clients," Anton said, emphasizing the word smart. Anton was smart, and thanks to Chase and me, he was starting to believe it. He had a social intelligence and a perceptiveness that he never gave himself enough credit for.

Silence hung in the air as Hollis took all this in. I didn't know what he was thinking, but I felt better. We came clean. We had nothing to hide about our relationship. And most importantly, Beverage Solutions *was* the better choice. If Hollis was going to let pride and prudishness get in the way, that was his problem.

"Thank you for your time." I stood up and shook his hand. Anton followed.

We waited one final beat before turning to leave. We didn't want to seem desperate.

The air changed when Anton and I entered the hallway. The energy we had leading up to the meeting dissipated. Anton gave me a chin up look.

"We tried," I said in a low voice as I hit the elevator button. "Onward."

I put my hand on Anton's shoulder and led him into the elevator. The doors closed. We would be okay.

"We're going to make one hundred cold calls today," I said. "We're going to find another Hollis, an even bigger Hollis."

The smile that I loved so much cracked onto his face. "Hell yeah."

Anton pulled me into a kiss as the doors opened into the lobby.

Where Hollis was waiting for us.

Shit.

He cleared his throat. We stepped out of the elevator and jumped back into business mode.

"Gentlemen," he said uneasily. But then a grin broke out onto his face as he handed over the signed contract. "I look forward to working with you."

I took the contract, but it didn't feel real. None of this felt real. Had the elevator plummeted us to our deaths?

"Set up a call with my admin for Monday morning."

"Yeah. Yes. Will do." I shook his hand, which again, didn't feel real.

"How did you beat us down here?" Anton asked.

"I have a private elevator." Hollis shrugged, as if it were the most obvious thing in the world. Clearly, we had a lot to learn about wealthy businessmen. "And speaking of elevators, no hanky panky in mine."

He pointed a warning finger in our faces. Then he broke into a laugh, clapped us each on the back, and was gone. Off to his secret elevator.

Anton and I walked to our car in dead, shellshocked silence.

"We did it," he said matter-of-factly, no emotion in his voice.

"Yeah, I think we did," I replied, just as confused.

———

THE NEXT NIGHT, Anton and I were still on the top of the world. And then we entered the kitchen.

"It says to broil it. What does broil mean?" Anton looked at me, then back at the steak simmering in the skillet, then back at me.

"I don't know. Is that a fancy term for cooking it?"

"Maybe it means boil it? Should I get a pot of hot water?" Anton asked.

"Who boils meat? Is that really a thing?"

Anton and I had conquered wrestling matches, starting a business, and landing our biggest client to date. Surely, we could handle making one meal.

It wasn't until we bought all the ingredients and began cooking that we realized just how tiny and unstocked our kitchen was. Our one skillet was too small for the meat, we had no appliances outside of a wooden spoon Anton's mom made us buy, and the only "spices" we had were the salt and pepper packets from takeout.

But we promised Chase a delicious steak dinner, and by golly, our nerdy boyfriend was getting a steak dinner.

"In Burger King commercials, they talk about broiled whoppers. Should we call someone at BK and ask?"

"Let's call the King himself." I rolled my eyes. Fast food employees weren't paid enough to care about broiling.

"I'm spitballing here!" Anton threw his hands in the air, and because of the tight quarters, he accidentally smacked me in the head.

The steak began to smoke, with a circle of black forming on the pan. Black was never a good sign in cooking.

"I'll Google," I said.

Anton smacked his own head. "Of course! The internet!"

I pulled up an article titled broiling for idiots. Very appropriate for the current state of affairs.

"It says to cook steak on the middle rack, then broil on the top rack." Our oven was so small would it even make a difference?

"The oven? We're roasting potatoes in the oven," Anton said.

"Shit. Did we set a timer for that?" I asked, just as a burning smell took over the cramped space.

"Relax. I set a timer on the microwave."

"But I used the microwave to melt the butter," I said. "Shit. I think I canceled your timer when I put in the butter."

We turned our heads to the microwave, which read the current time. No countdown.

"Do you know how long the potatoes have been in there?"

Just as with Beverage Solutions, Anton wasn't the best at the small details. He was a big picture guy.

"Uh, a while?" Anton put on a cow-shaped oven mitt and opened the door. A plume of smoke blew out, clouding the kitchen.

"Shit!" We yelled in unison.

Our eyes watered, and I couldn't stop coughing. With my lungs filling with smoke by the second, I reached out for the fire extinguisher. Visibility was low. My arm knocked into a rod, but why would we have a rod sticking out?

Unless that rod was actually the skillet handle.

The sound of the steak splatting on the floor rose above the din of chaos only to be outdone by the smoke alarm going off.

"Why didn't you use your iPhone timer like a normal person!" I yelled.

"Why didn't you Google broiling before we started cooking?" He yelled back.

We were both bad Gen Zers.

Anton pulled the fire extinguisher from under the sink. I found it strange that Savannah gave us a fire extinguisher as a housewarming, but now I understood just how well she knew us.

The white foam of the extinguisher sprayed across the stove and into the oven, adding to the cloud of chaos.

A few seconds later, the clouds of smoke and foam fell, leaving us with a clear view of Chase standing in the kitchen doorway, a bottle of wine hanging from his hand and a stunned look hanging on his face.

"I take it dinner will be a while."

———

FORTUNATELY, wine went great with delivery pizza.

"Congratulations on landing your biggest client thus far." Chase held up his wine for a toast.

Three glasses clinked in the center of the dining table, which we had set before the cooking fiasco. The fancy napkins were perfect at soaking up the grease on the pizza.

"I assume that the larger client load means longer hours for you."

Anton and I shared a look, our excitement colliding with cold, hard reality.

"It'll probably be intense," Anton said. "We gotta overdeliver for Hollis while serving our existing client base. He could call at any time with a problem."

It sank in how much work was waiting for us.

I rubbed Anton's arm. "We got this."

"We do," he said back. "Seb, thank you for taking this crazy risk with me. I never would've gotten this far without you." Anton reached for Chase's hand. "And Chasey, I'm grateful that you're along for the ride, too."

"If you need a helper at the office, I can pitch in however needed. Although I warn you, I can't lift heavy objects. I can barely lift chemistry textbooks."

Chase was underestimating his arm strength. But we'd work on that with him. *Get used to hitting the gym, dude.*

"Don't worry, Chasey. We'll be busy, but we'd never forget about you," Anton said.

I wiped my mouth with my fancy paper napkin. "I actually wanted to talk about that. I've been thinking about rules."

"Sebastian? Thinking about rules? I'm shocked." Anton laughed into his wine glass. That fucker knew me too well.

"We should have some ground rules about our relationship." I read articles about best practices for people in polyamorous relationships when I should've been reading up about how to broil. Every article mentioned the importance of communication. "Like for instance, I don't think two of us should fool around without the third person."

"Agreed. It's all or nothing," Anton said. "Leaving someone out would feel like cheating."

"I agree, too. Proposing a hypothetical situation, what if you were working late at the office, and you were inspired to have sex," Chase said.

"Have you ever had sex on a desk? It's not comfortable," Anton said. "No lumbar support."

"There was a time when that's what I would've wanted, the fact is that I don't want to do anything without you. We would never want to hurt you, and that's enough to keep us from that fantasy," I said.

Chase nodded. "If things change, let me know."

"They won't," said Anton. "But we can talk about it if they do."

"Next topic. Where do you stand on inviting other people into the relationship?" I asked.

"Hell no," said Anton.

"What he said."

"Same," I added. "We're in agreement."

"Are these questions meant to be foreplay, because they're not," Anton said.

"They're forming the basis of our bond," Chase said.

I put my hand on Anton's. "I know you're scared of things

getting boring. This is not boring. This is establishing rules so that we can be free."

"Think of it as the scientific properties that all matter on earth is beholden to," Chase said. "Within those rules, some very cool things are able to happen, like life and photosynthesis, and volcanoes."

"There better be lots of cool things happening tonight." Anton crossed his arms.

"I think we're at a good place," I said. I was out of rules.

"Good. Let's cuddle on the couch," Anton said with the same spirit our wrestling coach would tell us to hit the showers.

We retreated to the futon to watch some episodes of *Schitt's Creek*. Chase and I snuggled together while Anton got dessert. For that, we got a pint of ice cream. No cooking necessary.

"Chase, I meant what I said before. I know I came into this relationship with outsized feelings for Anton, but I would never do anything to hurt you."

"I trust you." He put his hand on mine, his blue eyes sparkling with certainty behind his thick-framed glasses. "I would've noticed warning signs well before our conversation. And likewise, I would never do anything without you. The pleasure it would bring would be outweighed by my guilt. Although, this precludes my desire to whoop your ass at darts."

"I'd like to see you try."

"I did try. And I was on track to beat you."

"I was in a heightened emotional state that compromised my performance ability."

"You sound like...me," Chase said, confused.

"Using lots of big words is kinda fun. I may do it more often." I tipped his chin and kissed him.

Anton listened by the kitchen doorway. A pint and three spoons were in his hand. He lazily smiled at us like he was seeing something we couldn't.

"What are you thinking over there?" I asked.

"Just how I'm the luckiest man times two." He gave us a serious look, the mood changing slightly. He didn't budge from his position.

"Are you going to watch with us?" I asked.

"Actually, I had another idea. I'm going to put this ice cream back in the freezer, and then I'm going to fuck the living daylights out of both of you. Seb, is that alright with you?"

Every hair on my body stood at attention. As did another appendage. Chase slipped his hand between my thighs, only making me harder.

I nodded yes. Tonight, I would get to feel Anton inside me.

"My guys," he said.

Yes we were.

29

ANTON

S ebastian and Chase walked into my bedroom holding hands. I turned off the light, the only illumination coming from the glow of street lights slashing through the blinds.

How lucky was I? I had these two gorgeous men all to myself, and they weren't going anywhere. Each day, their love made my insecurities fade further away until they were no bigger than specks of dust swirling in the air. Having Chase and Seb in my corner made me feel more confident, more loved, more alive. I was looking forward to being an old, boring couple with them.

But first, there was tonight.

Sebastian and Chase got on the bed and commenced making out. The sound of their lips smacking together filled the room. They caressed each other with tenderness, a hand sliding down an arm, a kiss on the neck. They were both getting into it, their soft touch turning to clawing. And every few seconds, they kept gazing over at me with heavy-lidded eyes, making sure I was enjoying the show.

I massaged my raging hard dick through my pants. Hell yeah, I was enjoying this.

I kept touching myself as they did the same to each other. Chase moaned and rolled his head back as Sebastian's lips kissed down his neck.

"Grab his ass, Seb," I commanded from my perch.

Sebastian palmed Chase's rear with two hands and pulled their bodies close. My breathing got caught in my throat. This was the hottest thing I'd ever seen.

"Now undress each other."

Sebastian pulled off Chase's shirt, smelling it before tossing it to the floor. Chase slid his hands underneath the tight fabric of Sebastian's shirt, then lifted. Sebastian gasped out a *yes* as air hit his chest.

"You two are so fucking hot." I gripped my cock, a drop of pre-come squeezing out.

Their bare chests rubbed together as their kisses became more heated. Chase flicked a tongue over Sebastian's pert nipples, his hands grazing down his pecs and the golden ridges of his abs. How had I spent years around Sebastian in a tight wrestling uniform and not fucked his brains out?

I stroked myself over my jeans with so much friction I could start a fire. I was going to have Sebastian's incredible body tonight. Whenever I slid inside Chase, I fucking melted. I had to mentally prepare not to blow my load on first contact. These guys were going to put my stamina to the test.

Chase and Sebastian met for a sweet kiss. They smiled and gazed into each other's eyes, two kindred souls that had found each other.

Chase had told me about what happened with his dad. It was eerily similar to what Sebastian went through. While I sometimes felt like an alien in my family of intellectuals, I knew how lucky I was to grow up in a loving two-parent household, where I never had to worry about my mom or dad walking out, leaving a gaping hole in my heart. My guys were strong as steel, but also fragile.

Being with them caused a protective urge to pulse through my veins, as sure as my beating heart. I would do everything I could to make sure they never got hurt like that again. They deserved all the love in the world, and I would provide it.

"Pants, too?" Sebastian asked me, knowing full fucking well the answer.

I shot him a look that emphatically answered his inquiry. *Don't mess with my foreplay.*

As they unzipped and pushed down each other's pants, I did the same to myself. My cock sprung from my boxers, engorged and growing increasingly impatient.

I held out my hand. "Spit."

Chase and Sebastian each spat into my palm, which I used to stroke myself. Fuck, I was already dangerously close to coming.

They knelt on the bed, stark naked, kissing, cocks sword fighting down below. I had died and gone to throuple heaven.

"Suck each other," I ordered, my breath rattling in my chest, my body tense with want.

I went to the edge of the bed so I could watch them sixty-nine. Their cocks filled each other's mouths as they pulled each other close. They moaned through full mouths.

"Just like that. My guys. This is quite a show." I walked around the bed, getting every view I could. Of Chase deep throating Sebastian. Of Sebastian spreading Chase's cheeks and tapping his pink hole.

Every so often, they glanced at me, making sure I was enjoying the show. I gave them nods of approval.

"You boys are hungry." I slapped Sebastian's ass, then went around and slapped Chase's, leaving handprints on both.

"Chasey, get on top of Seb. Fuck his face." I was the most powerful man in the world. My mind spiraled with scenarios of everything I wanted to see, and I knew they'd do it. Just as I would do anything for them.

Chase's ass moved up and down as his cock slid into Sebastian's willing mouth. I nudged my cock along his crack, smearing pre-come, a tease for later. On the other side of the bed, I took Sebastian's dick from Chase's mouth and gave it a few sucks myself, his hot length simmering on my tongue. Chase watched with bright-eyed lust reflecting in his glasses.

I stepped back and took in the spectacular view.

"That's enough. I don't want you blowing your loads. Sebastian, lie on top of Chase and kiss."

Sebastian combed a hand through Chase's wavy hair as they got lost in a hot kiss, the taste of their dicks on each other's mouths.

I knelt on the bed and slid my dick between their tangled lips. Their tongues twirled around my shaft, heat and moans pulsing against me. They continued kissing with my dick in the middle before dividing and conquering. Sebastian took my length, and Chase took my balls.

"Shit. You're fucking amazing. God, yes." I slapped Sebatian's ass hard, the sound echoing against the walls.

They switched. Chase deepthroated me as if a gag reflex didn't exist. Sebastian licked my balls. My whole body was one big wildfire, flickering flames devouring everything in its path.

"You're gonna make me come before I have a chance to fuck you. Shit, you feel so good." They passed my cock between them, taking turns.

I pulled away.

"Keep kissing," I said.

Their bodies tangled together while I removed the lube from the nightstand. I slicked myself up.

"Seb, get on all fours."

Sebastian did as ordered, sticking his ass up in the air. Chase lifted his legs up under him. Their two holes were lined up, one on top of the other, open and ready for me. I flicked a tongue over

Sebastian's puckered opening, then let it slide south to Chase's hot hole. Back and forth I went, satisfying my guys, their groans of approval making my dick impossibly hard.

I had Chase put his legs down. I was going to fuck Sebastian first.

I dribbled lube over his opening, massaged it around. I slipped my thumb into Sebastian's hole, working him loose. He was clenched and nervous.

"You ready, Seb?"

"So fucking ready. Give it to me," he said, a breathy mess of desire.

It was Fourth of July all over again because my vision lit up with fireworks when I entered him. I pushed through his tight ring of muscle slowly. I didn't want to hurt him, but I had an animal need to bury myself deep in him, to be closer to him than we'd ever been after years of intense friendship.

"Seb, how are you feeling? You okay?" I smoothed a hand over his back.

"Uh huh," he grunted out.

"Don't worry. I'm gonna go slow." I pulled out, then carefully made my way inside, every nerve ending catching fire again. "You feel so good. I love being inside you."

"Want it so bad."

"Are you grimacing?" I asked.

"No."

"Chase, is he grimacing?"

"Yes."

"Keep going. Please," Sebastian pleaded. "I don't want you to stop. I've wanted this for so long."

I leaned over and kissed Sebastian's neck. Chase smoothed sweaty strands of hair from his face. We were here for him. We were in this together. This was going to be earth-shattering.

"You tell me if it starts to hurt," I said. Sebastian had a habit of holding in his pain. He'd wrestled with a twisted ankle or gone on sales calls with a fever. "You don't have to be brave here."

He nodded, his body tense.

"This is my first time bottoming."

"Seb." His confession stole my heart. He had given me so much over the years. Now this. I dipped my face into the crease of his back, grateful for Sebastian coming into my life. "Baby, I won't hurt you. I promise I won't hurt you. Thank you for letting me be the first."

"You're doing great. You're so beautiful," Chase said, eyes beaming at him. He hugged Sebastian to his chest. It stole my heart.

"Are you okay? Do you want me to stop?" I asked.

"No," he answered, his voice strained.

"Because it looks like you want me to stop."

Sebastian looked over his shoulder. "Are you calling me a quitter?"

There was that competitive grin that I saw on the treadmill and on the wrestling mat. Sebastian wasn't someone who threw in the towel.

"Let's do it," Sebastian said.

"Okay, round two." I coated my cock and his hole with more lube, then pressed ahead. With each thrust inside, Sebastian became more relaxed, pain turning to pleasure. He loosened the vice grip choked around himself. I watched my dick slide in and out of his hole, opening him up, connecting to him on an even deeper level.

Soon, he cried out in moans of lust, arching his back to give me better access. I pulled him to my chest, his pulse and heartbeat vibrating against my skin. He was lost in abandon, a completely unbridled, wanting Sebastian that never came out in good company. It was a special Seb that was all for me and Chase.

Chase looked up at us with adoring eyes, taking in this beautiful scene and stroking Sebastian for even greater pleasure.

All those years of longing and pining brought us to this powerful moment. We would never be just friends again. We'd be something more special, some permanent.

"How you doing, Seb?" I asked.

"Don't stop. Please don't stop fucking me," he begged, his mouth struggling to form words. "Please, Anton…"

I wrapped my hand around his cock. He coiled under my touch, his body tense as I felt what was coming. He cried out as he came, a yearslong release which landed all over Chase.

I wiped off a streak from Chase's glasses and tasted it.

Sebastian couldn't say anything. He could barely breathe. I held him upright as I pulled out of his pink, stretched hole. He collapsed into Chase's waiting arms.

"I'm sorry, Chase. I should've given you warning."

"There were several warning signs that it was coming. Usually, I refrain from using Windex on my glasses, but I'll make an exception this time." Chase flung his glasses onto the nightstand. "You were incredible."

"You're next, Mr. M.," I said.

I lifted Chase's legs, revealing his luscious, waiting-to-be-pummelled ass. Sebastian rested on top of him, straddling his waist. I had a nice view of Seb's ass, too, but that thing needed a break.

I, however, was still raring to go. I slicked up Chase's hole, reslicked my rod, and pushed inside. Chase tightened around me, pulling me in.

I held his legs up as I pushed in, filling him up, and hurling myself closer to the edge.

"Yes. Feels so good. Give it to me," Chase muttered through desire-drenched sighs.

"Bad teacher." Sebastian teased Chase's nipple between his teeth.

"According to my annual performance review, I'm actually a good teacher."

I was amazed Chase could speak in full sentences considering the circumstances. That meant I had to fuck him harder.

No problemo.

After going slow with Sebastian, I was happy to unleash my full power, hammering Chase's hole with unchecked, insatiable need. My dick fit in Chase like a key for a lock.Sebastian looked over his shoulder and watched me in all my heavy-lidded, lust-filled glory. His eyes seemed to say he wanted some.

Fueled by the moment, I pulled out of Chase and pressed inside Sebastian. Despite his tenderness, Sebastian unleashed a guttural groan telling me he wanted more. He was stretched, he could handle it. I thrust into him hard, like how I'd wanted to, and would in the future.

Sebastian punched the bed, words unable to express his pleasure.

A few more pumps, and I slid out of his opening and returned to Chase. From one warm entrance to another. A loud, shocked gasp lurched from Chase.

"You good?" I asked.

"I'm very, very good." His head fell back onto the bed, absolutely dazed.

"You're leaking so much," Sebastian said. "I can feel it against me."

God, this was too hot. Like, the earth was going to combust if we kept up much longer. Though that meant I could brag about outlasting the earth.

Before I fully let go, I pulled out of Chase and plugged into Sebastian for one last trip. I jackhammered him hard, seeing how much he could take. Sebastian was no quitter. My guys were incredible.

"Fuck me, Anton." Sebastian hissed out breath. "Now finish Chase off. I want to watch him come."

His command sent my dick right to the edge. With delicacy, because one wrong move and I'd shoot, I pulled out of his now gaping hole. Sebastian rolled off as I slid back into Chase. I raised his legs off the bed and fucked him with every last ounce of strength, using all my willpower to get Chase to come before me.

Chase sang out a moan, going higher and higher. Sebastian watched with hungry eyes. Chase's entire body shook with orgasm as wave after wave shot across his already come-soaked body. It was enough to wreck me. I emptied myself into Chase, leaving him destroyed and quivering. But Seb and I were here to put him back together.

No one spoke for a good few minutes. We lay on the bed, staring up at the light, our bodies and souls united. There would be more nights like this, more dinners and breakfasts together, more secrets shared and wounds healed. I was never leaving these guys. My guys.

Chase was the one to break the silence.

"Whoever said three's a crowd never got fucked like that."

30

CHASE

While I hadn't been to many weddings, I knew from experience that a groomsman wasn't supposed to be the main attraction. And yet, as I walked down the aisle of Pop's wedding, the smoldering spotlight of two guests threatened to blind me.

Anton filmed me during the walk. Why he did so, I was unsure. A groomsman walking down the aisle arm-in-arm with a bridesmaid wasn't anything special. Was he actually going to rewatch this footage? I could save him the phone memory and walk for him in person whenever he wanted. Besides, Everett had a much more vibrant march, which he deemed catwalk ready.

When I got to the altar, those same two pairs of eyes were on me, watching me as if I were the most fascinating thing here. Honestly, all I did was walk!

Granted, Anton and Sebastian had never met Pop, so I could see why the actual wedding might not be of great interest to them. But still, it was tradition to focus on the couple, not a squirming groomsman whose sock was bunching at the base of his shoe.

I should've worn better socks. Amos insisted we wear gray

socks to be formal, but my dress socks branded with Einstein's face would've been loads more comfortable.

During the ceremony, the smoldering looks kept coming. I motioned for Anton and Sebastian to look at, y'know, the bride and groom. Pop had to walk down the aisle with a cane, but he was full of pep. He decided to wear tails with his suit, much to the chagrin of his bride who was luminous in a conservative blazer and dress combo. The guys watched the couple exchange vows, then returned their stare to me.

While it was against wedding protocol to focus on the grooms-men, I had to admit it was a thrill to be watched. I routinely caught Anton and Sebastian glancing at me, checking me out, an amused smile on their lips despite me performing mundane tasks like putting on my socks or cleaning my microscope. What was so engrossing about the minutiae of my life was a mystery to me, but I was glad there was someone (or rather, someones) out there who found me riveting.

Hutch served as the wedding officiant, and his prepared remarks about the beauty of love were very clearly written by Amos, who mouthed along here and there. I happily glanced back at my boyfriends, admiring those two lumbering, strong bodies crammed into formalwear. I'd spent most of my life being good with being alone. Having two large men constantly in my space was an adjustment. I had to clear out drawers in my dresser for their things since they slept over so often. And I often bumped into them in the tight quarters of our apartments.

But somehow, the upended routine and new living arrange-ment felt more comfortable than my old life. Maybe we were all made for love. Perhaps it was no different than the instinct all chemicals and organic life forms had to bond with complemen-tary particles.

I gave my boyfriends a stealth wink, then again signaled for them to look at the cute old couple.

"And by the power invested in me by the state of the New York and Internet Ministry dot com, I now pronounce you Pop and wife."

The couple shared a chaste kiss to the rapturous applause. My pants began to tighten with an oncoming erection because I would pass Anton and Sebastian on the procession out, and again I would be hit with those smoldering stares.

What was it about them? Or really, what was it about me?

The logic of this arrangement would always escape me. But I just went with it. Some things would have to remain a mystery.

———

THE RECEPTION WAS HELD at the MacArthur Community Center where Pop worked. They took over one of the party rooms, which overlooked a woodsy patch and the parking lot if you squinted closely.

"Mr. Bright, did you want me to get you a refill?" Anton asked.

"Please, you're dating my friend. Call me Amos."

I introduced my friends to Anton and Sebastian, and so far, everyone got along. Although, Anton kept calling all of them by the same name he used when he was in their class. I laughed at Amos being called Mr. Bright. Knowing what I knew about my friend and the things he posted on our group chat, it was hard to think of him as a mister.

We sat around a big table with a white floral arrangement at the center. The band was taking a quick break while we ate.

"This is a really nice wedding. I'm thinking we can do something like this for ours," Raleigh said as he tossed a piece of bread into his mouth. He clearly had no idea he set off a gossip bomb at the table.

"What...are you talking about?" Everett asked. "Who said anything about us getting married?"

"You don't think about it? It's a night where you get to be the center of attention and people give us gifts." Raleigh knew his boyfriend all too well.

"Wait, yo. Is this a proposal?" Seamus asked.

Everett was the most utterly confused of all of us. "It's not. He is not proposing because we aren't getting married. I thought we were gonna do the Goldie Hawn/Kurt Russell thing. Or as you wanted to call it, the Gurt Hustle." He looked to Raleigh to back him up.

"I don't know, Ev. I think I might see a wedding, marriage, and kids in our future." Raleigh had too much fun pushing Everett's buttons, but it was fun to watch.

"Sweet. Mr. Calloway and Mr. Marshall, you're getting married?" Anton asked, back with the drinks.

"Hold the phone." Amos held up his hand to silence all of us. "What's happening?"

"Nothing is happening," Everett assured, the tips of his ears turning red. "Raleigh's just being a tad dramatic. We aren't getting married, and we definitely aren't having kids. No way, no how."

"I don't know." Raleigh shrugged, getting a kick out of making his boyfriend blush.

"Babe, you do know that you can't accidentally get me pregnant, right? That's not how gay sex works." Everett gave Raleigh a polite pat on the lap.

"He has wedding fever," Julian said.

The band returned to the stage and immediately launched into a rousing rendition of *This Will Be*.

"Well, how about we dance then?" Raleigh asked.

Everett, for all his snarkiness, couldn't resist him. Raleigh did the impossible: he brought out Everett's sweet side. They folded into the couples on the dance floor.

Grandma Judy sidled up to Julian. "May I have this dance?"

"Absolutely, Grandma." Julian stood up and took her hand.

"Chase, are these your boyfriends?" Grandma Judy asked me while sizing up Sebastian and Anton with no shame.

"It's nice to meet you," Anton said to her, followed by Sebastian.

She motioned for me to bend down so she could whisper in my ear. "Nice work. I'm shocked you're still able to walk."

I stood up straight, suddenly understanding why syphilis was so prevalent among senior citizens.

"Grandma, what did you say?" Julian asked.

"Child, I lived through the Sixties. I've seen it all. Now spin me around that dance floor," she commanded. Julian rushed to her side, and off they went into the crowd of dancers.

Sebastian and Anton each turned and held out a hand to me.

"May I?" they said at the same time, before realizing what they were doing.

"We're still working out the kinks," Sebastian said to my friends.

There would be plenty more embarrassing moments like this to come, but no matter what, we could all laugh about them together.

"So what happens now? Do you pick, Chase?" Amos asked.

That was a good question. I could weigh the pros and cons of each man as a dance partner. Anton had more natural rhythm, but Sebastian likely had more technical dancing ability. I wasn't one for decision making. Having two Romeos would complicate that.

"You guys dance," Anton said. "I'll get the next song."

"See? We've worked out a dancing system," I said.

"So in this relationship, who's the alpha top dog?" Hutch asked.

The three of us shared a look, but we didn't have to think for long about the answer.

"Einstein," we said in unison.

EPILOGUE - SEBASTIAN

One Year Later

[Chase edit: Actually, it was eleven months and four days later]

Anton and I bolted out of our seats clapping and hooting, easily the loudest people in the South Rock football stadium. We screamed our support until our throats were sore. From the stage erected in the end zone, Chase gave us the simmer down gesture with one hand and accepted his award with the other.

Chase Mathison. Teacher of the Year. It had a nice ring to it.

"Mr. M., we love you!" Anton and I yelled. He wanted to paint a C on his chest. I reminded him this was a high school graduation. His shirt would have to stay on.

The audience felt our enthusiasm and jumped to their feet, too. Nothing less than a standing O for Mr. M.

"I like calling him Mr. M. in public because I know it makes him blush," Anton whispered to me. The only other place he called Chase Mr. M. was in the bedroom.

Chase gave the adoring crowd a modest wave, but in a moment of impulse, he held the plaque over his head triumphantly. The place went wild. Graduating students seated on the football field threw confetti in the air.

"Thank you, South Rock," Chase said at the podium. "It's an honor to receive this award. My friend and our drama teacher Mr. Calloway gave me pointers for a good acceptance speech. He said that I should act surprised even though I was notified in advance I'd be receiving this award. And despite knowing this was coming, I assure you I'm still in shock. He said that I should thank the director and crew, or else I could risk hurting fragile egos and getting myself blacklisted in this town. I'm realizing now that he didn't try and tailor his advice for this situation, but the sentiment remains. To everyone in the South Rock community, Principal Aguilar, fellow teachers, and my students, the only reason I'm successful as a teacher is because I love coming here every day. I love getting inspired by you."

He pointed at the students, which garnered him more cheers and confetti. In perfect Chase form, he picked a single piece of confetti off his blazer and studied it as if it were a questionable substance.

"Watching your brain work through challenging material, watching you grow, has been a highlight. The world may not always make sense, but that's part of its charm. We try to live orderly lives, but I believe life happens in the mess of things. That's where we really find out who we are and what we want. Never forget how capable and smart you are. If you can get through my notorious advanced chem midterm, you can get through anything. Thank you to all my students, past and present."

His eyes flicked to us for a flash before he returned to his seat.

Anton and I shared a look of sheer pride in our boyfriend.

"What a guy," he said.

I couldn't agree more.

———

AFTER THE GRADUATION, we had a surprise lined up for Chase. We weren't taking him to a fancy dinner. We made him one at home.

While Anton schmoozed with Chase and his friends at the graduation, I raced home and put the finishing touches on truffle mac and cheese and braised short ribs. When our leases were up, we moved into a bigger apartment in Chase's building. We got a two-bedroom space with a very large primary bedroom to accommodate our king sized bed. The extra room worked as a walk-in closet slash office.

The unit was on the ground floor with a lovely view of the communal garden. I missed living on the top floor. All those stairs were great for my quads and hammies. But this was the first place I lived in as an adult that felt like home. There was real furniture. No more futon, no more crate doubling as coffee table and ottoman.

As I was lighting the candles at the center of the table, Einstein hopped on, mischief in her eyes.

"Don't. You. Dare. You are not ruining this table setting with your hairballs." I stared her down. She might've run this apartment, but she wasn't the boss of me.

She narrowed her eyes at me, big cat eyes that would've been adorable under normal circumstances. A twitch of fear rose up my spine.

She arched her back and began to vibrate with the tell-tale, mechanical-esque sounds of trouble.

"Einstein. Why must you choose violence at every turn?" I

dropped her onto the kitchen floor just in time for her to let loose a nasty hairball.

And then she pranced back to the living room. She was not living up to her intelligent namesake.

Well, that was why they invented paper towels.

As I grabbed the roll off the counter, I spotted the anniversary card Hollis had sent to us hanging on the fridge. Seeing it always made me laugh. It was a very nice gesture to send, but he referred to us all as "gentlemen," something that we cracked up about randomly throughout the day. Still, Anton and I loved working with Hollis. Because of him, business was booming. He put us on the map with other local companies looking for vending machines. He would even chat with us on Friday afternoons and spit off free, invaluable business advice. It made Anton and me dizzy with future ideas. We wanted to install coffee machines and soft serve machines, expand Beverage Solutions to be the one stop shop for your break room needs. We had a hard time keeping up with our ambitions, wishing that God had created us extra hours in the day. We would conquer the world, one break room at a time.

The front door clicked open.

"Honey, we're home," Anton said. He led Chase into the dining room, where his special dinner was served, table fully set. His face melted with joy.

"This was why you had to come home early?" Chase asked. "Not because you thought you left the sink on?"

I nodded yes. A little white lie here and there was okay in a relationship.

"This is...wonderful."

"We both worked on it," I said. "Spent a good part of the day on those short ribs."

"We wanted to give you one helluva celebratory meal," said Anton.

He and I pulled out the seat at the head of the table for our award-winning boyfriend.

This past year exceeded all of our expectations. Managing a three-person relationship was surprisingly easy. It wasn't much of a struggle when there was love at the core. I got to spend my days with my favorite people.

We sat down to eat. Anton and I chowed down on our food, while Chase was the slower eater.

"Not to toot our own horn, but damn this food is good," Anton said. "Why don't we eat this good all the time?"

"Because then we'd have to spend the rest of our lives in the gym," I reminded him. The mac and cheese alone had three different kinds of dairy. It was the first time I'd ever bought whole milk.

"What do you think, Chase?" I asked.

"Brilliant. This ranks in the top five meals I've ever had," he said. That was a high compliment considering how thoroughly he tracked his eating experiences.

"Top five? That's impressive! Higher than that time you had the chicken pot pie at the Cheesecake Factory?" Anton asked.

"Yes, you've leapfrogged ahead of all franchise establishments."

"Did you hear that, Seb? We beat the Cheesecake Factory."

Anton and I clinked glasses. Take that, chain restaurants.

"Although, we'll have to see how your dessert compares to their titular cheesecake," Chase said.

Uh oh. I looked at Anton. He looked at me. Did we forget to make dessert?

We did.

"Actually, since you love dessert so much, we thought we'd go out and get ice cream at Sundae Fun Day," Anton said, in a brilliant cover. "Since it's your favorite."

"They still have their twinkie ice cream," I said.

Chase lifted an eyebrow, intrigued. Anton and I breathed a sigh of relief. One of these days, with enough practice, we'd get everything right. Entree and dessert.

"So how does it feel to be Teacher of the Year?" I asked.

"It doesn't feel any different. I didn't change or modify my teaching habits. I've been teaching as I always have, and it's merely a consequence of luck and timing that this award should come my way. But, it is pretty to look at." He gazed at the plaque sitting on the table beside him.

Einstein hopped on the award to sniff it out, and both she and the award tipped over and fell. Only one of them landed on their feet. Einstein darted back to the living room embarrassed, the same skittering she did whenever I pushed her off my desk while I was working. She had the annoying habit of resting on my keyboard.

"Maybe next year you can make it two in a row," Anton said as he refilled his plate. I doubted there would be leftovers. We had to carbo load for the gym in the morning, I told myself.

"I don't see that happening," Chase said. "I've decided to quit teaching."

Anton and I dropped our forks at the same time, the clanging breaking the awkward quiet.

"What? Why?" I asked.

"There's another place where I'd like to work, a start-up company with great energy." A coy smile sat on his lips. "From what I've seen, Beverage Solutions is, as you like to say, blowing up. You're expanding and can barely keep up with the work. I have a knack for being organized and efficient. I could help you establish business processes to ensure you can scale with minimal strife." He circled his finger around his wine glass. "What do you say?"

Anton had the same breakthrough look as I did. Why hadn't we thought of this before? Chase was super on top of things, and he would be awesome at handling all of the administrative stuff that trips us up. He was a very detail-oriented person.

"Are you sure about this? You love teaching," I said, noting the award currently on the floor.

"I do. I can always go back to it, but I'd like to give this a try. It's about time I took some risks in my life. Plus, if I can be perfectly honest, I'm a little tired of talking about chemistry all day. I do have other interests."

"Too bad you can't get a job putting together puzzles," Anton said.

"Unfortunately, not."

This felt like a momentous moment. Things were shifting, growing. Chase sparkled in the candlelight.

"Our first employee."

"Employee? Partner." Anton held up his glass. "We'll make this a true family business."

We all stopped what we were doing. We could feel it. Another shift.

Family.

Was that what we were?

Anton had said it, and we had heard it. The word sat there, opening us up. We were a family. No mess, no gaping wounds.

"To the family business," I toasted.

"To the family business," they repeated as our glasses clinked.

"Maybe after Chase joins, we can get Einstein on customer service," Anton said.

Einstein blinked at us from the living room and yawned. As per usual, she was not amused.

———

Thanks for reading!

For their first Christmas together, Chase decided to give the guys a special gift...a gift he might be having second thoughts about. Find out in the bonus epilogue scene *MMMerry Christmas,* available when you sign up for my newsletter: https://www.ajtruman.com/outsiders/

Outsiders always get the first scoop on new books, read bonus stories, and get exclusive access to other cool goodies.

Please consider leaving a review on the book's Amazon page or on Goodreads. Reviews are crucial in helping other readers find new books.

Join the party in my Facebook Group and on Instagram @ajtruman_author. Follow me at Bookbub to be alerted to new releases.

And then there's email. I love hearing from readers! Send me a note anytime at info@ajtruman.com. I always respond.

ALSO BY A.J. TRUMAN

<u>**South Rock High**</u>

Ancient History

Drama!

Romance Languages

Advanced Chemistry

<u>**Single Dads Club**</u>

The Falcon and the Foe

The Mayor and the Mystery Man

The Barkeep and the Bro

The Fireman and the Flirt

<u>**Browerton University Series**</u>

Out in the Open

Out on a Limb

Out of My Mind

Out for the Night

Out of This World

Outside Looking In

Out of Bounds

<u>**Seasonal Novellas**</u>

Hot Mall Santa

Only One Coffin

Fall for You

You Got Scrooged

<u>Written with M.A. Wardell</u>

Marshmallow Mountain

ABOUT THE AUTHOR

A.J. Truman writes books with **humor, heart, and hot guys.** What else does a story need? He lives in a very full house in Indiana with his husband, son, and cats.. He loves happily ever afters and sneaking off for an afternoon movie.

www.ajtruman.com
info@ajtruman.com
The Outsiders - Facebook Group